MORE THAN THRILLS

WATCHDOG SECURITY SERIES: BOOK 5

OLIVIA MICHAELS

FALCON IN HAND PUBLISHING

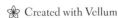 Created with Vellum

ONE

"**W**ell, that just figures," Elissa said out loud after Brett hung up on her. She bit her lower lip and closed her eyes against the oncoming tears as her heart sped up and her stomach plummeted through the floor.

"I am not going to cry," she went on. "Crying is stupid." She sniffled and opened her eyes. Her gaze landed on the cluster of potted succulents sitting on a table in front of the sliding glass doors leading out to her balcony. "I need a cat or a dog or something to talk to besides plants. People who talk out loud to their plants are pathetic. Or maybe it's just me who's pathetic." She shook her head. "I can't believe I trusted him."

Elissa looked at her phone. She contemplated deleting Brett's contact info from it but decided to text her bestie, Elena, instead:

You around?

She waited for a response, taking a moment to water her plants. When Elena didn't respond, she texted again:

Please respond. I'm talking to my plants. Out loud.

A second later, her phone buzzed with an incoming call. She hit the green receiver button.

"Oh, crap. Again, chica?" Elena sounded exasperated. Elissa heard kitchen sounds in the background—pots clanging, a cleaver hitting a butcher's block, and a woman's voice shouting a profound string of curse words.

"You're at work. I'll call you later."

"It's fine. You're the one talking to your plants again." Another even more colorful burst of blasphemy punctuated the background.

"Sounds like Delia's having a wonderful day." The chef/owner of her namesake restaurant had been friends with Elissa ever since the two of them had bonded over a quick and dirty meal of mac and cheese instant ramen in culinary school years ago.

"Yeah, we're in the weeds today, but what's new? Catering's really taken off since that profile ran on Bon Appetit's website after we did Jordan's party."

Elissa cringed at the mention of that event nearly a month ago. She'd been helping out Elena and Delia at the high-profile, high-society shindig—which was truly radical, except she'd had to see Nashville Jones there, up close and personal in all his security guard glory. Or more to the point, he had to see her elbows-deep in food prep and undoubtedly reeking of all the garlic she'd chopped earlier; Elena's little loser friend who was this close to ditching yet another job and was there to make a little extra scratch in case she couldn't find something else right away. At the time, she earmarked the extra money for her upcoming adventure, but that wasn't happening now, was it?

"Speaking of Jordan's party, are you and Brett still coming tonight?" Elena asked, making Elissa cringe even more.

"I...might. He's definitely not."

"That's why you're talking to a bunch of cacti, huh?"

Elissa heard Delia's voice grow louder in the back. "Tell that girl to stop talking to her damn plants and get her ass in here. We can use the extra help. I'll pay double for her trouble."

Elissa smiled despite herself. "Tell Delia I'm too broken-hearted right now and if I come in I'll taint the food with my bitterness."

"She says Brett broke up with her," Elena told Delia.

"Well, halle-frikkin-lujah! About time she dumped Sneaker Boy. Tell her to come in and I'll bake her a celebratory cake after we get through this real crisis."

"*He* dumped *me*," Elissa said, hating the sudden pathetic tone that crept into her voice. Thank God she was talking to Elena instead of Delia or else the woman would scold her for being so upset. She'd hated Brett on sight and didn't mind sharing her opinion.

"Chica, he's not worth the gum I hope he steps in with his most overpriced kicks, okay?"

Before Elissa could answer, Delia shouted, "She'd better not be pouting over that twerp." The cleaver *thunked* louder and Elissa imagined her friend chopping straight through a lamb chop and embedding it halfway into the butcher's block.

"Tell her I'm not pouting over *him*, believe me." Okay, she was, a little. More from her wounded pride and the grief she knew her family would give her when they found out—this was the first guy she'd dated in forever that they approved of. "In the end, I think I only wanted him for one thing."

"Chica, as good as he might have been in bed, no guy's di—"

"No, not for that!" Elissa's cheeks heated. She didn't even want to mention that she and Brett had never progressed beyond some heavy make-out sessions. "I was with him because...Oh, I don't know why."

Except that she did know why, she was just too embarrassed to say. For months, he'd talked up the Maui Challenge —a mini-triathlon that started with kayaking, then biking, and finished with a run until Elissa was dying to give it a shot herself. When he'd finally asked her if she wanted to partner with him, she was over the moon. Brett was a driven coach and perfect partner to train with for the race coming up in a couple weeks, plus, he had the racing kayak needed for the first event. Somewhere along the way, they'd sort of fallen into dating since they were spending so much time together. Probably too much, considering the fights they'd been having recently over just how far they'd go to win. But, Elissa never expected him to dump her.

Yup, Brett told her that after all their training together, he didn't think she was good enough and he was partnering up with someone else. Someone who wouldn't embarrass him by losing—if Elissa could even finish the race.

That's what had stung the most and brought tears to her eyes—the sheer doubt he threw at her after their months of training together.

No one believed in her—and she was starting to doubt herself.

"Chica?"

Elissa realized she'd missed what her friend had been saying. "I'm here, I just...tell Delia I am seriously not up for coming in to help right now. I'd probably chop my own finger off, that's how my day's going. I promise with all my heart I'll make it up to her on the next emergency. To both of you."

Elena sighed. "You'd better be at Jordan and Psychic's party tonight. That is non-negotiable."

Crap. Right. The party. "I don't know."

"I will come and get you. No, I'll send Camden to come and get you and you'll be subjected to terrible dad jokes all the way there."

Elissa smiled. "Since when has Camden stooped to telling dad jokes? He's the funniest guy I know."

"He's doing it for Tina."

"Oh my God." Elissa's heart melted right then and there. Tina was Elena's daughter from her previous marriage and Camden was doing everything he could to be the perfect dad to the little girl.

"I know, right? I told him he's going overboard again."

"I think it's wonderful."

"Elena! Is she coming in or not?" Delia interrupted.

"No, she says she'll chop off her own finger, she's so upset. But she'll make it up to us on the next one."

Thunk. "Okay, fine. But I need you to get off the phone and go help pack the van."

"Will do." Elena turned her attention back to Elissa. "I *will* see you tonight, Lis."

"You're using your mom-voice on me," Elissa complained.

"You bet I am." Elena disconnected and Elissa dropped onto her couch. She ran her hands through her long hair. Elena had it so good. She was in charge of catering for Delia's restaurant and working her way toward opening her own place one day—a dream she'd had all her life. She had a fiancé who supported both her dream and her daughter without hesitation. Elissa didn't envy her friend—she was very happy for her, especially considering everything Elena had to go through to get to the good place she was in now. But, she did wish she was in the same place in her life.

No wonder she uses a mom voice with me Elissa thought, looking at her bookshelf. Not a serious 'adult' book among them. Half her furniture was still from her early twenties right after she moved out on her own, heavy on milk crates and particle board and curbside finds. She could afford better but she spent her money instead on surfboards, paddleboards, cycles, and a stupidly expensive membership to a gym with a rock wall and Olympic-sized pool. Her computer was optimized for gaming and that was in addition to the three gaming systems cluttering up the shelves below her TV. She was on the third job of her fifth career and still didn't know what she wanted to be when she grew up, much to her family's chagrin. She'd never dated anyone for more than three months and her average was more like three weeks. She'd actually met and trained with Brett at the gym for the past six months and they'd been sucking face for the last two, making him a real contender for true boyfriendhood, even if she'd still seen him as temporary.

And why was that?

"Because I'm immature, just like everyone thinks," she told her stubby plants. Even now, she fought the urge to dive into an online computer game and forget herself, forget the party, forget that she was a twenty-something-pushing-thirty woman-girl and probably always would be.

She closed her eyes and an image of Nashville Jones popped up from the last time she'd seen him, looking sexy and mature in a suit coat and dark sunglasses, commanding a team of Watchdog bodyguards with a single word and a curt gesture. Elissa had been lusting after Nashville from the moment she laid eyes on the man. She was casually dating someone else at the time, so her immediate attraction took her completely by surprise. She'd stuffed her feelings down, telling herself it was just her weakness for Southern accents and his natural flirty nature that caught her attention. Elena confirmed later that he tended to play the field, so she congratulated herself on not falling for his charm.

But oh, that accent. Those broad shoulders. That sense of humor.

Her eyes popped open. Nope, she wasn't going to sit here and fantasize about a man who she'd thought didn't know she existed—until the last party at Jordan's estate when he overheard a conversation about Brett.

"His entire spare room is like a shrine to his shoes," Elissa had told Elena while they were in the kitchen setting up catering for the party. "He pretty much turned the whole thing into a giant closet with shelves and an air purifier so they won't get dusty. Not that most of them ever come out of their boxes unless he's showing them off. And he won't even let me touch them in case my hands are dirty, can you believe that?"

"Lis, why do you date these guys?" Elena had asked. "He sounds like an uptight prick."

Elissa laughed, but she didn't feel particularly happy. "Oh, I don't know. It's fine. It's not like I'm looking for anything permanent, you know? He's good enough."

"Good enough?" Elena sounded incredulous. She put one flour-covered hand on her hip. "You deserve better than *good enough*, chica."

"What? He fulfills my two requirements right now: he has a degree from Stanford so my parentals aren't getting on my case, and he's athletic. We're doing that race in Hawaii together."

They got no further before Jordan's obnoxious mother, Daphne, made her—and Nashville's presence—known in the hall outside. God, in retrospect, Elissa was even more mortified now than she was then that Nash had overheard that little tidbit. If she'd known Nash was right outside the kitchen door, she would've kept her mouth shut. She couldn't look away from him fast enough, trying to hide the blush that gave away her embarrassment.

But the worst was yet to come.

Daphne started a fight with Jordan at the party that led to them being physically separated. Elissa had been coming out of the kitchen with a fresh tray of food as Nash escorted Daphne away after she attacked Jordan. He was half-carrying her through the house, sweet-talking her in an obvious effort to keep the narcissist from exploding all over again. He caught Elissa's eye and she swore his cheeks reddened.

After he'd deposited Daphne in her room he came down to the kitchen. And there was Elissa again, grabbing something from the fridge.

"I'm getting a bottle of water for Daphne in her room." His jaw tightened, very unusual for someone who was so easy-going.

"Don't let me stop you." She stepped away from the refrigerator, her eyes downcast and her cheeks blazing. All she wanted was to disappear when she was so obviously in the way.

Then Nash said, "Jordan's outside, bleeding. I need to see to her too."

She looked up, shocked, then immediately composed herself and dashed across the kitchen. She opened a box on the counter. "First-aid kit right here. And I've had some paramedic training." She rummaged through until she came up with bandages and ointment. "Go on upstairs, I got this."

"Elissa?" he said before she left the kitchen.

She looked up at his unsure tone. Of course he thought she'd screw this up. "Really, I promise, I got this." She turned and started toward the door.

"I know that, sugar."

That stopped her in her tracks.

"Just wanted you to know you deserve more than good enough."

What? Mortified, she stopped and drew in a shocked breath. He was joking, right? If she turned and looked at him, she'd see a smirk, wouldn't she?

But what if he's serious?

Resisting the temptation to look back, she hurried out the door before she said or did something stupid.

She only moved faster to get away from him a few minutes later when he came outside to check on the situation. And she made sure she was long gone before he could talk to her again. Because she wanted to know if he thought *he* might be better than good enough. And that was a dangerous question. One she realized she'd already asked herself every time she caught Nashville Jones living in her thoughts rent-free.

Elissa groaned and covered her face. She'd see him this evening for the first time since then. And for once, Brett wasn't in the picture.

Nope. Not gonna think about that. That way lies more heartbreak and you know it.

Elissa stood up and went to her computer—her surest distraction. Nothing like toying with a scammer to make her feel better. She signed into one of her many fake email accounts and sure enough, someone had taken the bait.

Poor Edna Carter at Gmail, an eighty-six-year-old widow with a regular pension is in arrears with the IRS and all she has to do is call the number and give them her social security number along with her bank account number and password and all her problems will vanish. Elissa laughed out loud. She loved the 'IRS' scammers the most. She executed a homemade program that traced the email and sure enough, she'd dealt with this scammer before. She called the number through her computer and put on her best little-old-lady voice. Half an hour later, not only did she have the scammer on the other end frustrated and confused, but she'd siphoned five-hundred dollars out of their account and sent it back to the account where it belonged—with an actual widow who had fallen for the scam a couple of days before.

Spirits lifted and good deed for the day completed, Elissa checked out the chatter on one of the boards that discussed bigger scammers, the ones that attacked companies, not just sweet little old grannies. Everyone had been buzzing about a mystery server for a year now that no one could crack, though there were plenty of attempts, some more successful than others. Elissa had taken a few shots just for fun and wasn't surprised to fail. She scanned the new messages to see a few other attempts.

She wasn't surprised to see a message from Ulysses22. That guy always had killer voodoo and he'd posted code from his latest attempt. She looked over the code and felt that cool, prickly feeling on the back of her neck that she got whenever an idea was just out of reach. Ulysses22 had gotten close using a method similar to hers. What if she just made a couple of tweaks...

An hour later, Elissa had a modified version of her program scratching at the walls of the server's defenses. She'd check on its progress in the morning, or maybe when she got home from tonight's party. She started to post her progress to the group, then decided to send a private message off to Ulysses22 with her modified code instead. If he decided to share, that was fine. Then she went through her closet and looked for her sexiest dress for the party. *Go big or go home* she thought. She got dressed before she could change her mind.

TWO

Great. Nashville Jones was driving along the highway with his assigned watchdog, a Lab named Reggie, heading back to the last place he wanted to be right now.

Eden House. For *another* party.

It wasn't that he didn't like Jordan—he did, a lot, actually. She was one strong, sweet lady and he was happy for her now that she was out from under her mother's shadow. And it wasn't that he didn't want to hang out with his friends—he was always up for a good time. Except, he wasn't yet ready to socialize with his Watchdog Security partner, Elliot "Psychic" Costello. Psychic had let him down on their last assignment, which prompted Nash to take a work hiatus that was starting to feel permanent. Even though Nash forgave Psychic, he wasn't quite yet ready to forget. The whole incident had made him feel dumb, which just fed his hunch that everyone at Watchdog thought he wasn't as smart as the rest of them.

But the primary reason Nash was hesitant to go was that Camden and Elena would be there. And that meant Elena's friend Elissa would be, too.

The last time he'd seen Elissa was also at Eden House, in the kitchen. He was coming in one door and Elissa was coming in the other, and boom, their eyes met. She had the bluest eyes he'd ever seen under a fringe of hair the color of hot, sunny sand, light against her tanned skin. Yes sir, she fit the bill for a quintessential California girl. Which meant the quintessential *Nashville* girl as far as he was concerned.

Too bad she was always dating one loser or another.

Judging by the ones he'd seen or heard about, Nash did not fit her bill. These guys all ran to a type and that type was slick. Gelled hair; bodies sculpted, not built; and a wardrobe that rivaled any woman's. What the hell did a grown man need seventy-five pairs of tennis shoes for?

"Sneakerhead," Nash muttered under his breath as he drove. He turned up the SUV's radio as Blake Shelton sang "Some Beach" and shook his head. Sneakerhead—that was how Elissa had described her latest boyfriend. He hadn't meant to eavesdrop on that conversation, but he couldn't help overhearing how her boyfriend liked to show off his sneakers.

Now isn't that a fine way to show a lady a good time, hanging out in your closet with all your damn shoes? Nash could think of a thousand places he'd rather be with Elissa given half a chance, and there was no way he'd be showing her his *shoes.*

"And he won't even let me touch them in case my hands are dirty, can you believe that?"

He continued his imaginary conversation with her. *You can touch anything of mine you want, sugar, and just so's we're clear, I'm a big ol' fan of ladies with dirty hands.* Nash blew out a breath. If he kept those thoughts up, he'd be making his own hand dirty the minute he was alone.

He silently cheered when Elena put the guy down. *Fist*

bump, Elena! Remind me to buy you flowers or kitchen uten-
sils or some damn thing like that.

And then his heart sank when he heard Elissa's sad laugh.

"Oh, I don't know. It's fine. It's not like I'm looking for anything permanent, you know? He's good enough."

"Good enough?" Elena said. "You deserve better than *good enough*, chica."

Damn straight you do, sugar. Damn straight.

His ears perked up, hoping to catch her response and that she would agree. Instead, she told Elena that this loser was going to Hawaii with her for some race.

Hawaii? That sent a painful jolt to Nash's heart. *Why does it have to be Hawaii?*

And that was when Daphne had to alert the women to his presence, flirting with him and making him look like a fool as she asked him to zip up her little black dress.

Things only looked worse later as he escorted Daphne away from the party after she attacked Jordan. The woman draped herself on his arm like a dead possum. When Elissa spotted them, she couldn't look away fast enough.

But the topper was bumping into her again in the kitchen. He wanted to tell her that everything she'd seen was just not the God's honest truth—that he had less than zero interest in Daphne. The woman was a creep and there was nothing at all going on.

What came out was, "I'm getting a bottle of water for Daphne in her room."

Well, shit.

"Don't let me stop you." She stepped away from the refrigerator, her eyes downcast and her cheeks blazing.

You could have knocked him over with a feather when he told Jordan was outside bleeding and Elissa sprang into action, grabbing a first-aid kit and telling him she had paramedic training. So, the woman was a grade-A programmer, she went to culinary school, she surfed and was going to be in some sort of race, *and* she had paramedic skills? Not to mention she was kind, sweet, and funny. All wrapped up in a smokin' hot body.

He couldn't help himself. Before he knew it, he was telling her she deserved more than good enough.

After that, she did her best to avoid him. Nash hadn't seen hide nor hair of her since and that was fine. He didn't need the reminder that he'd blown it with Elissa. Not that he'd had a real chance.

Good enough.

Hell, he wasn't even that. Not for her. She was obviously not interested.

Now he had to face her again. Would she pretend he hadn't said anything? Would he? Nash groaned—what if she brought along ol' Sneakerhead to the party? He wouldn't be able to resist; he'd grab Jake and Camden and fill them in—hell, Camden probably already knew the sitch—and then pummel the shit out of him.

Verbally. Only verbally. Just because everyone thought Nashville was a hick from the holler didn't mean he was. But Sneakerhead wouldn't know his ass from a pickle barrel once the three of them got out a few one-liners at his expense.

Nash parked alongside the other vehicles on the wide apron in front of the estate, let Reggie out so he could join up with the other dogs, waved at the cameras, and walked through the open house to the gardens.

And there she was. Elissa was in a sky-blue slip dress that matched her eyes, sipping a glass of white wine and talking to Elena and Rachael. Her hair was down in the back and pinned up on the sides and she looked so good he could have eaten her up with a spoon. Then he noticed her usual smile was gone. She looked devastated.

Nash looked around for any strange assholes wearing tennis shoes that could lift a mortgage. Fuck pummeling him verbally; if that son of a bitch hurt her...

No one there fit that description. Nothing but friendlies as far as the eye could see.

"Hey, Nash." Camden walked up next to him, a bottle of beer in each hand. He handed one to him.

"Thanks, brother." He popped the top and took a swig. Now all three women looked upset—Elena and Rachael looked fit to be tied and Elissa was even sadder. Nash tipped the neck of his beer bottle toward the trio. "What gives?"

Camden grunted and shook his head like a bear with a hornet buzzing around it. "Elena's been in a mood all day because Elissa's latest douchebag went and dumped her right before they were supposed to go on this big trip."

Nash's heart sank. By the looks of it, she really did care about the guy. "So she's heartbroken over him."

"Over him? Oh, hell no." Camden took a swing. "She's heartbroken because now she can't go to Hawaii. She's been planning this..."

Camden's words faded into Nash's peripheral. *Hawaii. Shit. Well, here goes nothing.*

Before he realized what he was doing, Nash marched over to Elissa. She looked up, surprised, and her eyes locked onto his as her cheeks turned pink.

He poured the Southern all over his voice. "Howdy, Elissa. Heard you might need someone to accompany you to Hawaii. I'm on leave from Watchdog right now and would love to take you."

She continued to stare at him, those big blues widening as she blinked rapidly. She licked her perfect seashell-pink lips and said, "No."

"No?"

Elissa grinned. "I mean, thank you, really, but you can't."

"What do you mean I can't?" He'd reined his accent back in except it had slipped out on that last word, turning 'can't' to caint.' God, he was an idiot who needed to shut up right now. He knew she was out of his league so what had possessed him to continue to humiliate himself in front of all his friends by demanding an answer he already knew? Elissa didn't think he was good enough, simple as that.

Elissa took a half-step back and he realized his tone had been too harsh. And then she smiled and she was sunshine in a blue dress. "Really, it is so sweet of you to offer. You can't because *no one* can. It's over. Brett was the only one who could take me because we were signed up as partners for the race. *And* he has a racing kayak, which, let me tell you, are not cheap. I never dreamed I'd have a chance to go until he said I did." Her sunshine went behind a cloud. "I've been training with him now for months and he just told me that I wasn't progressing to the level of a winner." She paused, more storm clouds gathering in her eyes. "He only wants to be around winners, so he's talked the officials into letting him dump me and partnering with...someone else." She didn't need to say it was another woman—shame was written all over her face as she looked down.

"Then he surely made a mistake," Nash said. "Dumb son of a bitch Sneakerhead."

Her head snapped back up, eyes wide. "Wait, what did you just say?" A smile flickered across her lips.

"You heard me, sugar. Ol' Sneakerhead's spending too

much time in his closet playing with his shoes to know when a winner is standing right in front of him. Must be the fumes coming off the soles."

That got him a laugh. And not a cute little polite chuckle, either, but a laugh that made Elissa bend at the waist and spill the rest of her wine on his boot.

"Oh, shit!" She straightened up and placed her hand on his forearm. "I—" She stopped and looked at her hand as he felt an almost electrical throb where they touched. She quickly let go and stuttered, "I—I'm so sorry, that was dumb."

"No harm done." Nash tried to wave off a server who was already approaching with a towel. "Good thing I left my...let's see, Billy-Ogle three-sixty R-seven kicks at home."

She snickered. "Your what?"

"My fancy tennis shoes, of course. Don't that sound right?" He winked and was satisfied when the blush in her cheeks spread down across her chest. "You hit those bad boys with wine and whoo-whee, they just sorta disintegrate like an expired condom. Matter of fact, I think that's what they're made of."

Now he had her snorting. Looking mortified, she covered her face and grabbed the towel right out of the server's hand. As she bent to wipe at his shoe, Nash wrapped his hand around her upper arm to stop her. He was impressed by the hard muscle under his fingertips. She'd taken her workouts seriously.

"Stop. You're a guest tonight, sugar." He thanked the server as he took the towel and the empty glass from her hands and handed them back to the man. He didn't give a damn about the wine on his boot—that old thing had seen way worse than that. "You're the prettiest guest here, I may add."

"Oh, stop," she said, waving him off now as she looked

away. Great, along with making her spill her drink he'd managed to annoy her. He'd always used his humor to break the ice, but maybe he'd gone too far with the joke. *Smooth, Nash.*

Music started playing over speakers on the patio. She looked around, only to notice what he'd already observed— their friends had quietly retreated the minute he'd approached her. She looked even more nervous now, realizing she was alone with him. She was obviously trying to figure out how to blow him off without creating too much of a scene.

She surprised him when she laid her hand on his arm again. "Before you go find a woman of your actual caliber, would you mind dancing with me?"

My actual caliber? Ouch. "You don't need to do me any favors, shug." The words were out of his mouth before he registered her expression. Pure hurt.

"Never mind then," she mumbled. She turned and practically sprinted into the house. He started after her hoping to clear up, well, whatever this misunderstanding was, when Camden and Elena caught his eye. Camden looked confused while Elena shot Nash a look of pure pissed-off before dashing after Elissa. Nash changed course and headed for Camden.

"Brother, I suck at whatever is going on right now and y'all look fit to be tied. Gimme a status report."

Camden shook his head. "Did you get mad at Elissa for spilling her drink just now?"

"What? Hell no!"

"Well, that's the optics from here and Elena is *pissed*."

"No, that's not what happened. I gotta set this right." Nash started after the women and Camden grabbed his arm.

"Just stay here for now."

"But I—"

Camden tightened his grip. "Brother, I'm preventing you from stepping on a landmine. Trust me, stay here."

"But—"

"Landmine. Ambush. Not-so-friendly-fire. Am I making myself clear?"

Nash growled.

"Excellent. Now tell me what did actually happen and maybe I can help later once Elena's calmed down."

"Once *she's* calmed down? What about Elissa?"

Camden laughed. "Man, have you *met* women?" He took a swig of his beer. "It's all about tapping into the network the right way. I can't talk to Elissa and you sure as hell can't. So, I talk to you and get your side, then I tell Elena that you aren't a total bastard and the word gets passed on to Elissa once the fire's out." He shook his head. "You must not have grown up with sisters."

Nashville bit the insides of his cheeks and let that one go.

Camden looked up and Nash followed his gaze to see Rachael now scurrying up the patio steps and into the house. "See? Right there, I saved you from an ambush."

"I don't have time for your network thingamajig. I'm going in." Once again, Nash broke away from Camden.

And practically smacked right into Jake.

"Whoa, partner. Not sure what's up but my wife is not happy and I read your name in a text over her shoulder."

"It's a big misunderstanding...I think...but I can clear it up if y'all will just let me by." He tried to jog around Jake who blocked him.

Jake looked at Camden. "Why does Nash want to go on a suicide mission?"

Camden shrugged. "Beats me. I explained the network but he insists."

Jake crossed his arms and nodded sagely. "The network."

He nudged Nashville with his elbow. "Being a computer guy, I thought you'd understand the network."

"Elissa's not a computer to be hacked. She's a woman." *A smokin' hot, smart, strong, gorgeous woman* he added to himself. But what was the point of telling his friends he felt that way? As it was, they were treating him like a joke. "I like her. She's friends with y'all's women and she's a sweet gal. I know I'm not her type so I'm not even gonna try going there, so she's got nothing to worry about. That's all I'm trying to say."

Jake and Camden exchanged looks.

"What?" Now Nash was getting angry at them.

"She's not really your type, either," Camden said.

Nash put up his hands. "Okay. Message received loud and clear. I will stay out of her way."

Camden frowned. "It's not that, brother. It's just that you tend to..." he trailed off.

"Tend to what?"

Camden looked uncomfortable. "The women you date? They aren't always...they don't—"

Jake broke in. "What he's trying to say is that Elissa has a lot more going on upstairs than your usual arm candy, and that we've never seen you date someone for more than a few weeks."

"And...we don't want to see her hurt," Camden added.

So, there it was. Proof positive that his teammates thought he wasn't good enough for her, either. He'd already gotten the vibe from Psychic on their last assignment that he was considered less than intelligent, so hey, this just confirmed it.

Or worse—was that what they heard on the damn *network*? Is that what Elissa told them in the hopes they'd pass it on?

Only one way to find out.

"I'm not going to play y'all's stupid network game," he said as he headed into the house. Reggie broke away from the pack of Watchdog canines and bolted toward him, the perfect wingman. Nash quickly found the trio of women—now joined by Jordan, so make that a quartet—huddled together. Their heads snapped up and their eyes tracked him like heat-seeking missiles.

"Pardon me, but I'd like to say something." He focused on Elissa and let the other women fade into the background. "You and I, I think we had a misunderstanding outside just now. I would love a chance to start over from where you asked me to dance. I think if you gave me one dance, I could prove to you that I'm worth your time."

Elissa frowned. "*You* prove to *me*? But I—"

Nashville's phone decided it was the perfect time to interrupt, and not just with any call, but one from the most important woman in his life. He closed his eyes and sighed. "I need to take this." He pulled out his phone and hit talk. "Hey."

He was met with loud sobbing. "I'm...can you come over right now? I need you."

Great. Perfect.

"Yeah," he said as he watched Elissa's face fall. "I'll be right there." He hung up and realized he was deep in enemy territory. The women eyed him like a pride of lionesses just waiting for him to bolt.

Fuck it.

He grabbed Elissa's hand. "We're not done. I've got something I need to take care of tonight, but tomorrow, I'm calling you." He turned on his heel and strode to the door.

"Wait," Elissa shouted behind him.

He turned. "What?"

She waved her cell phone. "Number?"

Oh. Yeah. Dumbass.

Nash jogged back to her, tapped his phone against hers, and felt the withering power of her friends' stares.

He was glad he had Reggie at his side as he left; he was pretty sure his four-legged wingman was the only thing standing between him and certain evisceration.

THREE

The next morning came too soon. Elissa rolled over away from the sunlight peeking from behind her blackout shades and buried her face in her pillow. She'd tossed and turned all night after coming home from the party. And what hella-fun that was after Nash had left. All she'd heard was a woman sobbing over the phone and asking him to come over immediately. Was she a girlfriend who he'd conveniently forgotten about? Elissa didn't want to think that about Nashville. He was a flirt, but he seemed like a nice guy who wouldn't do that, one who would respect a woman. Though considering what had just happened to her with Brett, maybe there was no such thing as a nice guy.

Something had awakened her. She realized it was her phone vibrating in the bed beside her. Normally, she didn't take her phone to bed with her, but she'd hoped that she misunderstood what was going on with the phone call and that Nashville would call her after whatever emergency he'd had but the call never came. She grabbed her phone hoping that he was finally getting back to her.

Great. She realized it was her mom after she hit the talk button. *No way out, but through* she thought to herself.

"Hey, Mom, what's up?" She tried to keep her voice as chipper as possible, especially since she realized it was already eleven o'clock in the morning and she should have been up hours ago. Her mom had undoubtedly been up for several hours, having gone for her morning meditation walk and then eaten a healthy breakfast with her father afterward. There was a good chance she'd already checked in with Elissa's siblings and probably gotten the good news that one of them had won yet another award or registered another patent. Maybe Tamara was now the head of the political science department at Stanford.

And, what could Elissa tell her mother? Not much, except that she'd been dumped at a party after being dumped by her pseudo boyfriend, and that she was no longer even going to Maui to participate in the triathlon. She vaguely remembered she'd set up a bot to pick at the mysterious server the night before. Well, she'd check it after the phone call.

"Hello, sweetheart. How are you this morning? I was just calling to check in and see what's new." Her mother's tone of voice suggested that she really wasn't expecting much from Elissa.

"I'm great, Mom. Nothing really new here." She didn't want to talk about Brett right now.

"Well, I have good news. I just booked a room for us in Maui for your race."

Elissa blinked rapidly. "Wait. You and Dad are coming to Maui?"

"Yes!"

"To see...me?"

Her mother laughed. "Well, of course."

Elissa flopped back on her pillows. Of all the times her

parents took an interest in what she was doing, they'd have to pick the one event she'd been kicked out of. She debated coming up with some sort of excuse later for dropping out of the race. But then it would look like just one more thing Elissa had given up on. It was that or telling her mom that Brett had dumped her, which had its own flavor of embarrassment and shame. She decided the best course of action was to let her know now; it would save her trouble down the line.

"That's great, Mom, I'm so happy you decided to do that. Except that, um, Brett is partnering up with someone else for the Maui Challenge."

After a pause, her mother said, "So, he's left you?"

Wow. "*Left* me? It's not like we were living together."

"But he's not taking you to that race-thing."

Elissa rolled her eyes. "The Maui Challenge."

"Yes, that. Your father and I like Brett. We were looking forward to seeing you two in Maui. I guess I can cancel without too much trouble." The wistfulness and disappointment in her voice made it sound like Brett had called off a long engagement.

She gritted her teeth. "Really? Why do you like him?" Her parents had only met Brett once, on a trip down from their home in San Francisco for a conference in Los Angeles. They'd carved out an evening to see Elissa and she'd brought Brett along to dinner at Delia's restaurant. Her parents and Brett had spent so much time trying to impress each other, Elissa had gotten terminally bored and finally sneaked off to the kitchen to share a bottle of Delia's wife's homemade hard cider with Elena and Delia. It was the best part of the night.

"Well," her mother started in a bright voice as if she were bragging about her own son, not the man who dumped her daughter. "Brett's very successful. And he's had a positive influence on your life. He's motivated you to…" Her mother's voice trailed off.

"To what?" Elissa asked.

"Well, to make a mark, even if it's just in athletics."

Elissa could practically hear her eyeballs click as she blinked. But before she could end the conversation with some sort of excuse—the neighbor's cat is on fire. The houseplants are screaming. A meteorite just hit the kitchen—her mom changed the subject.

"Are you still with that company, that media place or whatever?"

Elissa suppressed a sigh. "Yeah, I am. I haven't really had a chance to look around for anything new—"

Her mother cut her off. "Oh, you mean you're looking for another job *again?*"

Oh good, more judgment. Just what I need this morning. "Yeah, It's just not the same since Elena left. It's no fun and I really despise one of the management people there." That was an understatement. Julia made life at work hell with her passive-aggressiveness. She'd lost her favorite target—Elena—and decided to double her efforts at making Elissa miserable.

"Honey, if you leave jobs for any little reason you're never going to advance in any career."

"Mom, this isn't really a career for me. Their IT department is actually really boring, Though it is fun to occasionally catch a glimpse of our clients. The other day I saw that actor from—"

Her mother cut her off again. "Sweetheart, I think you're focusing on all the wrong things. Maybe if you focused on your job instead of seeing who's coming in and out the door, you might find a little more satisfaction in it."

Elissa had had this argument so many times. She really didn't have the spoons for it this morning. "Yeah, I'm sure you're right. I'll just keep on at my freaking boring go-nowhere job for the rest of my life. Sound good?"

"Now, you're sounding a little bit grouchy. I don't think you've had your breakfast yet, have you? You know, you really should start out each day with some exercise, some meditation, and then you need to eat properly."

Yay! An out. "Yeah, you're right, I haven't eaten breakfast yet. Maybe I should go and do that right now, huh?"

"Is this your way of avoiding this conversation?"

Yes, absolutely. "Of course not. I'm simply following your wonderful advice, Mom."

"Elissa, darling, I'm just trying to look out for you."

"Look, I know I'm not like my brothers and sisters, and that I'm a huge disappointment to you right now."

Her mother gasped. "I have never in my life said anything like that, Elissa. And that's not how any of us feel."

"Well, that's kinda how I'm taking it." Before her mom could continue the argument, Elissa added, "I really need to get going. I actually do have things on the agenda today, even though it's a weekend. I'll talk to you later, okay?"

"Well, since Maui is off, your dad and I would still love to see you, dear. Please stop by sometime."

"Los Angeles isn't exactly around the corner from San Francisco, Mom. And, I do have a job and a life and everything else that prevents me from just picking up and going to see you. How am I ever supposed to be getting ahead if I'm constantly taking vacations?" As soon as the snarky words were out of her mouth, she regretted them. But today left her feeling brittle and snappish. She'd try and clear things up with her mom later. Maybe after she'd had breakfast and checked on the progress of her program. "I'm sorry, that came out harsh, and I didn't mean it."

"I'm just going to let you do your thing now, okay?" Her mother sounded hurt.

"Mom—"

"It's alright, sweetheart, I understand." And then her mom hung up on her.

Elissa pounded her pillow. She sucked at things like this. It felt like she could never say the right thing to her family and that they would never understand her. Some days, she wondered if she'd been adopted into this group of eggheads who seemed to achieve absolutely everything that they set out to do. She swore her oldest sister, Katheryn, knew exactly how to plan out her life from preschool on. She'd always gotten the best grades, she'd always been invited to all the right parties, she always met the right people. And of course, she went to the right college and got the right degree in bioengineering. Not only that, but while she was there, she landed the right man and now she had two adorable children. The same went for her brother, Stefan, the world-renowned surgeon who still found time to vacation in Hawaii every year with his lovely wife and their twin sons. And of course, her other sister, Tamara, ruled the poly-sci department at one of the most prestigious schools in the US, but still managed to raise three kids with her husband the architect.

It wasn't that Elissa was necessarily jealous. She didn't want that kind of life at all. And she adored her nieces and nephews, all Seven Dwarfs as she called them—but not around their parents. It's just that every time Elissa thought she found the thing she wanted to do and that she was ready to settle in, she'd start to get bored once she started at it. And once she was bored, her attention completely snapped and she couldn't help but look around for the next bright shiny thing to pursue.

The same went for men. They all seemed alike to her

once she got to know them—career-driven, self-absorbed, looking for a woman who was quiet and pretty to look at. If she didn't dump them first they either ghosted her, or at best sent passive-aggressive texts suggesting she might want to be a little less boisterous or outspoken with the next guy and maybe not talk so much about surfing, kayaking, or hacking.

Speaking of that, she had a program to check on. Elissa got out of bed and threw on a robe. She opened her curtains to let the morning light in. It was another beautiful day in Los Angeles. Well, at least weather-wise. Seeing so much sun all the time was a huge change from having grown up in San Francisco, where the fog seemed to be ever-present and summer lasted only a few days.

Elissa went into her office to check her computer. As soon as she got to the door, she could already hear the fans blowing like crazy, trying to cool her computer down. She sprinted the last few steps to make sure that she hadn't been invaded by a virus or that her computer wasn't melting down. She knew there were viruses that could cause a computer to actually melt and that could be deployed as defensive measures. She hoped she hadn't stumbled onto one as it was trying to break into the Outyard server.

She hit a key on her computer to wake up the screen. And what she found surprised her.

"Holy shit! This is the farthest I've ever gotten!"

A smile spread across Elissa's face, and she thought she must look pretty goofy right now. While she hadn't completely hacked the server—she hadn't really expected to— she managed to hack her way into a partition that had never been breached before. Now she was more convinced than ever that this must be some sort of CIA computer. She worried a little bit that maybe they were trying to catch black hat hackers and that she was going right into a trap. But they so often recruited this way as well.

"Do I really want a hacker job with the CIA though?" Because that's what this might turn into. Well, it would be better than her current job. And, it might even be interesting enough to keep her attention for more than six months.

Yeah. Yeah, she did.

Elissa checked her Surfboi65 email, and sure enough, there was a message from Ulysses22. She opened the email and read:

D ude, *your voodoo is brilliant. Let me know how far you get with this. In the meantime, I'm going to make a few little tweaks here and there and see where I get. High five, bro. Will share info but I'm still gonna beat you to the prize.*

E lissa never corrected anyone when they assumed she was a guy. It made things easier, kept the trolls away who would otherwise hit on her constantly and mercilessly. For all she knew, Ulysses22 was a complete creep and once he figured out that she was a woman, would never leave her alone. Elissa emailed back:

B *etween you and me, I made it into a new partition!*

S he deleted the exclamation point, thinking that it made her sound too girly.

. . .

I made it into a new partition, bro. I really think that we're both on to something here. Feel like shit for not sharing it with the others, but comes a time when you just have to run ahead of the pack. Am I right? That's what separates the sigmas from the alphas.

She added that last line just to be sure that Ulysses22 continued to think she was a dude. Now that she was going to be working with him exclusively to break into Outyard, she wanted nothing to be misconstrued between the two of them. That was her mistake with Brett. She should have kept things absolutely professional. She had a feeling the asshole probably found somebody way cuter than her who would put out and decided to dump her for that.

She copied the updated code she'd used the night before into the email to Ulysses22 and added a few screenshots of the partition she'd hacked into. Then she signed off, made a few tweaks to the program, and she started it running again after her fans stopped cooling down her computer. She went over and turned on the extra AC wall unit she'd installed just to make sure the room stayed even cooler than the rest of her apartment.

Finished, she headed toward the kitchen for some nice, sugary cereal. She had long ago stopped kidding herself that she only kept it around for the Seven Dwarves. If that were true, she wouldn't be buying a box every single week even when she wasn't going to be seeing any of her nieces or nephews. And Elena never ever let Tina have any sugary cereal. She made that clear whenever Elissa invited Tina for a sleepover at her apartment, and Elissa never wanted to put Tina in a position where she'd have to lie to her parents. The little girl had already been traumatized once from having to keep a secret from them. Elissa wasn't about to put her in the same position, even over something as innocuous as cereal.

Elissa had just added milk to the bowl when her cell phone rang. *Crap.* Now it was going to get all soggy unless she decided to ignore the call. It was probably one of her sisters or her brother calling anyway, having talked to her mom and sent like a flying monkey to speak to her. *Scold* her, was more like it. Since she was the baby of the family, she often felt like she had several parents, not just two. Out of all of them, Stefan was the worst about it.

She let the call go to voicemail and enjoyed her bowl of pure, unadulterated hedonism. After she picked up the bowl and tilted the last of the milk into her mouth, she checked her phone.

The name at the top of the screen was Nashville.

She debated hitting the callback button. The butterflies in her stomach were definitely trying to sabotage her. Elena, Rachael, even Jordan warned her last night that she should be careful, that Nashville was a love 'em and leave 'em type of guy and she was next on the list.

"How do you know?" she asked them.

Rachael answered. "He's using the trouser mouse accent. It only comes out if he's hoping to drop trow."

"What? Shit, he's used that on me every time we've talked." She grinned, unable to help herself. "To think, I could have gotten laid a long time ago."

Elena rolled her eyes and put her arm around Elissa. "You're still stinging from Brett. Go easy, chica."

Jordan held up her hand. "I've got to disagree. Thinking about everything you guys said to each other with the dance, I think it's a big misunderstanding." She smiled as she looked at the floor. "Happens to me all the time, and God knows, Elliot and I have had our share. I like Nash, especially after I got to know him while he was guarding me with Elliot." She glanced up at Elissa then away. "I think he's worth a chance."

A loud knocking at her door startled Elissa out of her thoughts. She brought up her front door camera on her phone.

Seriously?

There stood Mr. Trouser Mouse Accent himself in the flesh, big as life and twice as smokin' in his cowboy hat. He looked concerned as he shifted his weight from one foot to the other. Nashville looked around the hallway and then above the door where he spotted the camera—something no one ever did. He smiled and tipped his hat, then stopped fidgeting.

Hot, cocky bastard. Just her type and just the type she needed to avoid from now on. *Who comes to a woman's apartment unannounced?* But she couldn't very well leave him standing at her door. She pulled her silk kimono around her, ran a hand through her messy hair, and marched to the door. She opened it without a word.

"Elissa." To his credit, his eyes barely flicked down from hers before snapping right back. "Hope I didn't wake you up." His accent was molasses-thick this morning. Wait, make that early afternoon now.

"No, you didn't. I had things to do." She gripped her robe as she felt her face flush. "In my apartment. Not outside. I do busy things in my apartment." *Wow. Way to defend yourself.*

"Of course you did." Did he sound sheepish? "I wanted to apologize for last night, but you didn't pick up your phone. I guess I shoulda waited."

"No, no, not at all. Come on in." *Oh, God, now he's going to think I routinely let strange guys into my apartment in nothing but a nightie and a silk robe.* She weighed the consequences of letting him in versus slamming the door in his face and hiding in a corner in shame all weekend and figured he'd camp out on her doorstep if she did that. So Elissa stepped back to give him room to pass her.

He took his hat off as he stepped into her apartment. "I like that you have a security camera," Nashville said as he glanced around her front room.

"Yeah, I wouldn't answer the door in a robe without one." To her surprise, Nashville burst out laughing. "What?"

"Oh, shug, I just think you're a riot, that's all."

Elissa bit her lip. "Mind if I go slip into something less comfortable?" He caught her rolling her eyes. "Now I'm throwing stale lines at you. I'll be lucky if you're still here when I come back out of the bedroom."

Nashville grinned that slow, cocky grin that made chills gallop up her spine. He handed her his cowboy hat. "Here. Take this with you. I couldn't possibly leave without my hat, could I?"

"Oh, I don't know. I've had guys practically chew their arm off to leave me."

He frowned and crossed his arms.

"Smile, it's a joke."

"Sugar, nothing that puts you down is a joke to me."

Okay, knees going weak in three...two...one. "I'll be right back," she mumbled as she walked backward toward her bedroom. She practically slammed it shut and pressed her back against it. Her heart pounded as she gripped his hat and tried to catch her breath. What was it about Nashville that turned her into jelly?

What isn't *there about him that turns me into jelly?* Cute accent, swagger, body to die for, polite—well, until last night—and smart. She raised his hat to her nose and inhaled—leather, salt, pine, Nash.

You deserve more than good enough. His words stuck in her head.

Yeah, until you get to know me.

Elissa's eyes went wide. While she was hyperventilating in her room, Nashville had full access to the rest of her apartment. A perfect opportunity to judge her.

What if he sees my...

She kicked herself into high gear, grabbed a bra and panties, and threw on a jersey over a pair of cut-offs. Not her most sophisticated outfit, but at least now she was wearing actual underwear. She pulled her long blond hair back into a ponytail and grabbed a pink scrunchie. No time for make-up. She dashed back out of the bedroom just in time to watch him heading straight toward the last thing she wanted him to inspect.

FOUR

Well, I surely stepped in it again.

Elissa couldn't get away from him fast enough; hell, she didn't even feel safe enough to turn her back on him as she skedaddled to her bedroom. He shouldn't have come. When she didn't answer his call, he should've taken that as a hint that Elissa didn't want anything to do with him. But like the idiot he was, he'd talked Camden into giving him her address and come straight over.

He blamed his foggy, sleep-deprived brain on his bad choice. He'd been up most of the night offering comfort while his thoughts pored over every second from the party, everything he could've said or done differently that would've resulted in Elissa dancing in his arms instead of running into the house. Maybe the guys were right—maybe he was better off admiring Elissa from afar. Though, her blushes whenever he looked at her told him a different story.

Nash looked around the room to get a sense of her. The apartment had an open-floor plan with a small kitchen off the great room. Sunlight bathed the apartment as it poured in through a large skylight and sliding-glass doors opening onto a balcony. Her white walls amplified the light, making him feel like he was inside a large white seashell. On the walls hung large prints of oceanscapes. One depicted a surfer just entering a tube. Two surfboards leaned against the wall next to it. Beneath a wall-mounted screen was a credenza sporting several game consoles and a stack of games. If he didn't know she was a computer nerd already, that gave her away. Across the room was a bookcase packed full of colorful spines. Nash smiled. There was no better way to get into someone's head than to check out what they liked to read. He started for the bookcase when he heard Elissa's hurried footsteps behind him.

"Where's Reggie?" she asked. She sounded out of breath.

He stopped, turned, and tried not to stare like a rude monkey. Elissa looked incredibly sexy in her cut-offs and a loose jersey, her blond hair pulled back and her bangs spilling over her forehead. Her legs just did not end. Her ocean-blue eyes stared at him as if she'd caught Nash exploring her underwear drawer. She smiled but it looked a little forced, as if she were trying too hard to look relaxed.

Nash almost told her he'd dropped Reg off at Watchdog because he'd read online that her building didn't allow large dogs. *Way to sound like a real creeper.*

"Reg was lonely for better company than me, so I took him to Watchdog. Kyle's in town training his replacement for kennel master and I swear, that dog loves him more than he loves me."

Elissa's smile widened into something that looked more genuine. "Aw, don't say that! He's a sweet pooch. I'm sure he adores you the most."

"He adores any hand that feeds him," Nash answered.

"No way. I've seen him go after bad people and I doubt he'd show mercy over a dog biscuit."

Nash chuckled. "True, that. He's a pro."

Silence grew as they gazed at each other. Then Elissa's eyes widened again and she slapped her forehead. "Oh, I'm a terrible hostess. I haven't offered you anything to eat or drink." She made a beeline for the kitchen.

"You're fine, sugar. I'm a terrible guest for showing up at your doorstep without an invite."

Elissa rounded the counter dividing the kitchen from the rest of the apartment. "Not at all. When friends drop by unannounced it means they know they're welcome here."

Nash flinched inwardly. *Friends.* He caught Elissa's grimace just before she turned toward the fridge. What did that mean? That he wasn't actually welcome, but she was being polite? This whole thing was a mistake.

Still, he found himself walking toward the kitchen, admiring Elissa's backside as she explored the fridge.

"I have water, lemonade, some energy drinks. Um, Mountain Dew."

"The beverage of champions," Nash said.

"Spoken like a true gamer," Elissa answered with a laugh. She glanced over her shoulder as he reached the counter. Her smile dazzled him. "Do you want some?"

He bit back his gut response of *I've wanted some since laying eyes on you* as he rested his elbows on the counter. "I only indulge in the Dew when I'm playing."

"Yeah, me too. Wanna play?"

God, do I. She was not making this easy, especially when she flinched and blushed at her own double-entendre. Was she sending mixed signals or was he just too eager to read what he wanted into them? Dammit, if she was just any woman at a bar, some base bunny looking to score another notch in her bedpost, he'd be all over her like sawmill gravy on a biscuit.

But this was Elissa. She wasn't looking for that, and even if she were, she deserved much better. He remembered her voice when she was talking to Elena. The tone that said she didn't think she was worth a man's full attention and affection. It was as if she'd expected Sneakerhead to dump her, and that prophesy sure fulfilled itself, didn't it?

Had he been reading her wrong all this time? Did she think *he* was too good for *her*?

Jesus wept. No man on earth was good enough for Elissa as far as he was concerned. But Nash would do his damndest to try.

And that started with dropping the molasses out of his voice. The honey-trap accent he used on the bunnies was not good enough for her.

"God's truth, I'd like to talk about last night," he said.

The way she stiffened let him know she'd registered the change in tone. She grabbed two bottles of water and set them on the counter between them. Gone was the aura of bubbly effervescence that constantly surrounded her and he wondered if that was *her* 'honey-trap' style or something else.

"Okay," she said quietly. She took a deep breath and twisted the top off her bottle.

"Okay." Nash nodded. "I went into that party with a great deal of trepidation weighing on my heart. I was both hoping and dreading to see you there."

She tilted her head. "Why? I don't understand. We barely know each other." Her eyes widened. "Unless you think I want to get to know you better."

Well, that smarted. He twisted the cap off his water bottle and took a swig. At least he knew where he stood now. "Elissa, sugar, I think the world of you. Enough that we can keep this in the friendzone if that's what you want."

She nodded. "That's probably for the best, considering that phone call."

Nash tilted his head. "Phone call?"

"The one you got last night at the party that made you leave."

Oh. Did she think that he should have ignored something that important and stayed there with her? If so, this wasn't going to work out after all, not even at a friends-level.

He watched her swallow deliberately. "Your...girlfriend?" she added.

"My who what now?"

Elissa frowned. "The woman crying on the phone and asking you to come over."

"Oh. Oh! No, no, sugar." He smiled as his heart dropped a metric ton of weight, despite the sad reason for the call. Elissa had heard the crying over the phone, of course. And of course she would assume... "That's no girlfriend, that's my mama."

"Your...mom?" She covered her mouth as her cheeks flooded with pink. "God, I'm an idiot. I thought...never mind what I thought. It's not very nice. Is your mom all right?"

A boulder landed in Nash's stomach. "You thought I was at a party trying to hit on a woman while my girlfriend was back home crying over me."

Elissa dropped her head to the counter. Her ponytail splayed out over her head and across the countertop. "That makes me sound like a complete jerk, assuming something like that. And here you were, going off to help your mom. Jeeze, I'm so sorry," she said, her voice muffled.

Nash resisted the urge to run his fingers through her ponytail. "Shug, I think that might be more of a reflection on how you've been treated by other men. If they've all been like Ol' Sneakerhead, then you'd play a fool if you didn't suspect I already had a girlfriend, 'specially after that call." His desire to comfort her got the better of him and he trailed his fingers through her long, soft hair.

Instead of straightening up, Elissa turned her head to the side, pressing her cheek against the countertop as he continued to stroke her hair. "You're better than that though, and I know it. You didn't deserve my snap judgment. I really am sorry."

"I don't need an apology, but I'll accept it if it makes you feel better."

"It does. Thank you." She closed her eyes and sighed as he continued stroking her hair. Feeling brave, Nash hooked his fingers under her scrunchie and pulled it through her hair. Blond waves cascaded across the counter. He twined a lock around his fingers. Good Lord in heaven, she really was lovely. He'd wanted to play with her hair for so long.

Elissa's eyes opened wide and she lifted her head. Her hair slipped through his fingers. "Your mom, is she okay? What was wrong?"

And here it was, the thing he didn't want to talk about. "She's fine, shug. It's something that happened a while back, and she still gets upset over it from time to time." He swallowed the lump in his throat and pushed down his own latent grief. "When she gets like that, I just go and sit a spell with her and she feels better." His Tennessee accent pushed up through the flat Midwestern one he'd worked so hard to cultivate, the way it did whenever he talked about his family.

Elissa reached across the counter and rested her hand over his. No tingles this time, just warmth from someone who cared. "Do you want to talk about it?"

"Naw, shug. Not today." He turned his hand palm up and enlaced his fingers with hers. She rewarded him with a sweet half-smile as she looked at their hands. "Maybe another time."

Her blue eyes met his. "I'm going to hold you to that.

Being around you former military guys, I know that you're experts at bottling stuff up when you should talk through it instead."

Nash chuckled and shook his head. "I'm fine. Today, I'm fixing to figure *you* out."

Elissa rolled her eyes. "What's to figure out? I'm a simple surfer girl who's still trying to decide what she wants to be when she grows up. *If* she grows up." She mumbled the last bit under her breath.

"What's that supposed to mean?"

Elissa shook her head. "I just have a lot to live up to is all, and so far, I'm not."

"Live up to?"

She took a deep breath and blew it out. "I come from a family of overachievers and I'm the dumb one."

Anger uncoiled in Nash's stomach. Elissa must have seen it on his face because she quickly added, "My assessment, not theirs."

"Don't ever call yourself dumb, you hear? I can't believe all the things you know. You went to culinary school—"

"And dropped out."

"—you said you had paramedic experience—"

"Something else I walked away from."

"—you work in IT—"

"Okay, I'm still there, but I'm looking for the next thing."

"—and you have the discipline and strength to qualify for a big ol' triathlon thing in Hawaii—"

"Which is not happening now because I didn't make the grade in the end."

"—and those are just the things I know about you. I'm betting there's plenty more to learn." Nash shook his head, absolutely flummoxed. How could she not see how amazing she was? *By being surrounded by people who tell her she isn't, that's how.* "You made the grade, darlin'. Sneakerhead Brett's an idiot. I can only imagine how much work you put into qualifying. You must have trained at the gym all the time you weren't at work."

"Not *all* the time. I'm very well-rounded." Elissa pulled her hand back from his and counted off on her fingers. "I surf, I kayak, I snorkel, I dive, I paraglide, I sail. As long as it involves getting wet, I'm on it." Boom, her hand went to her mouth as her eyes got wide.

Nash laughed.

"I swear, I'm not trying to sound bad today," Elissa said through her fingers.

"You sure about that, shug?" Nash teased. "Because I gotta say, you are batting a thousand, lady."

"Must be the company," she said, her voice low and her gaze locked on his.

"Careful, or I might think you're flirting in earnest." Nash's tone matched hers.

"I might be," she purred.

He leaned across the counter and tucked a lock of hair behind her ear. She tilted her head to lean against his hand and he knew if he didn't pull his hand back he was a goner. When did they go from zero to sixty? She wasn't a woman he was picking up in a bar. As much as he wanted to sweep her up and carry her back down the hall to her bedroom, Elissa deserved more, deserved better. He grabbed his bottle of water and turned. Before she came out of her bedroom, he'd been intent on learning something about her. He walked toward the bookcase.

She sprinted ahead of him, her face turning a brighter shade of red with each step. She stopped and turned, blocking him from the case. "Where are you going?"

"To snoop on you, obviously." He peered over her head at the shelves. "Wait, are all those kids' books?"

Could she get any redder? "Yeah, guilty as charged. I do read grown-up books, too but I keep the kids' books out here in the bookcase so that when my nieces and nephews stay with me they can choose what they want and we can read them together. But honestly, that's an excuse. Truth is, I love kids' books. They always cheer me up."

Looking resigned, she led him the rest of the way to the bookcase. As they got closer, Nash could see that the books ranged from middle-school chapter books to picture books. *The Wizard of Oz* series, *The Secret Garden*, *The Giving Tree*, *Where the Sidewalk Ends*, *The Gashlycrumb Tinies*, *Sara Crewe*, *The Alligator and His Uncle Tooth*. Elissa ran her finger along the thin, colorful spines on a shelf of picture books until she found the one she wanted and tipped it out until she could pull it free. She handed it to him as she fought back a goofy smile. "See? Just look at the cover."

A cartoon stark-white fish floated in the air above a fish-bowl. "Lemony Snicket. Illustrations by Lisa Brown. *Goldfish Ghost*," he read. There was something off about the fish besides the color. Nash got it after a second and he snorted out a laugh. "It's floating upside-down."

Elissa grabbed his forearm as she lost it. "I know! I did the same thing you did and died laughing when I first saw it. Lisa Brown's a frikkin' genius to draw the ghost fish upside-down." She tilted her head, admiring the cover with a wistful look. "It's a good story, too—funny and comforting, especially if you're a little kid who just lost their pet goldfish. Or maybe even a family member." She glanced up at him.

Nash ignored the weight in her stare. He opened the book and flipped through the pages. He tried to read it, but with Elissa so near, the warmth of her hand on his arm sending electricity all along it, he couldn't even concentrate on a basic kids' story.

"You probably think I'm extra-immature now." Her tentative voice sounded dismissive, full of self-judgment under the lighthearted tone.

"Not at all." He closed the book and gave her his full attention. "I think it takes an extra-mature person to openly admit to what she likes, even if she thinks she'll be laughed at. Which, in this case, absolutely will not happen." He gave the book one last glance as he replaced it in the narrow gap on the shelf.

Her cheeks pinked further and she looked away from his face to the book. "I think it takes a lot of talent to write a good kids' book that isn't derivative. Elena's daughter Tina can see right through those. I take her along when I go book shopping because she's got great taste and she's a perfect excuse to browse the kids' section. I end up buying double copies of books that way, one for her and one for me, but it's totally worth it." She looked back up at him and grinned. "I call it her curator's fee." Her voice trailed off as she studied the look in his eyes.

He couldn't wait another second. He took her hand in his and pressed a kiss to her palm. Her eyes glazed in the sexiest way as she stood on tiptoe to meet his lips with hers. He pulled her in, wrapping his arms around her as she slid her palms up his chest to meet at the nape of his neck. God, he loved how she touched him there, stroking the tips of his hair until he shivered, his cock coming to full attention. He groaned into her mouth and she pressed harder against him, giving him exactly what he wanted, what he needed.

What he had no right to take. Yet.

Nash broke their kiss. Elissa kept her eyes closed and

licked her lips like she'd just tasted the sweetest thing in the world.

She blinked rapidly as she looked up at him. "Why'd we stop?"

"We stopped because I want to savor you. I don't want something quick and shallow, and that's where we're headed if I keep kissing you like that. Told you, darlin', I want to get to know you better." He ran his thumb over her cheek. "I'd hoped to take you out to lunch today, your choice."

"Oh." Elissa glanced down at herself. "I'll need another wardrobe change."

"Why? You look great."

She stepped away from him. "Whatever you say. Besides, I left your hat in the bedroom. I should get it."

"You should leave it so I have an excuse to come back for it." He winked. "After we know each other better."

She rolled her eyes and shook her head. She started to turn to head back to her bedroom when the first muffled strains of "Flight of the Valkyries" started playing from somewhere down the hall. Elissa gasped.

"I need to get that."

"Your phone?" Nash asked, then remembered he'd seen her phone on the kitchen counter.

"No, it's, um." Her head whipped back and forth between Nash and the hall and she groaned. "Oh, whatever. You said you wanted to get to know me, so here's your chance. Just don't judge."

"Judge? Shug, have I done that yet?" he asked as he followed her down the hall.

"Give it time." She opened a door into a spare bedroom she'd set up as an office. The first thing Nash noticed was that the room was at least ten degrees cooler than the rest of the apartment. Elissa crossed the room to her desk and the source of the music—her computer.

"Whoo-whee that's quite a rig you got there." And Nash would know—when he wasn't on bodyguard duty, he'd been one of Watchdog's IT guys before his hiatus, and that place did not skimp on the electronics. At a glance, Elissa's setup rivaled anything that Watchdog owned.

"Thanks, I built it myself." Already her voice sounded distracted as she sat down, turned off the sound, and studied the screen. "Ho-ly shit. We did it."

"So, what'd y'all break into?"

Elissa's head whipped around. "Before you call someone to arrest me, let me explain."

Nash pulled up a spare office chair and sat next to her. "I can't imagine you wearing a black hat, shug, so if I called for an arrest, they'd have to haul me in too for my hacking."

"Gray hat."

Nash raised his eyebrows. It wasn't the idea that she was a gray hat; his job at Watchdog required him to be one at times. The fact that she'd come right out and told him that the hacking she was doing wasn't entirely on the up-and-up shocked him. He'd assumed she was either freelancing as a white hat hacker or tasked with hacking into her own company's system to test for weaknesses—totally common and legal. But gray hats were a different story. They bent the rules and sometimes broke the law—though without malicious intent—breaking into computer systems without the owners' knowledge. Some did it as a calling card, finding holes in a system then alerting the company and offering to fix the hole for a fee or for a job in the security department.

Was that what Elissa was doing? He knew she was looking for another job. Maybe this was her way of finding one.

She cleared her throat but kept her eyes on the screen as she typed. "I've been working on this server now for the better part of a year. Others have been trying to hit it for longer than that. It's a mystery, an open challenge. No one knows who it belongs to or what's hiding in its sweet nougat center, but the voodoo protecting it is beyond top-notch. It took the early responders months just to get a name for the server —Outyard."

"Never heard of it."

"Not surprised. There's nothing concrete about it anywhere. Lots of rumors though. It's a CIA recruiting tool. It's a Russian recruiting tool. It's marketing for a new gaming company or a TV series that'll drop when the puzzle's solved. It's alien technology." She laughed. "That's my favorite one. E.T. hack home."

Lines of code filled the screen and Nash read it over Elissa's shoulder. "Impressive stuff. No—*real* impressive stuff." This was damn near Shakespeare-level coding. Elissa's fingers flew, but she wasn't typing fast enough for all the code to be appearing.

"Wait. Are you working with someone right now?"

"Yeah. Guy named Ulysses22."

The hair on the back of Nash's neck rose. "Tell me you know this guy."

"Don't be jelly." Clickety-clackety. Nash was barely in the room to her.

He gripped her upper arm. "Elissa, darlin'. I'm not jealous, I just don't want you tangled up with some troll."

"He's not a troll. And he thinks I'm a dude anyway. Now, let me finish. We're almost past the last firewall. I think. God knows. But I'm about to find out."

As concerned as he was, Nash couldn't help but admire Elissa's determined spirit. He found himself caught up in her excitement and in the code itself. She and this Ulysses22 were using some out-there voodoo, things he'd never think up. Totally unconventional, which was saying a lot. Her computer's fan was screaming, trying to keep up as the computer threatened to overheat. Nash jumped up, went to the AC unit in the window, and cranked it up all the way.

"Thanks." Her beaming smile was all the reward he needed. "We make a pretty good team."

"You're the one doing all the work." He leaned in again, watching the attacks and counterattacks. They had to be close considering the onslaught. "This ever happen before?"

"Nope. And if we don't get in, it's gonna brick my rig." Now she was biting her lower lip, her eyes narrowed, determined to keep her computer from turning into an expensive paperweight.

"Almost...oh my God!" Elissa pushed her office chair back from the desk and raised her arms over her head in victory. "We did it!"

She wheeled herself back to the desk. An open chat box on a different screen erupted with celebratory emojis from Ulysses22. She quickly responded with more of the same, then went back to the task of looting their prize.

"It's a video file. No, wait, a live camera." She turned to Nash, her eyes wide and unsure for the first time. "I'm almost afraid to look. What if it's...something bad?"

"Too late for that," Nash responded. He pointed at the screen.

Ulysses22 was already activating the camera.

FIVE

Elissa dragged a French fry through a smear of buffalo wing sauce. "I can't believe that's all it was, some stupid timeshare pitch. And of course because it's me, the place looks like it's somewhere in Hawaii. Nice of the universe to rub it in." She'd never felt so frustrated.

Nash sat across from her at a table on a rooftop bar with a view of the Pacific. The place was a little pricey but it did have a great view and the fries were cooked in duck fat, which Elissa thought made them the best in the world. After the letdown, she was in the mood to spoil herself a little.

Nash shook his head as he studied her face. "There's got to be more to it, shug."

Elissa's shoulders lifted and fell. "You saw the live cam. All it did was pan the scenery from a lanai, which, yeah, is absolutely gorgeous beachfront and garden."

"But that sign," he said before he shoved a wing in his mouth and then pulled out nothing but bones. The camera had stopped on a white sign with red letters nailed to a wall before panning back across the lanai and the ocean beyond it.

"What? The sign made it obvious it was a timeshare.

'Welcome to your destination, your dream, your turnkey to the future!' It's a vacation condo for rent."

Nash shook his head, his brow furrowed. "Can't just be that. There was no website, no phone number, no address on the sign. Why would you put an advertisement for a rental at the center of a near-impenetrable server and then not even provide a way to contact the owner?"

"Have you *met* computer nerds? We're sick, twisted misfits. Someone did it for a laugh, that's all. Joke's on me. And on Ulysses22. He blew that pop stand as quick as he could. Smart."

Nash blew out a breath. "Whole thing's not sitting right with me, I tell you what."

And the truth was, with Nash's hackles up, Elissa's rose with them. Or, maybe it was the weight of one more disappointment. She had to admit it, if only to herself; she'd been hoping for something like an eccentric billionaire giving away a treasure trove of cryptocurrency. No, even that wasn't true—though she wouldn't have been *that* disappointed to suddenly find herself a multi-millionaire, duh—what she hoped for in her heart of hearts was that she'd stumbled onto a secret recruiting site that wanted her for her top-notch skills. A job that would be exciting and fulfilling, that wouldn't have her looking for the next thing a week into it. A career that she could only allude to vaguely to her family because it was so top-secret and important.

Maybe then she'd feel like she measured up.

Okay, so aliens would have been cool, too.

Nash reached across the table and did that thing where he tucked her hair behind her ear. Such a simple gesture, and yet it sent shivers pinging all around her body as the barest edge of his finger brushed her cheek. All the times Brett touched her during training and then the kisses he gave her once they were kinda-sorta dating never made her feel like this, like her skin was a conduit for electricity. Nash's touch never failed to short-circuit her brain.

"Let's talk about something else. I can see you need some cheering up. I think our original plan was to get friendly," he said.

"Get *friendly?*" She looked around at the other patrons. "Right here? Well, okay." She pretended to sweep the dishes off the table and laughed when he roared.

"I mean, we've known each other a long time, but we haven't gotten to *know* each other." Nash's features softened. "I want to do that with you."

Wow. Breathe, Elissa. "So, how do you want to do it?" she asked.

"That's a loaded question."

"Not sorry."

Nash laughed. "It's a good idea though. How about twenty questions?"

She sat up straight. "Isn't that a nice way of saying interrogate each other?"

"Sugar, no." He laughed again. "This won't hurt a bit." He quirked an eyebrow and she giggled.

"All right. I'm game." Elissa folded her hands on the table. "Ask away."

Nash thought for a moment. "What's something that, no matter how many times you do it, you never get tired of it?"

Elissa burst out laughing. "*Now* who's asking the loaded questions?"

Nash raised his eyebrows as if to say, *who, me?* "You can answer it however you wish. Take it where you want."

Elissa grinned. "All right. Flying. I love it every single time. First time I ever flew, I was only three, so I didn't really appreciate it. I was too distracted by the flight attendant mixing up my drink order with the man next to me and that he didn't care. How can you not care that you're drinking cola and the kid next to you is stuck with your lemon-lime?"

Nash's expression turned mock-serious. "Very important stuff when you're three."

"Damn straight!" Elissa and Nash both laughed. "But the second time I ever flew, I was seventeen, which is the best age to do anything good because it stays with you." Her voice turned serious. "I had a window seat and I watched the ground drop until it looked like a patchwork quilt, and I thought of how many millions or maybe billions of people who've lived never got to fly or ever dreamed of flying, and here I was in the air, living out something impossible. I felt... euphoric. I remember looking around at all the people taking this miracle for granted and then I felt detached. Like, I couldn't understand how no one else felt the same way I did. I wondered if maybe they'd flown so many times they just forgot. So, I swore I'd never forget that euphoria or take it for granted. To this day, whenever I'm in an airplane I say to myself, *respect your takeoffs and your landings.* I take out my earbuds and I stare out the window and I really feel it, like I'm seventeen again. Every time."

Elissa's cheeks flushed as she wondered if Nash would think she was childish or corny. But when she met his eyes, all she saw was warmth mixed with a touch of wonder.

"That is one hell of an answer." He nodded. "Sure is."

"So, my turn? Let's see." She drummed her nails on the table. Now that she actually had Nash sitting across from her, she couldn't think of a single thing to ask him, at least nothing that would keep the mood light. There were plenty of things she wanted to know, like why his mom was so sad. And why he'd decided to take a break from Watchdog. But those topics were way too heavy to get into right now. "You know what?

I'm going to fire that question right back atcha, because it's such a good one. What do you never get tired of?"

"Easy. Music. What was the—"

"Uh-uh, no." Elissa waved the next question off. "You can't just give me a one-word answer and then expect me to tell you another story. What's your favorite music or song and why?"

"That's two questions, shug."

"Nope. Same question, just expanded."

He chuckled. "I'll give you this one, but only this one. Country, obviously, is my favorite." He leaned in as if imparting a great and ancient secret. "You can tell by my lucky cowboy hat. You know, the one that's currently residing in your bedroom."

Elissa smirked. "You wore your lucky hat to my apartment?"

"No, shug. It wasn't lucky before today." He winked.

"You are terrible." She laughed. "Okay, so what type of country music?"

"You just keep adding on the questions. I don't think you know how to play this game."

"And you're dodging. Come on, tell me." She drummed her hands on the table.

"Okay, props for realizing there's all types of country music. I tend to go old-school, though I do love a good Blake Shelton tune."

"I like that song "Some Beach" by him," Elissa interjected.

Nash grinned like she'd won the lottery. "My favorite of his."

"Mine, too. But what's your overall favorite country song?"

He tilted his head. "Darlin'. Ain't it obvious what my favorite would be?"

"No, actually, That's why I'm asking you." She folded her hands on the table again and leaned forward.

"The greatest country—no, the greatest song of *any* kind—ever written is Dolly Parton's "I Will Always Love You.""

"Oh! Sure, of course." She slapped her forehead. "Elena told me all you guys are like obsessed with that movie, *The Bodyguard*."

"Look, that may or may not be true—"

"Totally true." Elissa smirked.

Nash grinned back. "Whitney does that song justice and then some. But, I love the original version on account of it's the best version, and I'd be going against my kin if I said otherwise."

"Your family would go after you?"

"Sugar, Dolly Parton *is* my family."

"Wait, what? You are not related to Dolly Parton."

Nashville covered his heart. "Swear to God and hope to die, I am related to Dolly Parton."

"No way! Have you met her?"

"Of course. She's kin."

"Wow. Okay." Elissa shook her head. "Is that how you got your name?"

"May I have *my* turn now, or are you gonna play all twenty questions at once?"

Elissa snorted. "Yes, yes, take your turn. But nothing I can say will come close to being related to Dolly Parton."

"All right then. What's the worst date you've ever been on? Better not say this one."

Elissa snickered. "Oh, God no, I'm having a blast. Worst date ever? Okay, I had this coffee date where the guy spent an hour explaining to me how an orgasm is just a sneeze for the genitals. And that's exactly how he phrased it," she added when Nash started laughing, "a sneeze for the *genitals*. So, even though he was really good-looking, when he asked me if I wanted to sleep with him, I took a hard pass, because for the rest of the afternoon, all I could think were the words, *dick snot*. And I did *not* want any of that noise. As a matter of fact, I don't think I even went out for coffee with anyone else for a solid month after that one."

By now, Nash was guffawing. "Oh, darlin', that's terrible."

"I know, right?"

"I don't even know if I can stop laughing long enough to answer your next one."

"I don't think I can stop laughing long enough to ask."

"You got to ask. Them's the rules."

Elissa blurted out, "How do you like your coffee?" Then slapped her hand over her mouth.

Nash snorted. "I can tell you how I *don't* like my coffee now."

"Oh, God." Elissa was laughing so hard she started hiccupping.

"Okay. I like my coffee strong enough to walk into the cup by itself, maybe do a couple push-ups along the way."

"Good answer, good answer." She hiccupped. "God, I'm a hot mess. Next question, please."

Nash grinned the hottest grin she'd ever seen. "Why'd you really ask me how I like my coffee?"

She tilted her head. *Is he implying...?* "You think I'll be making you morning coffee anytime soon?"

Nash leaned back in his chair. "That's not an answer, that's another question."

Elissa bit her lip and looked down at the decimated platter of wings and fries. "That would not be the worst thing." Her heart skipped a beat.

Nash reached across the table. He tilted her chin up with one finger. Hazel-green eyes captured hers. "I'm gonna pay up, then I'm taking you back to your place. When we get there, I'm going to kiss you for a very long time. Maybe we'll talk coffee after that."

The door to Elissa's apartment opened hard enough to bang against the wall. Nashville pressed her against the wall on the opposite side of the doorway. Clutching her wrists, he moved her hands up over her head as they kissed—hot and hard and deep. She dropped the keys she still held and Nashville transferred both her wrists to one hand as he reached out and closed the door with the other. Elissa pressed her body against him and he groaned into her mouth. He moved his leg between hers, giving her a lovely place to grind for the time being. At this rate, they weren't going to make it to the bedroom.

A dog sneezed behind them.

Elissa's eyes flew open as Nashville broke the kiss and whirled around. Out of seemingly nowhere, a gun appeared in his hand. He pointed it straight at a figure sitting on the couch across the room while blocking Elissa's body with his.

"I thought that was your hat, Nash." The woman's calm voice sounded familiar but still took Elissa a moment to place.

"Gina?" Every last trace of Nashville's accent had drained from his voice. His body relaxed a fraction, enough for Elissa to look past him and confirm that Gina Smith was indeed parked on her couch, Nashville's hat in one hand and a copy of *Harriet the Spy* in the other. Her ginger-colored dog, Fleur, sat on the floor beside her.

Nash lowered his arm and tucked the gun away somewhere behind his back. "You got some kinda nerve tracking me down here. I told Lach I was taking a leave of absence. If y'all needed me back so bad, this was not the way to let me know."

Gina tilted her head, a half-smile playing on her lips. "As sad as I am that you've decided to take a break, who said I was here for you?" She switched her gaze to Elissa's. "Good evening, Elissa. Sorry to intrude."

"No. Way." *Could it be true?* Elissa ducked under Nashville's arm as he protested the move. "I knew it!" She had to stop herself from bouncing up and down as she hugged her arms. "That was a CIA server, wasn't it? You're here to recruit me."

Gina set the book on the couch. She pursed her lips as she stood, Fleur taking her cue from her owner and standing too. "Not quite, but you're close." She looked from Elissa to Nashville and back again. "I need to speak to you in private."

Nashville crossed his arms. "Uh-uh. Consider me back on the job. I'm not going anywhere." He put his arm around Elissa's shoulders. "You don't have to answer any of Spooky's questions if you don't want to."

Gina looked genuinely hurt before she schooled her features into a placid expression. "Believe me, this is the last place I want to be right now, because I'm here to protect you, Elissa."

Elissa felt like she just swam through a cold current in an otherwise warm ocean. "Oh, God, I didn't mean to do anything illegal. I mean, okay, even though it was open-season, I knew it was probably not legit legal to hack Outyard, but—"

"If you'd broken the law, I wouldn't be here because that would mean Outyard was a normal server and you'd have to deal with the authorities, not me." Gina walked toward them and Fleur trotted at her side. When she came within arm's reach, she plopped Nashville's hat onto his head.

"A gentleman doesn't wear his hat inside," Nash said as he reached up to take it back off.

"I put it on your head because you're going outside. Now." Gina pointed at the door.

Nash tightened his arm around Elissa. His whole body tensed. "I'm staying here."

"You're on a leave of absence so this doesn't concern you."

"And I said I was back on the job as of five minutes ago."

"Guys," Elissa said as she stepped between them. She hated nothing more than to watch two people she liked arguing and she'd had enough. "Please, Gina, whatever it is, you know you can trust Nashville. And Nash, this is Gina, not some Cold War Russian spy—"

"CIA spy," Nash said.

"I can neither confirm nor deny—"

"*Guys!*" Elissa crossed her arms. "We're all on the same side here." She looked at Gina. "Seriously, I *am* on your side, okay? Yay, America. Please, just tell me what I did, and let Nash stay and listen too."

Suddenly, Gina cracked a smile. "Now I see why I'm here." She turned and headed down the hall with Fleur toward the office. "Are you coming?"

"Both of us?" Elissa asked.

Gina stopped and turned. "Both of you." She looked at Nashville. Elissa saw an agreement pass silently between them, but she didn't know if the truce was permanent.

Then Nash grinned. "You know dogs aren't allowed in the building." He pointed at Fleur.

"There's no dog here," Gina said. "And you're talking to yourself."

They entered the office. Elissa's computer was sleeping, its fans quiet. Gina took a device out of her pocket and hit a switch. She set it down on the desk. "Now we can talk without being overheard. I checked your apartment and there were no bugs, but that doesn't mean no one's listening now."

Elissa shivered. This was getting real, real fast.

The three of them sat down in a semi-circle in front of the computer. "Like I said, Outyard is not a CIA server, nothing of the kind. Though, they have been watching it because they were alerted to its existence over a year ago. And they aren't the only interested party."

"If it's not a CIA recruitment tool, then what is it?" Elissa asked.

Gina looked at her. "That's what I'm here to ask you."

Elissa's eyes got wide. "I don't know what it is."

"But you should know, you breached it."

"I did, yeah. I mean, *we* did."

Gina's gaze flicked to Nashville, surprise on her face. "*You're* the other hacker?"

"What? No. But I saw what happened."

"You know about Ulysses22?" Elissa asked Gina.

"I know *of* Ulysses22, but not who he is," Gina answered. "Do you know?"

"He's the guy who's been working with me to break in."

Gina leaned toward Elissa. "So, who *is* he?"

Elissa shrugged. "I haven't a clue. We're not in the habit of revealing our true identities because you never know when you might walk into your apartment and find someone from the government waiting for you." She grimaced. "That came out harsh."

Gina waved it away. "I get that a lot. Well, if you have any way of finding out who he is and you give the slightest damn about the guy, you should reach out and warn him. If it isn't too late already."

Elissa let out an exasperated sigh. "Warn him about what? Can you please just tell me what's going on?"

Gina stood up and began pacing. "From what we can tell, Outyard is a renegade server. We don't know who owns it or where their loyalties are, but we do know they're dangerous and they want to sow chaos."

Nash raised an eyebrow. "Capitoline?" Elissa had never heard the word before.

Gina paused as she glanced at Elissa as if weighing options. She seemed to come to a conclusion and then said, "It's not them, no. They're actually one of the other interested parties."

"Well, shit," Nashville said. He looked at Elissa. "Pardon my French."

"I can take it. What's Capitoline?"

"A group I hope you never have to tangle with, shug," Nash answered. He looked at Gina. "But that's not an option anymore, is it?"

Instead of answering him directly, Gina continued pacing as she asked Elissa, Does the phrase, 'the key to discord' mean anything to you?"

Elissa shook her head. "I got nothing. Wait, it did say something about a turnkey."

Gina stopped and looked at Elissa. "What did? The prize you found on the server? I assume it's some sort of virus or Trojan horse."

A virus or Trojan horse? "We didn't find anything like that," Elissa said. "Here." She turned and woke her computer. "Once we got in, we left a back door. It was stupidly easy to do that. I shoulda been suspicious." A few clicks, and she should've been back in Outyard's server unchallenged, but now the server appeared to be down.

"Weird," Elissa mumbled.

Gina swore. "Did you tell anyone on the message boards that you made it in?" she asked.

"I didn't, no. I was too embarrassed to have fallen for a timeshare. At least, that's what I thought it was."

Gina frowned. "Try getting in again."

Elissa did, and still, the server wasn't there. Gina looked like she might puke.

"It's cool. I made a quick video of what we saw." Relief immediately flooded Gina's features as she came over and leaned in. Elissa opened the file. "There. This is what we found."

The movie clip showed the camera panning slowly back and forth across the lanai, ending with the spammy, red-lettered sign.

"Welcome to your destination, your dream, your turnkey to the future," Gina read aloud. "But no computer coding? No executable program?"

"Just what you see. That's what we found. I have screen-shots and video both."

Gina nodded absently. "How long did you watch the video? Did you see anyone on it?"

"Not long, and no. Like I said, I thought it was a joke." She buried her face in her hands. "God, I'm dumb."

Elissa felt Nash's big hand on her shoulder. "No phony has your mad skills."

"He's right, Elissa." Gina's voice was surprisingly warm and gentle. "It took amazing skill to hack in. You and Ulysses22 are the only two who've accomplished it."

Elissa lifted her head as a cold shiver ran down her spine. "How'd you know it was me? And so fast?"

Gina placed her hand on Elissa's other shoulder. "You're not going to like this. We'd been watching you already, Elissa. Because of your association with Watchdog, you're automatically a person of interest."

From Nashville's flinch, Elissa realized this was news to him.

Gina continued. "We thought we knew all your handles, but we missed Surfboi65. We were alerted to that one last night and have spent all this time trying to find out who that was. Thank God we had a head start."

Elissa felt like she might barf. Or faint. One or the other. "How did you find out about Surfboi65?"

"I'm sorry, but I can't tell you that at this juncture."

"Fuck," Nash swore.

Gina stood. "The good news is, as far as we can tell, no one else has breached the server or connected you to your handle. And we took steps to make sure no one will. You're under my protection. You're safe, Elissa."

Elissa shook her head. "Safe from what?"

"That's yet to be revealed. This might be nothing. A prank, like you said. Or it could be something big." Gina sighed. "All the same, I'm afraid your computer now belongs to my friends. And you're coming with me to Watchdog."

Nash stood so quickly his office chair rolled backward into the wall. "Then so am I."

Gina tilted her head. "Does this mean you're back on with us?"

"Damn straight it does."

SIX

After Elissa agreed to go with Gina, four goons entered her apartment and packed up her computer, which was like stealing a baby out of a mother's arms. At least Elissa didn't have to stand there and watch, since Gina gave her five minutes to pack a bag with her important papers and all the irreplaceable valuables she could cram into a duffel along with a couple changes of clothing—business and casual. Elissa eyed her surfboards and sighed as Gina hustled them out the door, only to be stopped by the same four goons coming back in with her computer.

"Not *your* computer," Gina explained. "An exact copy, at least externally, just in case someone comes looking."

"Awesome," Elissa said. "My computer has a stunt double." She looked at Gina before they stepped into the hall. "Wait, do I have one too?"

Gina grinned. "You might."

"Oh, God, I'm putting someone in danger." Elissa covered her mouth.

"It's her job," Gina said. "And you need to let her carry that," she added to Nash, who had started to grab Elissa's bag from her at the door. Right, there had to be no mistaking that the duffel was Elissa's overnight bag. Though Nash had the feeling the pink and blue tropical print sorta gave that away.

When they got to the elevators Gina said, "You two, go down to the parking garage and get into your truck. If you see anyone, make sure you kiss or grab each other's asses or something. Elissa, as far as anyone knows, you're spending the night with your new boyfriend."

The elevator doors opened but they didn't get in. "Um, wait," Elissa said. She looked up at Nashville. "We're not...are we?"

"I now pronounce you girlfriend and boyfriend," Gina said. "Nashville, protocol three. Fleur and I are right behind you."

"Yes, ma'am." Nashville tipped his hat to Gina and laid his hand on the small of Elissa's back to escort her into the elevator. Once the doors closed, Elissa opened her mouth to undoubtedly ask what protocol three was, when Nashville leaned down and kissed her. He knew there was a ninety-nine percent chance with a one percent margin of error that Gina's people had commandeered the cameras in the elevator and probably throughout the entire building, but it never hurt to go along with the cover. Plus, it gave him an excuse to kiss Elissa.

"For the cameras," he breathed against her lips. He felt her shiver as she gave the slightest nod, then kissed him back passionately.

This both sucked and did not suck simultaneously. Was she putting on an act or was this how she felt? He didn't have time to ponder and he couldn't afford the distraction. From this moment on, she was his client.

Who he was kissing against all regs. And yet, he had no choice.

Ironic, considering he'd taken a leave of absence to protest his partner doing the same damn thing on their last assignment and consequently putting them all in more danger.

Last time I'll throw a stone in a glass house when I don't even know I'm about to live in one Nash thought.

Sure enough, when the elevator doors opened, a woman was standing there with a tote bag of groceries slung over her shoulder.

"Oh!" the woman said, startled.

Elissa broke the kiss. "Oh, hey, neighbor." She grinned and her face turned a shade of red Nash thought of as DEFCON Two. "Just, um. Going out. See ya, um, tomorrow?" She scooted out of the elevator and past the woman with Nash in tow as if she were doing a speed-walk of shame.

"How was that for looking embarrassed?" Elissa murmured to Nash.

"That was fake?" Nash was genuinely confused.

Elissa grinned. "I can neither confirm nor deny—"

"Darlin', don't even." The last thing he needed was Gina's antics rubbing off on his woman.

My woman?

Oh, hell, why even deny it? He pulled Elissa closer as she giggled.

When they got to Nash's truck, he beeped the alarm and took Elissa's bag as he opened her door for her and helped her in. He tossed the bag on the bench in the cab behind Elissa and circled the truck to the driver's side. He opened the door, reached into the molded plastic pocket, and pulled out a mirror attached to a telescoping arm. He was about to extend the arm when he spotted a guy in the sports car facing his truck. The guy nodded and signed the letter 'G' for Gina. Nash put the mirror away—no need to check the undercarriage for a bomb when your truck was under the protection of a goon squad.

Huh. Maybe that's what the 'G' stands for. Nash grinned. At least now it did in his head.

When Nash got behind the wheel, Elissa asked, "Can we talk now?" He glanced at her and she looked serious—at least more serious than when they'd skedaddled to the truck.

"Yeah, shug, we're clear." Nash started the truck. He'd follow the first step of protocol three which was to make sure he wasn't being tailed. If he did have a tail, he'd identify it, and then the tail would have a tail.

Instead of saying anything, Elissa watched out her window. *Great, maybe it's all sinking in now and she's scared.* After a minute, Nash prompted her with, "Looks like you're wool-gathering there, shug. What'd you want to say?"

She jumped a little as if startled. Then she smiled. "Oh, no, I was watching in the rearview for tails. Do we have one? I don't see one."

"Oh good Lord." He glanced at her. "This doesn't upset you?"

"Nope." She even bounced a little in her seat. "So do we have one? Which car is it?"

"First, we don't have a tail."

"Aw." She slumped.

"Second, you're not supposed to be excited that someone might be after you."

"But—"

"Darlin', this is real, okay? This is not *Harriet the Spy.*"

Wrong thing to say and Nash knew it immediately. Elissa deflated. She looked at her hands in her lap. *Idiot. You probably took away her coping mechanism.*

At the next red light, he reached over and tilted her chin

up. "Hey. I'm sorry. That was rude, and if my mama was here, she'd slap me upside the head and I'd deserve it."

"No, she wouldn't."

"You're right, she wouldn't. She's the sweetest lady ever walked God's green earth. But, she'd think real hard about it."

That made her smile. The light turned green and Nash drove. "How'd you know my mama wouldn't do that? You never met her."

Elissa shrugged her right shoulder as her head tilted that way. "Nobody mean could raise someone as good as you."

That felt better than moonshine. "I really am sorry about what I said."

"No, you're right. I'm treating this like it's a video game. It's my immaturity showing again."

"There's nothing immature about you."

He saw her shake her head out of the corner of his eye and she went back to watching her rearview mirror. Which, he needed to focus on. Just because they weren't followed immediately didn't mean they wouldn't pick a tail up on the way. Nash took one of the meandering routes they'd all memorized to the office and saw no one. He knew he had eyes on him at Watchdog and that if any of them saw something suspicious through the traffic cams, they'd contact him as well. So far, so quiet, so good.

Was it legal for them to have access to those traffic cams? Nash had long since stopped asking questions like that. Usually, the answer was "Gina's friends." And at the end of the day, they all stayed safe thanks to those friends.

Didn't always sit right with him though. *What happens if your friends turn on you?*

Elissa looked away from her side mirror. "The white Toyota Corolla. That's following us now, right?"

"Sure is, but it's a friendly." He glanced at her. "Good eye."

She smiled.

After that, the ride to Watchdog was quiet. Nash tried to get a read on Elissa's state of mind, but she kept mum. He concentrated instead on what he'd say to his boss and owner of Watchdog, Lachlan. Would he have to eat crow? Or, was he back on with no reservations?

An hour later, they pulled into the underground parking garage at Watchdog. Elissa hadn't said another word and Nash wasn't sure how to break the silence. He'd give anything to have back their easy conversation from lunch. She was so much fun, so energizing, one of those people who radiate positive energy. Now she was closed up, like someone had flipped the off switch. And that person was Nash.

It's for her own good. I'm protecting her and she wasn't taking this as seriously as she should.

It still sucked.

He went around the truck and opened her door, then grabbed her duffel.

"I can carry that," she said.

"And deprive me of a chance to try and be a gentleman after I offended you with the *Harriet the Spy* reference? I don't think so."

"You didn't offend me. Truth hurts sometimes."

"First, it isn't the truth. Second, I never, ever want to say something hurtful to you." He rubbed his thumbs over her smooth, warm skin. "I admire you so much. Look at all you've accomplished in your life."

Elissa rolled her eyes. "My life is a game of leap frog from one shiny thing to the next." She grinned ruefully. "And now this."

"We'll get through this, whatever it is." He led Elissa to

the parking garage doors. A retinal scan allowed Nash through the door leading into Watchdog.

Gladys, one of the receptionists, met them almost immediately, Reggie on a leash at her side. She kept a smile on her face, her voice even and light. "Mind coming with Reggie and me?"

"I don't really have a choice, do I?" Elissa responded.

"It's always polite to ask, dear," Gladys answered.

The last Nashville saw of Elissa, she was looking back at him over her shoulder as Gladys and Reggie led her to one of the small waiting rooms.

"You are most definitely *not* back on with Watchdog," Lachlan told Nashville when they met in the conference room. After the whirlwind of Gina infiltrating Elissa's apartment—and her life—Nash was not having this.

"What do you mean I'm not back on?" Nash demanded. He stood up and pounded his fist on the conference table. Lach's old dog Sam, who'd been lying under the table, got up and moved closer to Lach. Gina stopped leaning against the conference room wall and took a step toward Nash. "I'm the *only* man for this job."

"Sit. Down," Lachlan said. Nash complied with his boss's command. "I don't disagree," he continued as he scratched Sam's ears, then crossed his arms.

"You don't?" Nash asked, confused.

"Which is why you're staying on leave. As a matter of fact, you're so pissed at us, you just might not come back."

"Boss, you're being clear as Mississippi mud right now."

Gina paced. "Here's how it is. You're Rebound Boy for Elissa—"

"Excuse me? I am not Rebound Boy." Nash was relieved that Elissa wasn't in the room.

"You are now." Gina smiled. "You are on paid leave. Since Elissa was dumped by her coach, in order to impress her, you're taking her to Maui for the race."

"Do what?"

"It's your cover, Nash." Gina dropped a folder on the table in front of him as she passed behind him. "Until we know what sort of mischief Elissa's gotten herself into, we're getting her out of the lower forty-eight while we have the chance. And, considering that sign from the live cam, we might want her there anyway."

Nash's blood ran cold as he realized what Gina was saying. He stood back up and turned around. "You're not doing this."

"Yes, I'm afraid we are." She stopped pacing and folded her arms.

Nash turned back to Lachlan. "She's a *civilian*. We're not turning Elissa into an operative!"

He shrugged. "It's not up to me. This is Gina's op."

Nash turned back to Gina. Her eyes said it all—it was happening, and she wasn't happy about it, either. "Nashville, I'm sorry. My friends have been monitoring that server for over a year. We are beyond fortunate that the hacker was someone we know and were able to bring into custody so quickly."

Whoa. "What aren't you telling me?"

"It might be nothing. Or, it might be something big, we just don't have all the data yet." She glanced at the conference room door as if expecting someone. "Let's discuss your role."

Nashville gritted his teeth. He remembered all the frustrations from his time as an active SEAL whenever his team was given murky intel at best, and downright incorrect intel at the worst. He knew the consequences could be deadly. But so far, in all his interactions with Gina, he'd grown to trust her, as far as he could trust anyone from the alphabets. He knew she cared, even when her job required her to be distant, even cold. He knew she genuinely liked Elissa and that she'd do everything possible to keep her safe the way she'd do the same for anyone at Watchdog. But the idea of using Elissa as an operative didn't sit right with Nash and never would. So, the best thing he could do was to go along and keep her safe.

"I'll do whatever y'all need, you know that."

Gina nodded. She touched his arm. "I do. You're a good man. Elissa's lucky. And we're lucky to have her. She's got the right attitude, I can tell."

High praise from Gina. "She's still a civilian," Nash said.

"I know. But, she's got a wide skillset, she's smart, she's brave, she's athletic. If this turns into something, Elissa's going to need all of that. But chances are, this is an elaborate hoax." Gina grinned. "Right now, just think of it as getting a paid vacation to Hawaii with your girlfriend."

Nash's stomach rolled over. *If this turns into something.* Why did Nashville have the feeling it would?

SEVEN

Elissa waited in a small room at Watchdog, Reggie at her side. The dog was as protective as Nash, if a bit more...drooly. She scratched the black Lab's broad head and floppy ears as her knee bounced up and down. She didn't like being parked off to the side while people who knew way too much about her were discussing her future. Worse, she couldn't call Elena, or Delia, or Rachael, or Jordan, or *anyone* and tell them that her life had just been turned upside down and dumped out like a purse. Gladys had confiscated her phone.

Ugh! It's been an hour, at least. Elissa glanced at the wall clock—to see that only ten minutes had gone by. But there was not a word, just a reassurance from the receptionist that it wouldn't be much longer when the woman came in and offered her more coffee. Still, Elissa was starting to feel like a mushroom—kept in the dark and fed shit.

"Okay, that's enough." She looked down at the dog who gazed lovingly back up at her. "Play along, puppy, and there's a whole tray of gourmet dog biscuits in it for you the second I have access to a kitchen again. Deal?"

Reggie thumped his tail against the floor.

"Good enough." Elissa stood up and clipped Reggie's leash back onto his collar. She turned the knob and opened the door. At least they hadn't locked her into the little waiting room or she would have seriously freaked. She walked Reggie out into the hall and tried to reorient herself. Who knew Watchdog was such a warren? She closed her eyes to reorient herself, took a deep breath, and then knew which way to go.

Less than a minute passed before she encountered someone else. She didn't recognize the older man but presumed he was one of the bodyguards since he was built like a tower made of muscle and easily passed the Hottie Test she was certain Watchdog required of every hire. The Malinois he had on a leash was another dead giveaway.

Before she could open her mouth with her prepared excuse, the guy smiled and said, "Hey, I wonder if you could point me to the kennels?"

Elissa straightened up. She wished for the business outfit she'd packed in her duffel, but oh, well. It was the weekend, right? She could work with that. "Sure, I'm heading that way myself. Just, uh, follow me." It wasn't entirely a lie. She would be going through the kennels to get to the courtyard where the dogs trained. She knew the conference room everyone was meeting in had a window opening onto the courtyard And, Elissa also knew American Sign Language and could read lips thanks to spending a childhood summer with a cousin who was hearing-impaired.

"I'm Malcolm," the guy said as he extended a hand.

"Elissa." She shook his hand—a nice, firm but not bone-crushing grip. "Nice to meet you." They started walking.

"I'm new here, obviously," Malcolm said.

"Yeah, me too. Don't mind my, um." She gestured at her informal clothing. "Weekend casual, right?" Elissa picked up the pace. She didn't want to get into too deep of a conversation. *How do spies do this all the time?*

"Bodyguard?" He barely kept the doubt out of his voice. He was at least a foot taller than her, but still, what if she were a master at Brazilian jiujitsu? What if she could throw the guy over her shoulder without a second thought? Okay, no, it was pretty obvious she wasn't there to protect anyone.

Go with what you know. "IT department, actually."

"Oh." He glanced at Reggie. "They issue everyone here a dog?"

"Oh, yeah, no. Just you guys, I guess. This is um, another guy's dog." *Wow, definitely superspy dialogue here.* "He has to go potty."

Malcolm's lips twitched but he said nothing.

"Here we are." Sure enough, her directional instincts were correct. Elissa reached for the handle on the door leading to the kennel. Malcolm quickly reached past her and opened the door for her.

"Thank you," Elissa said as she quickly scooted past. She had to tug Reggie's leash, since he was more interested in checking out the other dog.

"Thought he had to go potty." Now Malcolm was outright trying not to laugh.

"Well, you know. Dogs. They get distracted. Come on, Reg." With her luck, she'd miss the entire meeting, and then they'd see she'd escaped her little dungeon, and then Gina would snap her fingers and the men in black would disappear her. *Crap.*

Stop it. Gina's your friend. Kinda.

"Nice meeting you," Elissa waved her fingers at Malcolm and continued down the hall to the courtyard.

"Still going your way," Malcolm said as he and his dog caught up.

Lucky me. Elissa gave him a tight-lipped smile.

"How long have you been with Watchdog?" Malcolm asked.

"Not long. At all."

"So IT? Security for the company, or...?"

Ugh! Why do military guys slash bodyguards have to be so nosy? "Or," she said dismissively and hoped that would cover it.

Wait. What was a new guy doing here now? "They make the new guys work weekends?"

Malcolm opened the next door that led to the courtyard. Several dogs were already out there. "I volunteered," he said as he unleashed the Malinois. "I was hoping to get a feel for the place when it wasn't so crazy. Seems like a nice company."

"Yeah, it's great." She unsnapped Reggie's leash thinking *Where's that window? Which one is it?* Then she spotted Gina pacing behind glass. *Bingo!*

"Isn't the, um, doggie bathroom over there?" Malcolm pointed across the yard to a fenced-off area with a pole and a box of plastic bags attached to it. Of course it was far from the window she needed.

"Oh yeah, right." *Shit.* "Reggie! Come here, buddy!" But the dog was already off exploring. He ran up to a standard-issue Watchdog hottie Elissa had never seen before who appeared to be working with the other dogs. She quickly looked around for Kyle and breathed a sigh of relief when she didn't spot him. He'd definitely want to know what she was doing there.

Malcolm put his hand on the small of her back—not her favorite move. "Let me help you get your dog where he needs to be."

"Nope, that's fine, I'm good." She stepped away from the

towering hunk and tried to turn back toward the window, but by now they'd gotten the dog trainer's attention.

"Hey!" he called out. "This is Nashville's dog, right?" He was giving her a warm, friendly smile. And standing up. And walking toward them.

"Marc," Malcolm called out. "We have another newbie here." Malcolm placed his hand on her back again, giving her no choice but to walk toward Marc.

"Nice to meet you." Marc extended his hand.

She gave him the briefest of handshakes before turning again. No sign of Gina—or anyone else—in the conference room. *Shit, shit, shit!* "Do you mind taking Reg from here? I really need to get back to work." She turned and started for the door.

"Wait, I didn't get your name," Marc said.

"Elissa St Clair." She tried to move past Malcolm but he smiled and stepped between her and the door. Now this was getting sketchy. "Can I leave?"

"In a minute." Malcolm gripped her upper arm. Marc closed in behind her.

Oh, God. What's happening? Elissa tried to pull away. The door behind Malcolm opened but the guy was too big for her to see around.

"Hey!" Elissa called out, hoping it was a friend or at least someone familiar.

And it was.

"Gina! Who are these guys? I don't think they belong here."

"Let her go," Gina said, her voice even but firm as she looked at the men, eyebrows raised.

Malcolm dropped his hand to his side and Elissa scooted around him toward Gina who continued to walk toward them.

"How'd she do?" Gina asked Malcolm.

What?

Malcolm broke into a huge grin. "She was out the door in less than fifteen minutes, as expected. Pretended that she was a new hire, matching my story. Said she was in IT, which was smart in case I'd asked some in-depth follow-up questions about her job. Pretty convincing, actually. I'll give her props for that."

"But she gave me her full name without having any idea who I was," Marc added.

"And once we got out here, she let me run the show," Malcolm said. "Marc and I were able to cut her off from her escape route."

Elissa felt like she was watching tennis, the way her head swung back and forth between the men and Gina. "What the hell is this?" she asked Gina.

"So why did you head for the courtyard?" Gina asked. "I was expecting you to eavesdrop outside the conference room door."

Wait, what? "First, tell me what's going on." Elissa looked back at the men. "Are these...friendlies?"

"Yes, they are. Good job, by the way." She smiled at each man before turning her attention back to Elissa. "Malcolm is a friend who I stationed to keep an eye on you. Marc is our new kennel master." She clapped her hands together once. "So, why the courtyard and not the conference room?"

"Wait, aren't you mad?"

Gina laughed. "Of course not. I'm delighted, actually. I was hoping you'd break out. You've got the instincts, I'll give you that, but we need to work on your technique. Rule one: never, ever give anyone your real name on an op."

"I'm not on an op." *Am I?*

"No, but let's pretend you *are* on an op. You were trying to gain information about the meeting...from the courtyard?"

Gina looked around. "Ah, the window. Did you think you could listen in from there? It's soundproof glass."

"Yeah, I figured because otherwise, all you'd hear inside would be dogs barking. I wasn't going to try and listen with my ears, but with my eyes. I know ASL and I can read lips."

Gina laughed again. "You are full of surprises." She laid a hand on Elissa's shoulder. "Class dismissed. For now. Let's debrief inside." She thanked Marc and then she and Malcolm flanked Elissa as they walked toward the kennel doors. "Maybe you can get Nash out of his bad mood."

"Bad mood?"

"I don't appreciate you playing your old CIA mind games on Elissa," Nash told Gina. He'd stood up the second the three of them entered the conference room. Lachlan was seated at the head of the table. He stood up as well, but more as a courtesy to Elissa and Gina. Nashville was just plain old pissed-off.

"Nash," Lach started.

"No." He crossed the room to Elissa and laid his hand on the small of her back. It felt good there as he pulled out her chair then sat down beside her. Malcolm sat across the table and Gina remained standing.

Nashville continued his tirade. "I'm against all of this."

Gina started pacing. "We have no choice. Elissa, you're still off the radar so far, but that could change at any moment. And if this is serious, we're going to need your help."

"Hell no. She's a civilian and should go into hiding," Nashville said, "until all this blows over."

"*If* it's anything. If not, we've disrupted her life for nothing, so that's not happening," Gina shot back.

"Oh, but going to Hawaii isn't disrupting her life?"

"Not if she was already planning it—"

"Can you please talk to me as if I were actually in the room since *I am*, and tell me what it is I'll be doing?" Elissa demanded. Anticipation made her stomach twist into a knot. Would she be helping them somehow? Could she finally say goodbye to her boring old life?

Gina ran a hand through her shoulder-length bob. Her tawny-gold eyes flashed at Elissa. "We've been lucky. And I can't tell you how much I hate luck. So, we're getting you out of Los Angeles just to be safe. Until then, you're going to go into work like nothing happened."

Elissa clunked her head on the desk. "I don't like that." She turned her head and looked at Gina.

Gina shook her head, a look of faint disbelief on her face. "Wait, I thought you'd be happy not having to live in hiding. Most people are."

Elissa sat back up. "Then your intel's bad. I've been wanting to quit my job for a while. This seemed like a great opportunity to do that."

Gina folded her arms as a look passed between her and Nashville before she focused on Elissa again. "Well, then. You are full of surprises. How fast can you pack for Hawaii? Because as of today, you are back in the Maui Challenge." She shifted her gaze to Nashville. "*With* your new boyfriend and coach, Nashville Jones. Who will be teaching you more than just how best to paddle a kayak."

That wasn't loaded. Elissa fought back a grin. "Wait a minute. How'd I get back into the Maui Challenge and why?"

Nashville crossed his arms. "This is the part I don't like. I do *not* want to take her to Maui."

Well, that hurt. Shocked, Elissa couldn't help looking at

Nashville. All she saw reflected back was anger. Then his expression softened. "She's not trained for it."

For a moment, Elissa thought he was talking about the Maui Challenge, and that hurt doubly. But of course that wasn't it. "Trained for what?" Elissa asked as she looked back and forth between Gina and Nashville.

Gina answered, "You were planning on it anyway, so it's minimally disruptive and it checks out if any interested parties are looking into you." She paused. "And...we *might* need you in Hawaii to finish the hacking job you started."

Yes! "Tell me what I need to do and I'll do it!" She looked at all of them one by one, her heart pounding. As scary as it was, this felt right. She finally found something to do that was important and that could make a real difference. And she wasn't about to let anyone take away her chance. Not even Nashville Jones.

EIGHT

Nashville and Elissa drove in silence after their meeting. The plan was to have her spend the night with him. Nash kept a white-knuckle grip on the steering wheel.

God, what is wrong with me? he thought.

What man on God's green earth would ever bemoan the opportunity to accompany a woman as gorgeous, as funny, as smart, as *right* as Elissa St Clair to Hawaii?

Even better? She was spending the night with him. He should've been in hog heaven but instead, he was fit to be tied. *This was not how I pictured starting a relationship with the woman of my dreams—worrying that one wrong move, one slip of my attention, and she'll be gone.*

Elissa broke the silence first. "It's going to be fine. I'm excited, really." She side-eyed him. "Unless you aren't too crazy about spending time with me in Hawaii?"

He couldn't help the heat flooding his cheeks, or his cock. "That is the only thing that excites me about this assignment. A little too much."

It was Elissa's turn to blush. She was quiet for the rest of the drive. Every mile piled on the doubt. He thought back to earlier, the way he'd thrown her against the wall the minute they stepped into her apartment. The way she'd responded, he was sure she wasn't about to let him leave until they'd explored each other. But now? Everything had changed.

He drove up the twisting roads into the hills and noticed Elissa's eyes grow wider. *Here it comes.*

"This is Laurel Canyon," she breathed. "Do you...live here?"

"I do," he mumbled, then quickly added, "House has been in the family since the Sixties." Sometimes admitting that made it better, sometimes worse. No way could he have afforded to buy one of the million-dollar-plus homes in the Canyon these days, but then it opened up questions about his family that could go on for hours. Laurel Canyon had been both home and playground to a whole mess of folk and rock musicians back in the Sixties and Seventies—The Byrds, Gram Nash, even The Beatles were known to drop in.

"So, you said you were related to Dolly Parton. Was your family in the music business?"

"One branch was, yeah. Still are. On the business side 'a things, though, not the talent. Managers, handlers, accountants."

"Your family hung out with all those people though." He knew she was dying to ask more. Maybe it would work to his advantage and he could distract her all evening with stories. Show her the piano where Joni Mitchell supposedly sat one night and debuted songs from *Ladies of the Canyon*. Or the obscene doodle Frank Zappa drew on the wall in one of the bedrooms during one of many infamous parties.

"They did," was all he said, suddenly tongue-tied. Would she think he was trying to show off? "You're gonna have to excuse the dust though. Place is finally undergoing some deferred maintenance. It's how I managed to talk my way into living there. I'm fixin' her up."

"Groovy," Elissa said. He caught her grin.

Nash pulled into the long driveway past the wooden fence and made his way down into the trees obscuring the house. He loved the fact that the house was hidden from the road—making him feel safe. He had cameras up of course, but the natural cover always put him at ease. Now that it was dark, he felt even more secure, knowing that if Elissa was under any threat, she'd be hard to find here.

Elissa waited while he let Reggie out of the kennel in the back, then they made their way to a side door. He disarmed the security system and opened the door. He locked it up behind them and rearmed the system as Elissa slipped her sandals off in the alcove serving as a mud room. He set the duffel down on a bench and waited for her to stand, then gently placed his hands on her upper arms, fighting the urge to just pull her into his body.

She stepped closer to him. "This has been one hell of a date, but I wouldn't call it bad though." She tilted her head up as she lowered her eyelids, expecting a kiss.

Nash leaned down until his lips were an inch from hers, which was when the voice in his head calling him a hypocrite kicked in. He groaned. "I shouldn't do this."

"And yet you're not pulling away," she whispered. She ran her hands up his arms.

I take back what I thought earlier. I don't want to go back to our lunch conversation. I want to go back to that kiss against her apartment wall.

"I'm not, am I?" He wrapped his arms around her.

"It's just the two of us alone here at your house."

"Sure enough." His lips brushed featherlight across hers. Then he pulled away.

"Now what?" Elissa's expression told him she was getting more than a little annoyed. "Wait, don't tell me." She looked around. "Gina? You here?" She looked back at Nashville. "You think she teleported in here ahead of us using super-secret spy gear?"

Nash folded his arms and smirked. "You watch too many movies, shug."

Elissa folded her arms in turn. "No such thing as too many movies. And tell me I'm wrong. She did it before."

Nash laughed. "Okay, okay, you have a point."

Elissa turned serious. "So now I'm your client or whatever. Which further means you have to be all professional and not kiss me, right? Is that really what's going on?"

Nash let his head drop forward. He nodded vigorously. "As much as I am positively dying to kiss you. And do more. *All* the more. Every last bit of it. But you're my principal now."

Elissa was quiet a moment. "So, which version of "I Will Always Love You" should I sing, Dolly's or Whitney's? Though I gotta say, there's no way I can hit all of Whitney's notes."

Nash looked up. Elissa was grinning at him. But try as she might, her grin wasn't quite reaching her eyes.

I love you. The feeling came not as a rush but as a quiet certainty. It hit Nash hard all the same.

So this was how Psychic felt when he was falling in love with Jordan and trying to protect her. No, scratch that; Psychic was already in love, had been in love for a long time, and so had she. Their story was incredible. So how much harder had it been for his partner to resist temptation with Jordan than it was for Nash to resist picking up Elissa, carrying her to the bedroom, and ripping off all her clothes right now? Because everything in his body, heart, and soul was telling him that was the best idea he'd ever had.

Maybe he'd been too harsh on Psychic, and on Watchdog.

"What?" Elissa asked. "I can see the gears turning so hard there's steam coming out your ears."

"I'm thinking you're all right. I'm also thinking this is gonna be a tough assignment." He held up his hand when her face started to fall. "Not because of you. Because of me. It's going to be very hard to keep my hands to myself."

That put a mischievous spark back in Elissa's eyes.

"And, you just made it ten times harder."

"What? I didn't say anything."

"You didn't have to."

She smirked, and damn if that didn't make her even more tempting.

"Still didn't—"

"Darlin', hush." He winked. Just as he was about to go over the protocols and give her a tour, they heard a car drive up and park. Elissa stiffened and turned around, all her playfulness gone.

"Don't worry, that's our team." Sure enough, it was Kyle with Camo. After Nashville let them in, the dog gladly accepted a treat from Nash's pocket.

Kyle blinked a couple of times when he saw Elissa. "What?" He looked at Nash. "I'm not supposed to ask, so I won't. But..."

Nash grinned. "Sorry, Pup. So I take it you're my backup?"

Kyle shook his head. "Not on this one. I had my orders just to make sure you got here in one piece. I'm happy to report we weren't followed. Other than that, I have no idea what's going on." Kyle hugged Elissa. "You take care of yourself, whatever this is, okay?"

She gave him a smile they both saw through, one that said *shit's getting real.* "That's what I've got Nash for, right?"

Kyle looked back at his teammate. "Yeah, you're in good hands." He slapped Nash on the arm. "Anything you need that I can do, just ask. I'll be in town a while longer."

"Appreciate that, brother. Not sure what all they'll *let* you do."

"Understood." He and Camo left.

Reggie left Nash's side and trotted to Elissa. She went to her knees and quietly petted the dog before pressing her face into his side.

"We need to go over safety protocols," Nash said quietly. "And then I'll give you the house tour."

She nodded into Reggie's fur.

"You're gonna be all right, shug."

"I know," she said, her voice muffled. Then she stood up. If anything, she looked excited. He wondered if it was real or if her fear was tucked back behind her smile. "Let's do this."

After going over the same protocols he'd use if they were in one of Watchdog's safehouses, he gave her a tour of the house. She stared up at the fifteen-foot cathedral ceilings lined with pine boards stained to look like redwood, and laughed at the Frank Zappa doodle as he'd hoped she would. The house wasn't overly large—just two bedrooms, one set up as Nash's office for the time being. He reassured her that he'd be sleeping on the couch and that she could have the bed. Then he saved the best for last—the wide deck out back that overlooked a ravine. House lights twinkled on the hills across the canyon like the stars above them.

"Beautiful," Elissa breathed. As he studied her, Nash couldn't agree more.

They had the rest of the evening to themselves. Suddenly, they were like two preteens at a school dance—shy and quiet and barely making eye contact. He led her back inside.

"I'm really tired all of a sudden," Elissa said. "I think I'm going to head for bed." She turned toward the hall.

"Elissa."

She stopped and turned back around. "Yeah?"

Hell with it. Nash spread his arms. She walked into his embrace. Her hair smelled like sun-warmed citrus. "We're gonna get you through this."

"I know. I'm more excited than afraid."

And that's what worries me he thought. Instead, he said, "Let me know if you need anything. I'll just be right out here."

She ran her teeth over her bottom lip—an infinitely enticing gesture that drove Nash to distraction. "This might be too much to ask since you're supposed to be all professional now, but...can you sleep beside me tonight?" She looked up at him through her lashes. "Just sleep. I don't want to get you in trouble."

Nash couldn't resist her. He ran a hand through her long hair. "My pleasure, shug."

Torturous pleasure, holding her all night. And of course, Elissa was a snuggler. He woke several times with her body pressed up close, his erection pushing against her, and had to turn onto his back for both their sakes. But he never took his arm from around her. As far as he could tell, she slept soundly. *Mission accomplished.*

The next morning, they ate a quick breakfast and took separate showers—much to Nash's chagrin. He tried not to think about her wet, soaped-up body just behind the bathroom door and failed miserably. He knew every contour of her lean, athletic body from holding her all night and his imagination did the rest. To distract himself, he logged in to check his work email.

"So, what's next?" Elissa asked as soon as they got into his truck to head for her apartment. "Am I still in the clear?" Her eyes widened. "Do I have to cut off ties with my family?" Did he detect a hint of glee?

"Slow down, sugar. Good news is, no one suspicious has been near your apartment or my place. We think you're still in the clear."

"That's good." She wiped her hand over her face. "I'm worried about Ulysses22."

"That old boy can handle himself. Gina's friends are already looking for him. My concerns are all about you right now." He reached across and tucked a stray lock of her hair behind her ear. "Seems like you slept well, though."

"Only because you were there. I think I would have paced all night otherwise." Her eyes rounded. "Did I snore? Sorry if I kept you up."

Nash stifled a grin. Yeah, she'd kept something up all right.

"I can see what you're thinking there," Elissa said. He saw her smile out of the corner of his eye. "Bad, bad, bad."

"I didn't say anything."

"Didn't have to."

Yes sir, she sure wasn't making this easy.

NINE

It's Monday morning. I just had the weirdest weekend of my life. And I'm sitting at my desk at my crummy job listening to Julia talk about writing me up for my granola and yogurt breakfast.

Elissa stared at a spot between Julia's eyes where a tiny black hair grew. The woman droned on about office culture, being respectful of other people (her), and how granola and yogurt somehow didn't fit into that paradigm.

You know what? I'm done.

"I need to pack." Elissa stood up.

Julia quit speaking mid-sentence. She rocked back on her stilettos. "Excuse me?"

"No, excuse *me*. You're in my way. I need to leave right now and go pack." Elissa grabbed her tote bag which she'd already stuffed with all the little knickknacks and photos she'd accumulated at her desk since starting with the company. She raised her eyebrows in expectation of Julia stepping aside.

"You can't just leave," Julia said. "Your vacation isn't scheduled to start yet. Which, by the way, is a huge burden on the company."

Elissa shrugged. "So write that up, too."

"How about I write up your resignation?" Julia put her hand on her bony hip.

Elissa bit back her smile. "Like the one you wrote up for Elena Martinez?"

Julia fumed. "You know we don't talk about certain former employees *ever*."

"Boy, she really got to you, didn't she?" Elissa's bestie had finally stood up for herself to Julia when she quit under the threat of being fired and the woman had never forgotten it—or missed an opportunity to take her anger out on Elissa.

"She was rude and ungrateful."

"She's doing great now, by the way. I think I'll swing by the restaurant and say hi today while I'm at it."

Julia scowled. "You can stay at that restaurant, because as of now, you don't have a job to come back to."

"Awesome! Thanks." Elissa saluted and sauntered past Julia. Even though her knees were shaking—Elissa really didn't like conflict in general—she kept her head high and waved to the team in IT. She didn't think she was imagining the envious looks on most of their faces.

"HR will be expecting you for an exit interview," Julia shouted at her back.

"Sure thing. I'll be kayaking in Hawaii if they need me."

And that was that. Elissa was out of yet another job.

Won't my mom be proud? she thought and sighed. Nothing to be done about that, at least for now.

As soon as she got to the lobby, her body started trembling as reality set in. She couldn't tell if it was excitement or fear—maybe both. Or maybe it was a delayed adrenaline rush.

Once she got to the street, she felt eyes on her. She spotted Malcolm sitting on a bench ostensibly looking at his phone. Without glancing up, his lips moved and she lipread the words *Surfer girl is* before he covered his mouth. She walked past him and he stood up a few seconds later to follow her. She really was headed to Delia's like she'd told Julia. Best to stick to the plan she'd stated out loud. Good practice for later when anyone could be listening just in case her dreams of espionage came true. Plus, she needed something to ground her—familiar territory. Elissa looked around as she walked down the sidewalk, feeling other eyes on her—Gina or Nash? Probably both.

Elissa opened the door to Delia's and breathed in the welcoming aromas of roasted chicken and fresh tomato sauce that promised a good meal. Waving at the maître d', she headed straight back to the kitchen where Delia and her crew were getting ready for the lunch rush.

"What the heck are you doing here mid-morning?" Delia asked as she paused from chopping a tomato.

Elena had her back to the kitchen door but when she turned and saw Elissa, she smiled big and said, "You quit, didn't you?"

"I did!"

Her smile got impossibly wider. "Straight to Julia's face?"

"She actually staggered backward."

"Ha! Chica!" Elena wiped her hands on her mono-grammed Delia's Catering apron, then spread her arms wide and crossed the kitchen for a hug while the rest of the staff applauded. They'd all heard the horror stories about Elena's—and now Elissa's—former boss.

"So, does that mean you're finally coming to work here?" Delia asked.

Elissa bit her lip. "Well, first I have the Maui Challenge to do."

Elena's eyes got wide. "Wait. Tell me you are not back with Brett."

Elissa stopped herself before she said anything else. *This was a bad idea coming here.* How much could she actually tell Elena and Delia? It was true that Elena had been at the party when Nashville offered to accompany Elissa to Maui when Brett dumped her. So, she wouldn't be revealing anything new, would she?

"No, there's no way in hell that I'm back with Brett. Actually, I'm going to Maui with Nashville."

"Get out!" Elena said. "You told him yes? Is that why you didn't return any of my texts this weekend? Spill the tea *now.*"

Here goes nothing. "Yeah, Nashville came over and we sorta spent the weekend together." Elissa shrugged, but her lips twitched while she tried holding back a huge smile.

Her eyes got wider. "What about that phone call he got at the party?"

She pressed her lips together. "I think that's kind of private, but it wasn't another woman. Obviously."

"Go back to the part where you quit your job," Delia interjected. "And this time finish with, "Sure did, Delia, and I'd love to come work for you now.""

Elissa laughed—it was an old argument and Delia knew it was hopeless but couldn't help needling her. "Sorry, Hawaii beckons."

Delia glanced at Elena. "I should send you there to pick up some new recipes."

"Twist my arm."

"I'm gonna scoot out," Elissa said. "Let you guys work in peace. But I had to share."

Delia waved her toward the little table set up to the side of the kitchen where honored guests were welcome to be used as tasting Guinea pigs. "Sit and eat."

"No, really, I gotta go." Elissa headed toward the dining room.

"Why? You don't have a job to get back to." Even though it was meant as a joke, Elissa felt the tiniest sting.

"Gotta pack. And shop. And pack the new crap I shop for. See ya." She skirted out the door before anyone could stop her. She felt like her legs had a mind of their own and couldn't wait to be on the move. She both loved and dreaded this anxious feeling that propelled her forward. Would it ever let her settle? And settle for what?

Don't think about it, just keep moving she told herself.

Nashville was waiting for her right outside the restaurant entrance, an easy smile on his gorgeous face. Did she really sleep with him last night without mauling him? Just remembering the soul-scorching kiss he'd given her after lunch made her knees go weak. She liked having a good time with a hottie as much as the next red-blooded woman, but Nash's kisses alone took things to an all-new level. And, he was a perfect gentleman. *Dammit.*

He quickly swooped in for a very public kiss and her knees got weaker. "You on break, shug?" Full-on sexy Southern accent and a lighthearted smile to match, but on closer examination, his eyes held worlds of concern.

"More like a permanent vacation," she answered, smiling. "I quit."

Nash's eyes darkened further and he leaned in. "What happened to sticking to your routine?"

"Oh, quitting out of practically nowhere is pretty routine for me," she answered as she patted her tote bag. "At least this time, I remembered to pack up my knickknacks first."

He shook his head and his lips parted. Then it looked like he thought better of speaking. "Well, all right then. No time better than the present." He offered her his arm and she took it.

"Where we going?"

"You'll see," Nash said as they walked to his parked SUV.

E lissa finished stretching in the Watchdog gym. "Look, not gonna lie, I have almost zero self-defense training."

"Good. That'll make this easier."

That surprised her. Reading her expression, Nash added, "It means I don't have to undo a lot of bad training you might have learned. There's a lot of misinformation out there about self-defense, especially when it comes to women. Those internet videos showing women holdin' their keys between their fingers should be banned."

"What? I do that."

"Well, stop." He grabbed a set of keys off a bench and held them between his fingers. Then he took his other hand and pushed back against the keys, which folded easily into the back of his hand. "Do like that and you can see how your enemy can push 'em all back and cut your hand." He readjusted the keys. "Do it like this, see? One key out along your thumb to stabilize it. You can get a good jab in with that if you're unfortunate enough to have an enemy that close to you. The whole idea for you though is to keep you far away from an enemy. I don't have time or inclination to turn you into a soldier, so we're gonna work on your evasion skills today."

"Aw! But what if I want to flip you over my shoulder?" Elissa teased. "Then pin you?"

Nash went stock still, then his cheeks puffed up and he blew out a long breath. "Woman, you are not making this easy."

"Nope, I'm trying to make it har—"

"Do not, if you care one iota for me, finish that thought, shug."

Elissa giggled. But Nash didn't play along.

"I mean it, darlin', you need to take this seriously."

"What happened to the fun-loving, easygoing guy I thought I knew?"

"I put him to the back of my mind so that he doesn't fuck things up by distracting me and making me lose..." his voice trailed off.

Elissa stepped closer. "Making you lose what?"

His gaze went to a level of intensity she'd never seen, making her realize just how serious he was. She suddenly felt truly seen, cherished, wanted. Then he looked away and those feelings evaporated. Who was she kidding? Sure, they had chemistry, but she knew his reputation as much as he knew hers—love 'em and leave 'em fast. But in her case, she tacked on, *before they can leave you*. She sincerely doubted any woman ever willingly left Nash. Which meant she needed to keep her feelings in check before she fooled herself into thinking any of this was real or had a chance of evolving into something permanent.

Oh, God. I think I want *something permanent.*

"I get it," she said. "You'd hate to lose a client."

He whipped his head back around. "That's...true." Nash grimaced. "Let's just get started."

Yup. Not a trace of an accent. No flirting now. All business as they trained.

Well, it was nice while it lasted.

'Serious Nash' as she'd started thinking of him, touched her respectfully and distantly, keeping his movements to a minimum as he physically corrected some of her moves. Everything that came out of his mouth related to what they were doing and only what they were doing—not the slightest hint of innuendo or double-meaning. By the time they finished and Elissa was wiping the sweat off her body, she was convinced she'd imagined every last bit of flirting the previous day.

Until he took her home and left her breathless from another toe-curling kiss just outside her apartment door. She couldn't be imagining his passion in the way his lips consumed hers, or how his fingers gripped her back and moved up to tangle in her hair. Nor in the sounds he made in the back of his throat that soaked her panties right through, or the hardness between his legs as he pressed her against the wall.

Then with a smile and a tip of his cowboy hat he was gone, leaving her breathless and utterly confused.

TEN

"Look, I know how much you want to be with me," Nashville said, his heart breaking as he looked into those loving eyes so full of hurt and confusion. "But it ain't happening. That call is out of my hands. Believe me, if I could do this differently, I would. But trust me when I say this will all be over soon." He blinked back sudden moisture that took him by surprise.

"Now be good and get in the cage."

Kyle clapped a hand on Nashville's shoulder as Nash stood up and Reggie turned and somberly dragged his feet into the kennel. "I get it, brother. Feels like you're leaving a part of yourself behind. These dogs get under your skin quick."

"Truth." Nashville took a quick swipe at his eyes, hoping Kyle wouldn't notice. But of course he did.

"No shame in that game, either," Kyle added. "Sorry he can't go to Hawaii. Even though he's up to date on his vaccines and he's got a fresh OIE-FAVN test, everything needed to be submitted weeks ago and there's no way around the quarantine since he's not technically a service dog. He'd end up staying there in quarantine longer than your visit. But I promise that Reggie's going to be spoiled rotten while he's staying here. I've got his back, and then Marc after me when I head back home to Colorado."

"I appreciate it," Nash said, though his own personal jury was out regarding the new guy. He understood Marc had had a role to play when Elissa snuck out to the courtyard, but he also didn't like *anyone* messing with her.

"Did I hear my name?" Marc walked in behind the two men.

Kyle nodded. "Nash here has to leave Reggie behind. I was just assuring him that we'll spoil that good boy rotten."

"Sure will," Marc said. He immediately took out a treat and gave it to Reggie, which scored him a few points with Nash. "Hey, sorry about the other day with Elissa. I didn't know who she was. I seriously thought she was training here or something and doing an exercise. Didn't realize she was your...girlfriend?"

Nash studied him, noting genuine confusion in his eyes. Yeah, this whole situation was a mess. "No harm, man. We're good." He shook the man's hand without elaborating further.

After dropping off Reggie, his next mission was to pick up Elissa, take her to dinner, then spend the night at her place. Since they'd be leaving for LAX at oh-dark-thirty, it made sense. And, that was about the only thing that made sense between them right now.

Nash wasn't sure how much longer he could keep up his double-life, which ironically, shouldn't have been double at all. He wanted nothing more than to show Elissa *exactly* how much he cared. His feelings for her had only grown deeper as their week of 'posing' as a dating couple flew by. In public, he was constantly touching her, sneaking kisses, wining and dining Elissa the way he'd wanted to do for so long. And she responded to every touch with overwhelming warmth and passion. She'd already learned how much he loved feeling her nails scraping lightly down his back, or when she sucked his earlobe between her lips and teased it with the tip of her tongue.

It was their time alone that was the problem.

He couldn't let himself go, didn't dare continue their touches and kisses because they inevitably would lead to bed. She was a client until they got the all-clear that she wasn't in any danger. Nash did *not* sleep with a principal, no matter how tempting. And there had been some tempting ones in the past, women who just went ga-ga over his y'alls and his boots and his cowboy hat. He'd remained a professional then, and he was determined to remain one now, especially after going on leave in protest of what he'd seen as Costello's reckless behavior when he'd fallen for Jordan.

So to keep from sweeping Elissa off her feet and carrying her to the nearest flat surface where he could lay her down, strip her naked, and bury himself inside her, Nash resorted to talking about anything and everything. The minute she'd start to cozy up to him, he'd ask her what her favorite movie was (*Spiderman – No Way Home*, which of course raised his esti-mation of her up twenty notches since he loved that one too) or about her favorite music. On that count, their tastes varied wildly, but that only made it more fun to introduce her to some of his favorites—which she ended up liking—and listening to some of hers that he'd never heard—with the same result.

As Nash turned the corner to the hall leading to the parking lot, he nearly collided with Costello. The other man had already started backing up before Nash careened into him—Psychic at his best.

"I was hoping to catch you," Costello said.

Great, the last person I hoped to see wants to talk. "I was fixing to leave right now since I'm running late," Nash said. "Can this wait?"

"No, it can't," Costello said as he moved to the middle of the hall, effectively blocking Nash's path. "We need to clear the air, Nash. I know why you took a leave of absence. Our last assignment went sideways. That's on me. I fucked up and it made you doubt, well, everything. I've nearly cost Watchdog a good man. So, let me apologize."

"Apology accepted. Can I go now?"

"No," Costello said, crossing his arms. "That's only half of what I want to say. You and Elissa—"

"Are none of y'all's business, and I'm fed up with everyone talking about us," Nash snapped, surprised at his own sudden anger but unwilling to stem it. "Everyone's got an opinion about me, that I'm just gonna play around with her and then toss her aside—"

"That's not what I—"

"I imagine y'all think I'm using her to go to Hawaii, when to be honest, that's the last thing I want to do, the last place I want to go..." He got a hold of himself before he started down the road on a subject he didn't want to share. It was no one's business why Hawaii haunted him.

"I would never accuse you of using her like that." Red crept up Costello's neck. "What I'm trying to say is," he lowered his voice. "I know she's your client."

Nash's eyes went round. "Damn gossips. This place leaks secrets like a sieve."

Costello shrugged. "Can't argue that. I remember walking in on a certain conversation between you and Jake once."

Oh yeah. Costello had once caught him telling Jake he was pretty sure something was going on between Costello and Gina of all people. Nash was just as big a gossip as anyone. All his self-righteousness drained away and he actually chuckled. "Got me dead to rights, brother. Guess I owe you an apology right back."

Costello's shoulders relaxed and he dropped his arms to his sides. "That wasn't what I was looking for, but I'll take it." He smiled. "I just want to give you some advice." The red returned to his face. "Seeing as I was in your shoes not that long ago."

"All right, and what's that?" Now it was Nash's turn to cross his arms. Here's where Costello would assume Elissa and Nash were already sleeping together and tell him to cool it.

"Go with your heart as much as your gut. There's more to life than this job, as important as it is. No one's judging you, Nash. That's where I fucked up—putting too much importance on how everyone around me saw me, about keeping up the illusion of being perfect, and it almost cost me everything. Thing is, I was wrong. I was projecting my own insecurities onto other people and it affected my job. I nearly lost Jordan that way. I don't want to see the same thing happen to you."

Costello's sincere words took Nash aback. He never would have guessed he'd hear Psychic admitting to his failures. Then again, Jordan had changed him, loosened him up and made him human. "I appreciate what you're saying, Psychic, but I know I'm being judged. Jake and Camden said as much, that I'm a dirty dog who shouldn't be sniffin' around Elissa. That all I'm gonna do is break her heart."

"So are you going to break her heart?"

"Oh, hell no." That thought alone set his stomach to churning.

"Then who cares what they said? They're wrong about you. I see it. Jordan sees it. She knew you were solid from the moment you walked through the door to protect her."

Well I'll be. He had no idea she held such a high opinion of him. He figured she thought the same way as the rest, especially at the party. "I am surely humbled by that. But the other thing is, so long as Elissa's a client, Lachlan would skin me alive were I to sleep with her," Nash said.

"Looked like the two of you were already heading that way long before she retained our services. Seems like your relationship would be grandfathered in, so to speak."

Nash shook his head—more scuttlebutt about their skirting around each other. "You might have a point. We were definitely starting something before this."

"So, it looks like you're the one who's standing in the way."

Direct hit. Nash pushed the truth of that down deep for now. No way was he about to talk about that here in a damn hallway at Gossip Central. But one thing Costello said needed correcting. "Elissa didn't exactly come to us though. Gina came to her."

Costello frowned. "Wait. Gina thought Elissa was in some sort of danger?"

"*Potential* danger, brother. I can't say much more'n that. Except, one of the reasons we're going to Maui is to get her out of harms' way."

"I'll see if I can't make myself useful here," Costello said.

Nash grinned. "I appreciate that too, brother, but won't that give away that you know too much?"

Costello chuckled. "Did you forget? I'm Psychic."

Nash laughed. That was new, too—Costello embracing his handle. Jordan really was good for him. As good as he was for bringing her out of her shell and giving her confidence.

Nash wondered if he'd ever find that with a woman. But he didn't wonder long—his gut told him yes and his heart told him who.

Starting tonight.

E lissa answered his knock at her door moments after he heard her checking to see who it was. Damn, she was gorgeous with her hair pinned up off her tanned shoulders, her blue eyes sparkling as bright as the sun on the ocean, her mini-dress caressing every curve down to her long legs. The only thing he hated was the look on her face—open attraction quickly swallowed by guarded anticipation. That wasn't her at all. No—*he'd* put that look there by giving off mixed signals.

He took off his hat and set it on the little table beside the door. This should've been the part where he took her in his arms and kissed her down to her soul—no hesitation, no guarded walls, just pure pleasure. Instead, she smiled and said hello before backing away and giving him room to come in. As she turned her back on him, she said, "So, for dinner, I was thinking we could go to—"

Nash grabbed her arm and spun her around to face him. Surprise filled her gaze as she looked up at him, her mouth a perfect and inviting 'O'. He pulled her to his chest and wrapped his arms around her. Her arms went around his waist but there was hesitation in her movements. She held him loosely, with a look of uncertainty on her face.

That quickly changed when he bent and claimed her mouth with his. She rewarded him with a sweet-as-molasses little moan and melted against him. Her sun-kissed citrus scent enveloped them as he turned and pressed her back against the wall the way he'd done what felt like a million years ago. Before the danger. Before the charade. Before the thought of how the tips of her hair brushed the tops of her shoulders when she laughed kept him up at night. Before he couldn't get the desire to touch her bare skin where her waist flared out over the strong curve of her hip out of his mind. They were back where they belonged as if no time had passed, and he had no intention of wasting one more second on a farce.

So he devoured her, starting with her sweet mouth. She tasted like wildflower honey as he explored her lips, twined his tongue around hers until they gasped for air. She was kissing him with abandon and he could taste her desperation there along with the honey. Her hands moved up from his waist to his shoulders and she held on. He'd remember that it was her idea first, communicated through her clutching fingers, when he slid his hands down her hips and lifted her until she wrapped her legs around his waist. One hand kept hold of his shoulder while the other explored his hair and Lord have mercy if that didn't feel *good*. Her nails lightly scratched against his scalp, sending shivers down his back. He pressed harder against her and realized that if he didn't carry her to the bedroom this second he was in danger of sending her straight through the wall. He needed her under him *now*. Needed to take that little white tease of a dress off and look her over before he went exploring.

Just as he readied to carry her across the apartment by moving his hand up and spreading his palm across her back to steady her—hardly needed because she was so strong—she pulled her head away and broke their kiss.

"Did they install a camera in my apartment?" she asked.

"Do what now?" The warm fuzzy haze in his head wouldn't let him parse her question. He leaned forward again to recapture her lips but she angled back.

"Is that why you're doing this? We're being watched inside my apartment now?" She loosened her grip to slide back to the floor.

"Wait, shug, no." He tightened his arms around her, turning them to steel bands holding her in place against him. "We're not being watched. It's just you and me right now. This isn't for show. This is how I feel, what I want to do— what I've *wanted* to do for a long time. Long before I approached you at Jordan and Psychic's party. Hell, before I even knew your name. From the minute I saw you bustling 'round the kitchen with Elena at that political shindig, I thought you were the bee's knees. Camden only had eyes for Elena, but I couldn't see her at all past your light. I thought you were perfection." She started shaking her head but he continued. "Now having spent time with you, getting to know the warm, sweet, amazing person you are, I *know* you're perfection."

"I'm not," she protested. "I'm such a hot mess, I can't even settle into a job I like, and I can't wrap my head around what we're doing here."

"That's my fault, shug. I've been hitting both the gas and the brakes with us. Tryin' to be two people at once. The professional who sticks to the rules, and the man who sees his chance with you and grabs it before someone better'n me comes along and you realize I'm not good enough for you."

"Okay, what did you just say to me?" Because *I* keep waiting for *you* to figure out *I'm* not good enough." She tipped her head until it rested against his chest, her warm breath teasing him through his shirt. "I thought that's why you've been keeping your distance when we're alone." She tipped her chin up until she was staring up at him through her black lashes and blond bangs. "That the more you got to know me, the more you realized what a flake I am. But you're telling me that it's all just you being a professional?"

"Most, shug. The rest is me just guarding myself for the day this assignment is over and you wizen up and move on."

"Okay, so we're both flakes." She looked dead serious until her lips curved up into a smile and she couldn't hold back her giggle. Which in turn made him laugh. She held on tightly as he twisted his waist, swinging her back and forth. She pressed her cheek against his chest and he buried his face in her hair.

"Oh, I like you so much, Mr. Jones," she said.

"I'm sweet on you too, Miss St Clair." He nuzzled the top of her head. "Damn my job, I'm fixin' to show you how much, in all the ways I can."

She looked back up at him, her eyes at half-mast. "I'm looking forward to it."

He'd been wondering about her tan lines—specifically, the lack of them. No matter what dress or shirt she wore, tank tops, spaghetti straps, midriffs, he never saw a pale strip of skin. Her tan seemed to be even all over. Did she use a tanning bed? That didn't seem like her style. He couldn't imagine Elissa lying still long enough in one of the lighted coffins to get a tan. As he slowly undressed her, sliding her minidress down and exposing more of her body, he had yet to see a pale inch of skin. He reached around and unhooked her lacy bra, revealing her perky breasts tipped with pink-brown nipples. So *perfect*. He ran his thumbs over them until they pebbled under his touch and she mewled. He knelt and hooked his fingers under the silky fabric of her panties and down they went.

"Mercy me, no tan lines," he murmured. "I'd been wondering about that."

She laughed. "Were you?"

"I was, shug. You never struck me as the type to use a tanning bed."

She laughed again. "Got that right."

"So?" He let his question hang there.

"I sneak up to the rooftop of my apartment building with a book, a towel, and an inflatable raft." She grinned.

Nash laughed. "You are one for a thrill, aren't you?"

"You could say that." She winked.

And then she closed her eyes when Nash pressed his lips to her secret, most sensitive place. She was already wet for him, slick and musky and sweet all at the same time. He ran his tongue through her soft folds and over the tight bud of her clit while she held his head, almost directing him where she wanted him. So *damn hot*—he'd never had any woman who was so forward with him.

He pulled back and she protested, actually pushing his head back toward her. "Spread your legs for me, sugar," he said as he placed his hands on her inner thighs to 'encourage' her to comply. She grabbed one of his hands and slid it up to her entrance. "I need you inside me, too," she panted. "While you...while you...yeah, *that*." He'd gone back to lapping her up like honey from a biscuit while he slid his finger into her hot, tight core. She squeezed around his finger which sent an electric jolt straight to his cock right when he thought he'd gotten the upper hand. Damn, damn, *fucking* damn she was hot. As he caressed and stroked her with his lips, he felt his cock weeping in his jeans, begging to get in on the action. He added a second finger and she squeezed again as she moaned. He bent his fingers until he found the hard bundle of nerves inside her walls and pressed.

That did it. Nash held her up with his other hand as her knees started to buckle and her squeezes went from being under her control to fluttery, growing stronger like waves hitting the shore from a storm out to sea. She gripped his shoulders tightly as she came hard against his mouth. He slackened his tongue lashings as she pulled back slightly, realizing she must be very sensitive after an orgasm and adjusting his game plan accordingly. He'd give her a minute to recuperate, then it was back to the races.

"Oh, my, God," she breathed. Her eyes opened and she blinked several times as she smiled down at him. "That was lovely. Thank you."

Nash smirked as he stood up. "Lovely? You make it sound like I poured you a cup of tea."

She cracked up. "Okay, fine. It was mind-blowing. Cosmic. Earth-shattering. Better?"

"Well, I don't know about that." He kissed the tip of her nose.

"No? You don't believe me?"

"Oh, it's not that, shug. I know it was good. I felt how good it was for you." He watched her focus go fuzzy and her cheeks pinken up. "I just think I need to give it another try."

She sucked in her lower lip. "I'm all for that. But it's your turn first."

Elissa untucked his shirt from his waistband. But when he lifted his arms and she tried to pull it off over his head she realized she was too short, even standing on tip-toe.

"Need help with that?" He grabbed the back of his shirt and pulled it off in one smooth motion.

Elissa made an appreciative sound as her eyes went wide while she studied his torso. Her gaze went straight where he thought it would—to the hibiscus tattoo over his heart. When she touched it, he shivered. When she kissed it, he damn near lost his mind.

All the same, he hoped she wouldn't ask about it. Not yet. *The best defense is a good offense, so here we go.* Before she could open her mouth, Nash groaned and slid his hands down her back to her ass and lifted her up as he caught her lips with his. He headed straight for Elissa's bedroom, appreciating her taut body against his. He'd never realized what a turn-on it was to have such a physically strong woman in his arms. His type had always been softer, women who made a show of being impressed by his strength. Elissa felt more like an equal match, someone who could keep up with him.

Time to put that to the test.

When he got to her bedroom, she slid out of his arms and threw the comforter back. "Oh!" she said. "Wait. Do you have protection? I'm out. It's...been a while for me." Her cheeks went from pink to red.

That surprised him. He thought she'd been with Sneaker-head for months and they'd only recently broken up. Had she really never taken him to bed? "Yeah, I do." He reached into his back pocket and pulled out his wallet, then tossed a string of wrapped condoms on the bed.

He must have let his thoughts show, because Elissa's gaze dropped to the floor. "Brett wanted to. But, it didn't feel right for me so I told him no. Probably why he dumped me, huh?" Her eyes widened and her head snapped up. "Though, don't get me wrong. Brett dumping me is damn near the best thing that's ever happened to me."

Nash cupped her face. "You don't need to explain anything to me. He wasn't good enough for you and you knew it. I'm proud of you for not settling." Now it was Nash's turn to look away.

"What?" she said quietly. Her hand had already gone to his against her cheek and she threaded their fingers together then brought his hand to her lips and laid the sweetest kiss there. "Don't even *think* that you aren't good enough. I thought we'd settled that."

He gave her his tenderest smile. "So many areas in my life, I know I do a good job. I couldn't have been a SEAL if I wasn't bringing my best game every day. Same with Watchdog. Same with..." He'd started to say 'my family' but stopped. He'd failed there for sure. "Same with a lot of things. But sugar, when it comes to you, I'm never gonna assume that I'm good enough. I'm gonna strive for it every day. Every *minute* of every day that you'll have me. I'm going to let you know that I'm worth it because you are. You are so special to me, Elissa. So damn special." He pulled her close and wrapped his arms around her, his heart liking to burst against his ribcage.

He felt her heart pounding too as she stretched up to kiss him. Just before their lips met, she stopped and looked at him —*really* looked at him. "You actually mean it, don't you?"

"With all my heart."

She laid her hand over his chest and the hibiscus tattoo. "I care about you too, Nash. I'm not used to a guy like you." She looked into his eyes again. "Someone who I'm not just attracted to, but who I *like*. Who I *respect*."

Like.

He was going to have to up his game.

He kissed her deep and hard, pouring everything he had into it. Her arms dropped and her hands went slack before they went to his belt and fumbled with it. She barely gave him time to kick off his boots, pull off his socks, and step out of his jeans before she was pulling at the waistband of his boxer briefs, and soon those were gone too. His cock jutted out and she grabbed hold before he had a chance to snag one of the condoms. Her tongue circled the tip of his cock and he threw back his head and groaned.

"Lord have mercy," he growled. He undid her pinned-up hair and wrapped it around his fingers, playing with the long strands while she licked the length of him, pressing her tongue flat, then swirling it in tiny circles. He glanced down at her just as she looked up at him through those long lashes, pure mischief in her eyes, and he almost lost it. She knew exactly what she was doing and reveled in it. She took him in deep and hollowed her cheeks, creating the most incredible suction while tormenting him with her tongue.

"Darlin', you need to stop or I'm gonna make a fool of myself."

She ran her mouth back down his length and gave his tip a lick. "I don't think that's possible," she murmured.

"Which? You stopping, or me making a fool of myself?"

Elissa giggled. "Either. Both."

Before she could swallow him again, he grabbed a condom and tore open the wrapper. "I need to be inside you, right now."

As he reached for his cock, she took the condom. "Let me," she said. She pumped him as if he could get any harder, then slowly rolled the condom down his cock to the base. She backed up on the bed and he followed on hands and knees until she was lying under him. She grabbed his cock again to guide him inside her. *So, so sexy.* He loved that she knew exactly what she wanted and didn't hesitate to go for it.

He slid in balls-deep and found himself in heaven. So soft and warm and tight. As he moved inside her, she matched his thrusts with hers. He found her hard, wet clit again and rubbed until her pussy was squeezing around him.

"Nash," she moaned. "So close, baby."

"Come on, I want to feel you come around me. Wanna feel you lose it. Come for me." He rubbed her fast and light and she closed her eyes and arched her back.

"Look at me, shug. I wanna see it, too."

She opened her sky-blue eyes and locked her gaze on his.

No hesitation, no shyness, nothing but the intensity of the moment.

"So damn beautiful," he said as he felt her squeeze around him once, twice, then the uncontrollable flutters were back and he came fast and hard right along with her. When they were done he held her close, not willing to leave her body just yet. Wanting to stretch the moment all the way out to the far horizon. She lay still, not wanting to lose their connection, either, while he nuzzled her throat and she ran her fingers over the nape of his neck.

After ordering in, they made love two more times that night, each time better than the last as they got to know each other's bodies. By the time they fell asleep, Nash knew beyond the shadow of a doubt that he'd found the woman he wanted to keep by his side forever.

All he had to do was keep her safe over the next couple of weeks.

ELEVEN

LAX was its typical busy self when Elissa and Nash checked their bags, Elissa's bike for the race, a ton of her gear—and their surfboards. Nash had surprised her the night before when she saw his board strapped to the top of the SUV.

"I had no idea you surfed," she'd said as he unstrapped it to take up to her apartment for safekeeping before they went to dinner. He'd already packed it in bubble wrap and cardboard for traveling.

"Ever since I was a skinny-ass teenager who moved to the West Coast from Tennessee," he said. "Every place has its stereotypes, am I right? I was convinced that every single person in Los Angeles got up at the crack of dawn to catch the waves before they went off to their jobs as actors or waitstaff hoping to become actors."

Elissa snorted. "Okay, I wanna be offended by that, but you aren't too far off."

Nash chuckled. "So as the new kid, I reckoned I'd best learn how to surf as fast as I could just so I'd fit in and maybe dodge other people stereotyping me as some hillbilly from back in the holler the second I opened my mouth."

That went straight to her heart. "Is that why your accent comes and goes? You came here and got made fun of so you got rid of it?"

He tucked the board under his arm like it was a popsicle stick and they started for the stairs since the elevator was way too small. *God, he's strong* she thought. "Naw, shug, that came way before the thought of moving to LA was a twinkle in my Mama's eye." He put his accent on thick. "Growing up in Tennessee, my mama told me and...told me I best lose the accent if I wanted anyone to ever take me seriously. She even practiced with me from the moment I was knee-high to a tadpole. *War*shed the clothes became *wah*shed the clothes. Git became get. Flair became flower. Caint became can't." His accent faded out as he spoke until he sounded like he'd grown up somewhere in the Heartland. "And Nashville just became Nash." He chuckled. "By the time I knew we were moving out here, I'd even added 'Shiznit, man, that's righteous' to my vocabulary." The last words he spoke in the thickest stereotypical surfer accent ever.

Elissa shook her head. "I feel so sad thinking about you as a kid having to do that."

He shrugged. "You do what you have to do."

Elissa waited until they were up the stairs and back at her apartment to ask, "So did it work? Did you blend in, or did anyone ever make fun of you?"

Nash rubbed his chin. "Sometimes and sometimes. I learned to deploy the accent strategically." He winked.

Elissa rolled her eyes. "Vocal chick magnet."

He folded his arms in mock-affront. "Not just that. Sometimes, you get people who think the accent means I'm not smart and it pays to let them think you're dumb."

She frowned. "Not for me."

"What do you mean?"

"If you ever met my family, you'd understand." She closed the door on that subject as she opened the door to her apartment.

"Family troubles," Nash had echoed behind her. "That, I do understand."

She decided to let it go for now. After the knee-weakening sex they'd had, she wanted to keep things fun, light, breezy. She didn't want to think about how he made her want to sink roots down into the relationship and stay as long as Nash would have her. They had enough to worry about between the upcoming race and the idea that she might be under surveillance. And so she kept the conversation light through dinner, and then two more marathon-level bouts of sex before she fell asleep exhausted and satisfied in his arms.

Now Elissa watched Nash as he studied every face in the terminal while they waited to board the plane. She wondered what he was looking for. Was it somebody who looked suspicious? Or somebody who *didn't* look suspicious? She was dying to ask him. She wanted to know everything. She felt drawn to this sort of life, though she didn't know if it was short-term or long-term. Was it only because her life was in danger? Or was this a greater calling?

"Ladies and gentlemen, we'll be boarding flight 451 for Maui in just a few minutes."

"Oh my God that's us," Alissa said. She grabbed Nashville's hand.

"Are you ready, shug?"

"I've been ready for this all my life," Elissa answered.

"Me too," he murmured. His hand resting at the small of her back as they waited to board steadied her. They found their seats and she offered the window seat to him so that he didn't have to sit in the middle. He declined.

"This is your trip, shug. Enjoy the view." Then he leaned in close to kiss her ear. But he also whispered, "I don't want anyone sitting next to you. If anyone wants you, they'll have to go through me." At first, she thought he was being possessive, but then she realized he meant it literally. His body was tense and his attention focused on every person coming down the aisle. He only relaxed when their seatmate arrived—a teenaged girl whose parents and younger brother took up the three-seat row across the aisle. Another family sat behind them. She wondered if Gina's 'friends' had anything to do with the seating arrangements on the plane. The thought that came on the heels of that one sent a cold-water chill down her spine. If someone on the plane was targeting her and the seating around her had been manipulated to keep that person away, those 'friends' had no issue putting children in danger. She wished she could stand up and look everyone in the face, to try and read people the way Nash did. Maybe someone would give something away.

I'm not going to think that way. I can't. She popped her earbuds in and started her travel playlist to distract herself.

Nash grabbed her hand when the plane started to taxi toward the runway. She startled, thinking that he was about to tell her he'd located an assassin, but the smile on his face told her everything was all right. She turned off the music and he lifted his chin to the window.

"Time to respect the takeoff."

"What? *Oh.*" He'd remembered how she felt about flying. Her heart flipped over in her chest. Her smile threatened to spread until it touched each ear. Yes. This is what had always been missing in her romantic relationships. A man who understood and respected her.

She squeezed his fingers and together, they watched as the plane raced down the runway until the wheels left the ground and they were doing what so few people in history had done—sailed through the air on a dream.

After they were airborne, Elissa pulled out her lucky paperback which she took with her everywhere, and prepared to take advantage of the five-hour flight to immerse herself in Riley Edwards' world for the millionth time. Two chapters in, Jasper's speech was interrupted when she felt eyes on her. Yup, Nash was reading over her shoulder.

"Can I help you?" she teased.

"I'm just surprised you're not reading a kids' book." He tapped the cover with the deliciously bare-chested man on it. "Because this ain't no kids' book."

Elissa rolled her eyes. "You know, I do like adult books, too. Riley Edwards, Susan Stoker, Caitlin O'Leary, Raine Lewis. The list goes on." She started to grab her carry-on tucked under the seat in front of her. "This one's a signed copy to me so I don't let anyone borrow it, but I've got an Elle James in here and I think you'd like her."

"Nope, not if it has a cover like that one."

"Okay, suit yourself." She went back to reading. And Nash went back to looking over her shoulder.

"I could read it aloud for you."

Nash laughed. "Thanks, no." He stretched. "Never did like long flights. I've usually seen all the movies worth watching and I get antsy just sitting and waiting."

"I know the feeling. That's why I always bring a book." She turned a page. Things were just getting juicy.

"Teach me to sign."

She looked up. "What?

"Sign language. It's pretty cool that you know how."

"Ugh, fine." She closed her book and set it aside. "I'll teach you to sign the alphabet. That should keep you occupied for five hours."

It didn't take nearly that long. Nash was a quick learner and pretty soon they were signing the most obscene words they could think of and trying not to laugh too loudly.

"**F**un fact. Did you know the Hawaiian Islands are the most remote inhabited place on earth?" Nash asked.

"I believe it after this flight," Elissa said, gazing out the window. Nothing but ocean for hours, only the occasional cloudbank to disrupt the view. Eventually, the solid navy blue gave way to a growing spot of the darkest green she'd ever seen as Maui came into view.

"Unbelievable," she breathed. Nash leaned in and looked over her shoulder. She glanced back at him and he quickly looked away. Were his eyes just the tiniest bit glossy? *Weird.* The thought slipped back out of her mind as she watched the island grow bigger and bigger. The deep blue waters grew lacy white lines as the waves approached and broke on the volcanic rocks and reefs surrounding Maui. As they descended, the solid green broke up into individual trees—tall skinny palms, huge branching banyans, spiky evergreens. Mist shrouded the hills and clouds hung over patchwork fields. A rainbow flashed, then another, making her laugh with joy as she pointed them out.

Nash just smiled. He grabbed her hand and brought it to his lips, pressing her knuckles against his lips and holding it there. His eyes shone as she realized he was staring at her, not at the stunning view.

Then he lifted his chin, indicating the window. "Respect your landings," he said against her skin, and her heart about leaped out of her chest again. She turned back in time to see the ground rising to meet them as they passed through a wispy cloud and found the runway. The usual bump and the roar of the engines as the plane raced along the ground sped up her heart as it always did. And like always, she thought *Made it. I'm back on earth in a new place. One more everyday miracle.*

Just like the man sitting next to her who *got it.*

"We are in another country," Elissa said as they walked through Kahului Airport and another bird flew through the wide glassless window, circled above, and flew back out on a refreshing tropical breeze. She couldn't believe that an airport of all things would just be open to the air like that all the time. She wasn't even sure they'd gone back through security yet.

"Sure feels like it, don't it, shug?" He squeezed her hand as they followed the signs for baggage claim and the car rental desks past refrigerated vending machines where intricate leis hung.

"You want one?" Nash asked.

Elissa smiled, "No. It just seems, I don't know, anticlimactic to buy one for yourself from a vending machine like that. It's supposed to be an aloha from someone else, you know?"

Once they finished the rental car paperwork, they made their way outside, where a rooster and several chickens scratched and pecked at the grass under a squat palm tree.

"Oh my goodness!" Elissa looked around. "Did they escape? Do they belong to someone?"

"Nope. They run wild all over the islands."

"They're gorgeous." Elissa snapped several photos of the birds and the trees as they waited for the green train to take them to their vehicle. The lady behind the desk said they could pick out any vehicle in the row indicated on their receipt and she had a feeling Nash was going to go for the biggest truck he could find. The cute little train pulled up to the gathering crowd and the driver helped secure several surfboards. Someone said 'mahalo' and Elissa tried to remember what that meant.

"It means thank you," Nash said, reading her expression. "And more than that. A sense of deep gratitude, of respect."

"So, like how aloha means more than just hello."

"Exactly, shug." Nash and Elissa both told the driver mahalo then got into the shuttle.

As expected, Nashville picked out a hard-top Jeep that would accommodate their boards and her racing cycle and allow him not to give up his man card for a Ford Fiesta.

"Hungry?" he asked the minute they got in and buckled up.

"Starving. Where should we go? I just realized I spent more time researching the race than I did restaurants."

Nash grinned. "Leave it to me then." He started the Jeep and left the car rental without turning on GPS, just took a sharp left onto Airport Road, then a couple minutes later, a right on State Highway 36. Another right and they were at...a Costco.

Elissa frowned. She'd been hoping for something a little more...unique.

She stopped frowning when Nash drove around behind it to a group of food trucks and parked in a small lot beside them. Elissa gaped at the multi-colored trucks surrounding covered picnic tables. The delicious aromas nearly made her swoon.

Nash came around the Jeep and let her out. "Lots of choices here, but me, I'm going for the Big Kahuna Plate at Kalei's Lunch Box," he said before they'd even gotten to the trucks. "What are you in the mood for?"

She wondered how often Nash had visited Maui and when he'd found this place. "All of it?" she answered.

He laughed. "We can certainly do that, shug. That's why I thought this might be the best way to start." They made their way around the trucks, reading each menu. Elissa ended up ordering from two of them—an acai bowl from a purple, green, and yellow truck called Ma 'Ono and a Big Kahuna Plate right along with Nash because it looked and smelled so damn good.

"I just love watching you eat," Nash said as he watched her dig into the mushroom gravy-smothered hamburger patty.

"Is that supposed to be a compliment, because it's not," she said around her mouthful of food. She didn't realize just how hungry she was until she took that first bite. She was tempted to go feral—carry her meal off into the trees, forgo her fork, and just dive face-first into the meat followed by the rainbow of sweet fruit dolloped with lilikoi butter in the acai bowl.

"It is a compliment and I'm sticking with it. I'd hate to watch you sit there and pick at some lil' ol' salad when you could be eating that." He pointed his fork at her half-devoured hamburger steak.

"Eat faster or I might steal yours," she said and he laughed. It was so good to see him happy, not the guarded, almost moody Nash she'd been dealing with the week before. "So, what's the itinerary after this? When do I have to do actual things with other people?"

He tilted his head. "You don't have your schedule?"

"Yeah, I do, but it's in my bag and I figured you'd already have it memorized."

His eyebrow quirked up. "That's assuming a lot."

"But you do have it memorized, right?" She grinned back.

"Yes, of course I do."

"Because you're good at your job and minding your client." She took another bite.

"Sure enough, I am." She didn't miss his cocky smile before he took a sip of his POG, another delicacy he'd introduced her to—a juice mix of passionfruit, orange, and guava. "We have the next few days free since we got here early to train. First thing though is an informal get-together for folks showing up early. That's a cocktail party at the resort. Next is a private luau where the rules are laid down. Then comes the race immediately followed by the awards ceremony, then home a few days after that, which will give us some surf time once you've recovered."

She waved him off. "That won't take long."

He gave her that sexy, cocky grin. "Did you sign up online to train with anyone ahead of time like they suggested?"

"Trick question. You told me not to."

Nash smiled wide. "Good answer. For now, we can't trust anyone." His expression softened. "How you gonna feel, seeing Sneakerhead here with someone else?"

"Like a million bucks when they eat my dust."

That earned her a big laugh from Nash. "That's my girl."

They drove across Maui to the western shore and checked into the Fair Winds Resort north of Lahaina. Their suite on the eighth floor faced the narrow stretch of beach and the sound of rolling waves filled the rooms through the open windows.

Nash immediately unpacked some sort of electronic device. When Elissa started to ask about it, he put his finger to his lips and winked. He used it to search the room for any listening devices or cameras while Elissa followed along, eager to learn. Satisfied that the room wasn't bugged, they sat on a loveseat with a view out the lanai. He took out another device like the one she'd seen Gina use to create some sort of safe bubble so they could talk. Once he flipped it on, she felt herself relax, and Nash's broad shoulders definitely dropped.

"So tell me what this is and how it works," she said, tapping the device.

He chuckled. "You're curious as a raccoon."

She shrugged. "It's an electronic shiny that does cool spy stuff. Of course I'm curious."

She couldn't read the look he gave her, but he explained the device to her anyway while they unpacked. By the time they finished, the sun was close to setting, the light not yet turning orange.

"Do you want to walk on the beach before dark?" Elissa suggested.

Nash took her in his arms. "Sure, shug. Then I can think of a few things I want to do after dark."

She smiled as their lips met. *It would be so easy to forget that anything other than the Maui Challenge brought us here* she thought. *That we're just two people falling for each other while I have a race to run.* And yet, there was that thrill that ran around her belly whenever she realized she might be part of something bigger, something life-changing.

"What's that look?" Nash asked.

"If I tell you, you'll think I'm nuts."

"Never, shug."

She laid the palm of her hand against his cheek. "I'm so glad that you're here with me, and I wish it was under better circumstances. But..." She trailed off.

Nash covered her hand with his. "I think I understand. You really are a thrill-seeker, aren't you?"

"What was your first clue?"

He chuckled and turned her hand to kiss her palm. "Oh, I don't know. Maybe the hacking. The Maui Challenge. The sneaking out to spy on the meeting at Watchdog. No, wait." He shook his head. "It has to be the naked sunbathing on your apartment roof."

That made her laugh. "No guts, no glory, no tan lines."

Nash joined her laughter. Then he pulled her up off the loveseat. "You are fearless."

"I'm not fearless, that's the thing. I'm scared a lot, like when I'm out surfing and the water suddenly bottoms out and I just know that the ocean is sucking it up and that there's going to be a monster wave coming and I've got the choice of either chickening out or turning and catching it. There's that moment where I'm questioning my sanity. And then I just do the next thing. I turn, and prepare, and let my body remember what it's supposed to do and then I do it. I catch that wave and ride it as long as I can. I'm still scared, right up until that moment when I know that I've got it. I'm not going to wipe out, at least not this time.

"And then when I get to shore I think, *wow, I sure got lucky that time but I'll kill myself if I go back out there.* And then I do the next little thing that's going to get me back in the water, and the one thing after that, and before I know it, I find myself out at the edge of the breakers waiting for the next wave. I'm still scared, but I'm *there*, you know? I like the thrill, no doubt. It's why I do it, why I do anything significant, really.

But that little bit of fear never leaves me. It sits at the bottom of my soul like a layer of grit."

"Grit makes pearls."

She side-eyed Nash. "That is both really profound, and really corny."

Nash gave her a goofy grin. "Bless your heart."

"Uh-uh. That only works when it's coming from a Southern matron."

That got her another laugh. "Let's us head down for that walk, shug." He pulled her into his arms. "And after that, I'll race you right back up here."

TWELVE

The next day, Nash kissed Elissa awake well before the sun came up.

"Mmmurph." She rolled over and he hugged her back against his chest.

"Come on, sugar. Rise and shine. I've got a surprise for you."

"That's not really a surprise," she answered as she pressed her ass against his hardening cock.

Nash chuckled as he ran his hand through her sleep-tousled hair. "It surely is not." He rubbed up against her while he kissed the nape of her neck. "We've got just enough time to fool around a little, then we've got to go. You have a race to train for." He nuzzled into her hair. She really was delicious, even half-asleep. Just smelling her made his cock grow as hard as steel.

He scooped her up and carried her into the bathroom while she protested, then set her on her feet. While he adjusted the water temperature in the shower, she peppered his back with kisses. He swept her into the wide stall and watched the water cascade down her body. What he wouldn't give to be under a waterfall with her right now, without a care in the world. He'd texted Gina before waking Elissa and had gotten back the message that she was handling things and not to worry.

Yet.

Not the most reassuring message he'd ever gotten.

Elissa soaped up a loofah which he immediately confiscated.

"Turn around so I can soap up your back," he ordered. He liked the way her eyes sparked at his command, which she followed without question.

"Yes, coach," she said, turning and raising her arms, allowing him full access to her stunning body. He moved the rough loofah over her back until her skin turned pink under the tan. He filled his hands with suds and reached around to soap up her breasts, playing with her nipples until they were stiff peaks under his fingers. She squirmed back into him until his cock rested between her tight ass cheeks. At that point, she showed him no mercy, moving up and down until he was holding her tightly against him. The soapsuds worked in their favor, making their bodies slippery. It wasn't long before he was groaning and spilling himself all over the small of her back. He turned her around to rinse her off, kneeling and finding her wet beyond his wildest dreams. It only took a minute before she was crying out her orgasm against his lips.

Elissa rode her race bike south along the Honopi'ilani Highway which followed the shore, through the village of Lahaina, to Kamaole I Beach Park. She pushed it as hard as she could since this was part of the bike race route.

Nash followed close behind in the Jeep, his flashers blinking, providing her with cover from the other vehicles whizzing by on their way to board chartered boats for snorkeling excursions or to catch some waves. They'd started in the dark, but now the sky had lightened though the sun had yet to peek over the horizon when Elissa turned into the beachside parking lot beside a truck carrying a sleek tandem racing kayak. She smiled and covered her heart when she saw it. "Gorgeous," she whispered. "Is *that* beauty the surprise?" Elissa asked as she stretched. "I thought we'd only have a regular kayak until race day."

"Glad you like her," Nash said as he loaded her bike into the Jeep.

I never doubted you'd find us a good one."

Nash kissed her forehead then went to help the driver unload the kayak, unable to keep the spring out of his step. He really couldn't wait to get out on the water. The long needle-like vessel was lighter than it looked and could be carried by one strong person, but it was awkward getting it off the truck.

"Mahalo," he said as he slipped the driver a tip.

"Mahalo right back, bruh," the driver answered, smiling as he pocketed the money. "What time you need me to pick it up?"

"I'll text you when we get back. We're paddling down to Maluaka Beach and back."

The driver smiled. "You in the Challenge?" he asked.

"Me? Yeah, but only for the kayak race. The lady is doing the whole damn thing," Nash answered as he looked Elissa's way while she continued to stretch.

"Good luck with the race!" the driver shouted to Elissa as he got into his truck.

She stopped stretching and tilted her head as her concerned gaze darted to Nash then back to the driver before she smiled and waved. "Thanks!"

Nash headed for the Jeep to take out their gear for the day and she jogged up to him. "So what happened to keeping a low profile and not telling strangers anything?" Her eyes widened. "Unless something's changed?"

Nash kissed her. "All part of the cover. And what cover is better than the truth?" She gave him a look he couldn't quite read and wasn't sure he liked. "Here, help me put everything into these dry bags, then let's head out before the waves turn too rough."

They quickly got everything packed, then carried the kayak down the sloping gravel path to the narrow, sandy beach. The water was crystal clear, making it easy to see the black outcroppings of lava rock under the surface. Avoiding those, they pushed against the surf and were soon pointed south toward Maluaka Beach. The weather was with them, the waves not too bad as they paddled. Elissa was taking her training seriously, paddling as hard and as fast as she could, and Nash found it challenging to keep up with her. But they quickly established a rhythm and soon their needle of a kayak was slicing through the water and speeding on its way.

The waves sparkled as the sun rose. The surface of the water was broken now and then by a school of flying fish, which made both of them laugh with wonder.

"I hope one doesn't land in the kayak with us," Elissa shouted, her voice light and full of joy. The miles flew by faster than Nash expected and soon they were looking at Makena Landing. The beach was only a half-mile farther and the water ahead was dotted with other kayakers, paddleboards, and windsurfers.

"Nash, hold up."

"What?" He kept paddling. "We're almost there."

"I have to ask you something."

"So ask me while we're paddling," he said, glancing over

his shoulder and shouting over the wind. "I want to know our time."

She threw her head back in annoyance at that. "I think I already know what you're gonna tell me anyway." She paddled harder. "When did you talk to Gina?"

Nash grinned. That's what was bothering Elissa. Well, even if Gina's message wasn't the most reassuring, he'd put Elissa at ease. "About half an hour before I woke you up this morning. Gina says you're still in the clear, that she's got a team covering for us and for you not to worry, just enjoy the race."

Elissa didn't say anything. Nash wished he could see the expression on her face. He expected relief and wanted to see it in her eyes.

"Oh. Okay." The level of disappointment in her voice took him by surprise. They paddled the rest of the way in silence.

When they got to Maluaka, Elissa asked, "Time?"

"Fifty-seven minutes, eighteen seconds. Not bad."

"Not good, either. This is why Brett dumped me for someone better."

"Shug. I know that's not what's bothering you." Nash reached for one of the dry bags. "We have some time. Let's grab a bite, get rehydrated, and talk." He turned around in the kayak and handed Elissa a power bar and a water bottle. They let the kayak drift out from shore for privacy.

"Nothing to talk about. Everything's great. Like you said, I'm totally safe." She gave him a weak smile.

"Yeah, you are. And I'm grateful for that. It means you and me can just kick back and enjoy paradise. It means we have time together. It means I don't have to worry about..." He felt his throat damn near close around the sudden lump lodged in it.

"About what?" Her expression had gone soft and full of concern. Her gaze flickered to where his tattoo was hidden under his wetsuit then back to his eyes.

Fuck it. "About losing you."

Her smile brightened. "You aren't going to lose me, you big goof." She shook her head. "I'm just being weird."

Nash grabbed her hand. "You wanted to be involved, didn't you?"

"Yeah. I don't think I quite realized how much until now."

"My thrill-seeker."

Her smile faded. "It's more than that though. I want to make an actual difference in the world. I just haven't figured out how to do that yet."

"Elissa, you make a huge difference every day. Your nieces and nephews adore you. Everyone you come in contact with does. You bring out the best in people." *You bring out the best in me* he added silently. "You'll figure out where you belong because I know you won't stop trying until you do. You aren't going to get trapped in a mundane life because you won't let yourself settle for good enough anymore."

As he spoke, she looked down into the water, but at his last words, her gaze snapped back to his. "You're right. I won't. I'm going to figure out what I want and where I belong and I'm going to chase it down hard. But first, I'm going to kick ass in this race because I have the best partner I could hope for."

His heart lifted. "That's—" Movement farther out to sea caught his eye. Dorsal fins broke the surface as a pod of dolphins swam into view. They looked smaller than the ones he was used to off the coast of California. Which meant—

"Spinner dolphins." Nash laughed.

Elissa shaded her eyes as she watched them. "Why are they called that?" Not a second after she asked, one of their muscular bodies shot straight out of the water, spun several times in the air, then landed on its side, disappearing back under the waves.

Her shout was full of pure joy. Two more leaped straight up, closer to them. The pod was headed their way.

"What do we do?" she asked him. "We're supposed to stay away from the marine life, right?" She grabbed her paddle but hesitated before dipping it into the water. "I'm afraid I'm going to hit one."

She had a point; by now, dolphins were leaping all around them, some no larger than a German shepherd. *A pod of mamas and their calves* Nash realized as the spinners swam around and under the kayak. All they could do was hold still and watch in stunned, joyful silence. After a couple of minutes, the pod moved on to play with the next group of kayakers and Elissa turned her face to Nash. Her blue eyes shone brighter than the sun-kissed water and her cheeks were slicked with tears.

"Nothing like that's ever happened to me before," she said. *"They* found *us,* just came right up like they'd been waiting for us. We didn't even have to..." She looked back at the spinners.

"Maybe the rest of your life will find you just like that, shug."

———

They paddled back up the coast to Kamaole I Beach Park and anchored to do some snorkeling before turning their kayak back in. Elissa had been snorkeling along the California coast, but she wasn't prepared for all the turtles any more than she'd been ready for spinner dolphins. That was one for her personal history books.

"This water tastes so much saltier than off the California coast," Elissa said.

"I just noticed that too," Nash agreed. "Less freshwater runoff to dilute it, I imagine."

"I thought the snorkeling off Catalina Island was good. This is amazing," she told Nash.

"Sure enough. I am impressed. This even beats snorkeling in La Jolla Cove. Discovered that place living in San Diego as a SEAL. I'll take you some time."

There must have been an electric eel in the water, because Elissa felt a jolt go through her that made her heart skip a beat. He wanted to take her to San Diego once they got back. *This is real* she thought. *We have something real. Just so long as I don't go and do something stupid like run away from it.*

But for the first time in her life, she didn't want to run away. She didn't want someone else. She wanted to explore this relationship like it was a brand new world.

What makes him so different? she wondered. She thought she already knew the answer—he was easy to be around. She didn't have to pretend she was better than she was to impress him. He didn't keep moving the goalposts on her. He didn't brag, he didn't put her down to make himself feel bigger. No, instead, Nash made her feel comfortable in her own skin. Nash was everything she'd wanted and a whole lot of what she never knew she needed. He was drop-dead gorgeous and protective, funny and smart, which is what she wanted. But, he was also kind, compassionate, attentive—all the things she never thought she'd find. He believed in her as she was, not in someone he wanted her to be.

She needed that. And she was ready to give it right back to him.

"Whatcha wanna do now, shug?" he asked as he swam closer. "You look like you're ready to pack it in."

She was tempted to blow off training for the rest of the day, spend it relaxing with Nash. Instead, she pulled off her goggles and said, "I really need to check out the running portion of the race. That's where this thing is won or lost."

Nash grinned. "You're the boss." He followed suit and removed his snorkeling gear.

"But you're the coach," she said as she placed her hands on his broad shoulders and pulled herself against him.

"That's right, I am. So, let's get out of the water, get the kayak squared away, and check out the route. But first." He wrapped his arms around her and kissed her hard. "I just want to say how proud I am of you."

"Even if I don't win?" She couldn't help herself. Old habits die hard.

"Shug, it don't matter if you cross the finish line in first place or last. You're out here running your own race, which means you win no matter what."

THIRTEEN

Elissa ran the ten-mile route from Kahekili Beach to Punalau Beach in her own record time. She had to keep focused on running and not on the gorgeous peekaboo views of the ocean along Lower Honoapiilani Road. The air smelled sweet from countless blooming flowers and salty from the Pacific as she drew in every hungry breath. Of course, race day would be much more strenuous—no breaks for snorkeling or making out with your coach boyfriend between courses. It wasn't Ironman, but it was still a challenge. She pushed away the voice in her head that sounded an awful lot like her father telling her that this race was barely anything, that she could do Ironman if she really applied herself.

One look at Nash's smile when they completed the run took care of that. He knew her personal best time and that she'd broken it. And that was more than good enough for him.

So why not let it be good enough for me, too? she decided, and felt her chest swell with pride.

They got back to the resort sticky, sweaty, smelly, and looking forward to a long cool shower to wash away the grime. An evil mosquito sent by Satan himself had bitten her cheek at some point and she'd scratched at the bite before realizing what it was, causing the bump to redden and swell—not her best look. Nash promised her it wasn't that bad (so cute and deluded of him) and that he'd packed an ointment that would make it practically disappear overnight.

"I promise, sugar, it's not that bad. You're still the prettiest gal here."

His reassurances faded into the background when they got to the elevators—and ran smack-dab into her parents.

Oh no. No, no, no. What are they doing here?

She'd never called to tell them she was back in the race since she'd wanted to keep them safe if someone came after her. Yet, here they were, big as life and carting so much baggage on a bellman cart it looked like they were moving in. They'd been discussing something, a bright lei around each of their necks, her mother's hand on her dad's forearm as she leaned in and told him something that made him smile. She was wearing a Hawaiian print dress in muted colors while Elissa's dad's shirt was pretty loud.

"Mom, Dad. What are you doing here?"

Their heads snapped up and their eyes went round and shocked. They looked like she'd just caught them with their hands in the cookie jar.

"Elissa," her mother said. "We could ask the same thing."

Her dad's look of shocked guilt snapped into one of delighted surprise. He spread his arms wide and took a step toward her. "Well, now!" he boomed as his eyes darted around the lobby to take in whoever was listening. "There's my Ironman!"

Ironman. Not even close. Elissa's initial shock melted into her old, familiar sense of frustration flavored with anger and topped with a self-doubt cherry. Her dad had moved the goal-posts back yet again, and she was never going to score a point.

Even so, when he wrapped his arms around her, she hugged him back tightly. "Hi, Daddy. I'm not an Ironman by any stretch of the imagination."

He pulled away, still gripping her arms, and smiled down into her face. "Well, you will be after you've trained in this race and signed up for that one. You already qualify, right?"

"No, probably not. And anyway, I don't really want to dedicate my life to competing in it the way some people do."

His laughter belied the look in his eyes. *Yup, no hope of ever reaching those goalposts.*

Elissa started to hug her mom before remembering how grody she was after the run. Her mom gripped her upper arms and practically held her at arm's length while leaning in to give her an air kiss on each cheek.

"Sweetheart, what happened here?" She touched the mosquito bite, making it erupt into a new round of itching guaranteed to drive Elissa crazier than she already felt.

"It's just a mosquito bite, Mom."

"We're on our way up to put some ointment on it, ma'am," Nash said over her shoulder.

Oh. Right. I'm here with a new guy scant days after Brett dumped me.

Before she could introduce Nashville, her mom asked, "Elissa, who is this?" She looked Nashville up and down, taking in his ratty straw cowboy hat, old t-shirt, faded board shorts, and beat-up Tevas. "A...friend of yours?"

"This is Nashville Jones, and he's, um." *What? What exactly is he?* Her brain scrambled to answer that. "Well, he's competing with me in the kayak portion of the Challenge and coaching me for the rest," she finished quickly.

"Pleased to meet you," Nash said smoothly as he took off

his hat and inclined his head. His accent was non-existent. He extended a hand to her dad, who took it with the good-natured smile Elissa and her siblings had come to recognize as a total cover for his disapproval. *Oh, God, could this suck any harder?*

"I'm Tony St Clair, and this is my wife, Heloise. We're Elissa's parents. So, *you're* her coach in this race?"

"Yes, sir, I am. And it's my honor. She's remarkable." Nash glanced down at her, making her simultaneously heart melt and feel like it was about to burst with pride.

Her dad's smile turned a smidgen more sincere. "Well, of course we know that, but let's hear more about you. How'd she talk you into this?"

The elevator in its infinite mercy decided to ding and open just then. "Oh, there you go," Elissa said as she grabbed their bellman cart and practically shoved it into the elevator past an exiting family giving her the crusty eye. "We'll let you unpack. Looks like that might take a couple days."

"Why don't you come to dinner with us?" her dad said.

"Oh!" Elissa's mom interjected, her cheeks reddening. "We can't really do that tonight. Let's plan for another time. I'll call you." Now she was scooting into the elevator beside the cart as quickly as she could while her husband looked momentarily puzzled. She lunged back out to grab him by the arm and pull him in...and was her finger hitting the 'close door' button too?

Crap. Elissa tried to push the elevator door open while it fought her. "We'll ride up with you."

Nash backed her play, grabbing the doors and giving them a firm shove while she scampered in. In the cramped elevator, they closed barely an inch in front of his face.

"So, you have plans tonight?" Elissa asked. "That don't include dinner on your first night here?"

Her mom turned a little green while her dad said, "Oh, no, we're going to dinner with your brother and his family." He looked at her mom. "I don't see why we can't add two people to the reservations."

My brother? Elissa's stomach jumped out of the elevator and plummeted back down into the lobby. "Stefan's here? I mean, *here*-here right now? I thought they always went to that resort on Lanai later in the year."

"Well, they do," her mother started, her voice hesitant as she chose her words. "But I figured since your father and I already had reservations and everything, that it might be fun to have some family time on Maui, and your brother agreed."

Elissa barely had time to picture Stefan's surly expression throughout *that* conversation when her dad added, "Your sisters were too busy to come on such short notice, but your brother came through."

"You asked Kathryn and Tamara to come too?" She looked directly at her mom. "But not me?"

"It was a spur-of-the-moment decision," she answered, looking away. "I'm trying to be more spontaneous. And besides, I figured you'd be busy looking for a job anyway." The elevator dinged and she looked relieved. "That's our floor," she said brightly.

The doors opened and Nash stepped out first. "Let me help y'all with the cart." When he turned, Elissa saw how he was hiding anger behind his affable smile and the accent that had crept back into his voice. He grabbed the bellman cart, pulling it into the hall. Elissa followed, not done yet with this conversation, and her parents stepped out on the opposite side of the cart.

"Mom, Dad, let me help you." Her brother's voice carried down the hall as she heard jogging steps approaching.

Crap, crap, freekin' triple *crap.* She stepped around the cart in time to see Stefan trying to—oh, good God—hand Nashville a bunch of folded bills as a tip. Stefan looked up surprised when he saw Elissa and then there it was—the surly expression she'd just pictured on his face. *Wow, score one for my realistic imagination. But why is he aiming it at me? What the heck did I do?*

"Stefan," she said flatly. "Aloha, welcome to Hawaii."

"Elissa." He squinted at her cheek. "What's wrong with your face?"

"Mosquito bite. When did *you* show up?"

Her mother stared at the floor while her dad's loud and awkward laughter filled the hall as he wrapped one arm around Elissa and the other around her brother. "Look at you two, the gang's all here!" he said.

Stefan ignored their father. "We came in this morning. Question is, what are *you* doing here? You're not supposed to be here."

Their mother made a small, strangled sound.

"I'm sure it's no trouble to add two people for dinner tonight," her dad went on, oblivious in his own little whacked-out world.

"I don't think so, Stefan said. "It was hard enough getting that reservation to begin with."

Elissa ducked out from under her dad's arm. "Right, I'm obviously not supposed to be here. So, I'll just let you all make your plans and have fun." She backed into the open elevator which she thought had miraculously waited until she realized Nash had been keeping the door open.

"Nice meeting y'all," he said with a polite Southern Boy smile on his face.

Oh, God, what's he thinking right now?

As the elevator doors closed, she heard Stefan ask, "Why's she hanging out with the bellhop?"

Elissa closed her eyes and let her forehead collide with the elevator wall. Her mosquito bite itched and Nash undoubtedly hated her right now.

"Your brother's a good tipper, shug." Nash sounded amused.

"Don't you dare compliment *any* of them. The only thing they're good at is sucking my soul straight out through my chest." She opened her eyes and looked at Nash. He smiled back as he wrapped his arm around her and pulled her in for a kiss. After her toes stopped curling, she buried her face in his chest.

"You don't hate me after that?" she murmured against his pec.

"Sugar, I think I'm ass-over-teakettle for you after that. Now I understand where you're coming from a little better."

Elissa looked up at him to see if he was kidding. She was met with an easy smile and dead seriousness in his eyes.

"I think I'm ass over teakettle for you after that too." *Think I am? Hell, I know I am.*

He patted the chest pocket on his t-shirt. Paper rustled. "Dinner's on your brother tonight."

And just like that, Nash made it all better. Where she'd expected to feel devastated, she found herself laughing instead. She'd never, not once in her life, laughed after an encounter with her family like that one. She was more likely to dive headfirst into some wine or some ice cream or some wine ice cream and take her frustrations out on an unlucky online scammer.

Nash just made her laugh and suddenly she could appreciate the absurdity of it all.

The elevator door opened. Their room, a shower, and their bed were mere feet away. So they took full advantage of all three.

FOURTEEN

They spent the next few days training, as careful not to overdo it as they were careful to avoid Elissa's family, which they were successful at doing until her twin nephews spotted her walking past the pool to the beach and decided to pull her into the water. Sitting in a lounger, Stefan looked up from his tablet. She could feel him glaring at her through his shades. A quick glance around and she spotted her sister-in-law in conversation with her mom at a table under an umbrella, both studiously ignoring her. So she dunked her nephews a few times, noogied both of them, then got the hell out of there before her dad could shout something embarrassing.

The other two people they tried to avoid—and had been successful at it so far—were Brett and his new partner. By now, several competitors from the mainland and a few different countries had checked in. They recognized each other by their sports gear and from being up at ungodly early hours at the resort, then later training on one course or another. But so far, they hadn't run into Brett on land, at sea, or on a bike. They didn't show up at the cocktail party either, for which Elissa was both grateful and annoyed, since she'd spent the entire time coiled up and ready for their insults.

Despite the lowered risk of Elissa getting targeted, Nash still made sure to establish and maintain a safe perimeter around her during the party. Even as she talked to other racers, his eyes shifted from her to every entrance and exit, and he made sure to ask and note the names of every person who spoke to her.

"But I'm safe!" Elissa protested after he'd maneuvered her away from a particularly interesting woman from Ireland who asked if they wanted to train together the next day. "Gina told you just last night that she and her team have it under control, right?" Nash had been on the phone with Gina for close to an hour, and still came away with the barest of details but an abundance of reassurances that Elissa's identity remained protected and that they shouldn't worry on their 'free vacation' as she'd put it. Elissa had been taking an active part in her own protection as well, grilling Nash on how to spot a threat, and she never caught anyone she thought was suspicious. The hair on the back of her neck never stood up and she never had the feeling of being watched like she did in Los Angeles—ironically whenever someone from Team Watchdog was following her.

"I'm not taking any chances with you," he said. Then softened his verdict with an extensive make-out session in a hammock on their lanai later. She found it impossible to argue with someone whose tongue was flicking at warp speed across her clit.

But they couldn't avoid Brett forever. There was the mandatory 'informational luau' in Lahaina a couple days later where they'd pick up race numbers, swag, and receive instructions on rules, procedures, and regulations. Elissa dragged her feet as they headed for the Jeep. She hated meetings of any kind on principle—even if they did feature all the roasted pig you could eat—and she really wasn't looking forward to one where her ex would undoubtedly be gloating.

Of course, she had something to gloat over herself, and he was currently behind the wheel. Nash reached over and grabbed her hand.

"You nervous, shug?"

"Nope, not at all." She squeezed his fingers. "I'm excited because I get to show you off."

"Hey, that's my line." He grinned at her. "How are you feeling about the race?"

"Again, excited. We're gonna blow them away."

"Damn, you're sexy when you're confident."

"Now *you're* stealing *my* line."

As they queued up to go into the general area, Elissa looked around for threats, a behavior that had become an almost unconscious habit, but no one was paying any particular attention to them. Nash pulled her back against his chest and nuzzled the top of her head. God, she loved the way he was constantly touching her at every opportunity. She never had to question how he felt about her. It was in every kiss, every touch, every glance, and every cocky smile. He gave them all to her.

"Aloha." A beautiful woman greeted them when they got to the entrance. She dropped leis around their necks and handed them each a mai tai, then gave them the number of the table where they'd sit.

Nash looked at the drink in his hand like he thought it was going to bite him.

"What?" Elissa asked as they walked to their assigned table.

"This isn't a beer. I don't know what to do with it."

"Well, you can be adventurous and drink it."

He poked at the paper umbrella sticking out of the top. "Is this compensation for when my balls fall off?"

She rolled her eyes. "Real men drink umbrella drinks." Then there it was; the hair on the back of her neck stood up. She looked over the milling crowd and immediately spotted Brett, who quickly looked away from her. "Or, you can give it to me to drink. I might need it."

Yup, there he was in all his sneakerhead glory, making his way to the same table, of course. Somewhere, somehow, he'd managed to find a pair of crocodile-skin tennis shoes that probably cost more than the entire trip to Maui. He actually stepped over a wet patch on the concrete as if he were wearing tissue paper slip-ons that would turn to skin-eating acid if they touched water. At his side was a bouncy blonde hanging on his arm, as expected. She said something to him and he sneered. The perky smile disappeared from the blonde's face.

I. Dated. Him. How? How did I do that?

She couldn't help glancing at Nash to catch his reaction. No surprise—her man (*My man!*) was smirking, not the least bit intimidated. And that gave her confidence a much-needed boost.

"That him?" Nash asked, pointing his chin in Brett's direction.

"You know it is."

"We're gonna smoke them, you know that, right?"

"Of course."

They found their name cards at the nearly-empty picnic table—right across from Brett and his partner, whose place name read Stacy. *Figures we couldn't even be on opposite ends of the table.* She didn't recognize any of the other names or faces; no one she'd met in passing was sitting at their table, darn it. Fine, she'd just make new friends quickly.

"Elissa!" Brett said, the fakest smile ever plastered on his face as they stood across the table from each other. "Glad to see you made it after all." He nudged Stacy, who was looking at her like she was a giant upright cockroach. "Elissa and I work out at the same gym. I didn't think she was quite ready for this competition and I didn't want to see her get hurt, so I dissuaded her from coming. But considering some of the *other* competitors," his top lip curled up in a derisive sneer, "she probably won't come in last."

Asshole.

Brett looked Nash up and down. "Looks like she found someone halfway decent." How could she have overlooked his grating laugh when they were together? "I'm Brett Sorensen." He extended his hand across the table for Nash to shake.

Nash glanced at Brett's hand and crossed his arms. "Nash Jones."

"Come on, it was a fucking joke." Brett shifted his weight back and forth while he kept smiling. He looked at Elissa and Stacy as if to recruit them to his side. Elissa stepped closer to Nash while Stacy gave Brett a smile that looked like she'd just smelled a fart in an elevator, then sat down and took out her phone. Undeterred, Brett said, "Man, be a good sport and shake my goddamned hand. Unless you're afraid I'll crush it like we're gonna crush you in the race."

"Doubtful." Nash took Brett's hand. Elissa didn't think she'd ever quite seen that shade of red on a person's face before, or hear knuckles crack quite so loudly as she watched Brett try his best not to collapse. Nash looked like he was holding back a yawn.

He finally released Brett's hand and smiled. "Thanks for reminding me to use my manners. Have a drink on me." Nash set his drink down at Brett's setting and tipped his hat to Stacy, who was now trying her best to pretend she wasn't ogling him over her phone, and placed his hand on the small of Elissa's back. "Shug, let's head over to that bar and see if we can't scare me up a beer." As they walked away—Elissa's head held high and proud—he slipped his hand down to give her butt a quick squeeze. Oh yeah, by the quick little gasp she heard behind her, she was sure Stacy at least caught his move.

"Have I told you yet today that you are the hottest, sexiest, bestest boyfriend ever?" She batted her lashes at him as she did her best middle school girl impression.

He side-eyed her. "I can't tell if you're joking or not."

"A little. Except for the part about how you are hot, sexy, and the best."

"But I'm not your boyfriend?" He actually deflated a little.

"Aren't we a little old for the term boyfriend?"

"So, that makes me...what?" Now he was dead serious.

"Mine," she answered simply. "Just mine. I hope." She twined her fingers with his.

He snatched her up in his arms—nearly spilling her drink —and kissed her, then set her back down. "So long as you're mine, too."

"Oh, yes."

He gave her a cocky grin. "Ol' Sneakerhead hasn't charmed you back?"

"Remind me to do my best to step on his shoe at some point tonight."

Nash cracked up and wrapped his arm around her as they got to the bar. "You want something else, shug?"

"I'm good with this," she answered and took a sip of her mai tai. Not bad. "I don't want to drink too much before the race. Gotta stay hydrated, right?"

"Oh come now," a woman said behind her, her voice lovely and lilting. "We'll be in the water for a third of it and that's hydrating, right?" Elissa turned to see the competitor from Ireland she'd met at the cocktail party. She had a mischievous twinkle in her eye. What was her name again?

"Hey, Fia," Elissa said, remembering. "You have a point."

"For sure I do." She caught the bartender's eye and held up her empty plastic rocks glass. "And a little whiskey makes these events easier to bear. The crack at my table is dreadful."

"Crack?"

"C-R-A-I-C," Fia spelled. "Means conversation. My table-mates have no idea what it is, either. If I have to listen to one more person rattle off their BMI I'll go bonkers. What's the story at yours?"

"Way worse. Try sitting across from your snobby ex who's *also* competing." She pointed back at Brett.

Fia covered her chest and laughed. "Jaysus. Shall I sneak on over and sit beside ya? We can save each other that way, now can't we?"

"God, please. I would love that," Elissa said. She felt Nash bump against her. His expression had gone serious.

"Your fella isn't keen on that," she said, grinning at Nash. "I don't bite, I promise." She grabbed the whiskey the bartender set down. "I'll go grab my name card and dash back." Then she was gone.

"Elissa—"

"It's *fine*, Nash."

He grabbed his beer and steered her back to the table. "Can't be too careful."

"Yes, yes you can."

"Fia, was it?"

"You're gonna look her up online, aren't you?"

"Don't have to. Watchdog already did background checks on all the competitors. I'll be reviewing Stacy, too now that I know she's Brett's partner."

"Right. Because she's obviously an international spy."

"Elissa."

"Seriously. They're fine. Everyone here is fine. No one in the race is coming at me. I mean, people have been signed up for months, right?"

"Stacy hasn't been."

"Okay, yeah, she's obviously going to shank me during dinner and I'll end up face-down in my poi."

"Sugar. Be serious. We can't trust anyone."

They'd reached the table so Elissa said nothing back. She kissed Nash's cheek instead.

Fia jogged up, took one look at the name card at the empty place beside Elissa, then picked it up and tossed it over her shoulder. "Such wind we're having." She sat down beside Elissa and greeted everyone at the table with a smile. Stacy scowled back.

Elissa leaned over close to Fia's ear. "You are my new best friend."

"*Slaintè*," Fia said as she tapped her tumbler of whiskey against Elissa's mai tai.

By now, most of the tables were full as the late-afternoon sun hung low in a blue sky over the Pacific. The large dais at the center of the circling tables was empty except for several burning tiki torches and a mic stand. A group of three people lingered at the edge talking until one broke away and jogged up a short flight of steps to the mic.

"Aloha! If I can have everyone's attention before we get started with tonight's meal and festivities, we'll go over the rules for the race, how you can pick up your numbers, what gear is acceptable or not allowed during the race, and all that other good stuff." He was mercifully brief and everything seemed straightforward, most of it already outlined in the packet sitting beside each setting.

"Now, I'd like to highlight some of our racers. All of you are exceptional athletes who have been training hard. But for some, this race will be more of a challenge than for others. And the spirit of *ohana*—of family—runs strong with these competitors. Sitting at the front table here are a brother and sister, Jason and Cara Griegel, who will be competing in tandem."

Elissa's attention was drawn to the siblings, Cara sitting in a wheelchair that almost dwarfed her skinny frame.

"Cara has cerebral palsy but that hasn't stopped her from dreaming big. And Jason is here to help her fulfill that dream by competing with her using a specially-designed kayak, bicycle, and racing wheelchair. True athletes always find a way, and never give up. Let's give Jason and Cara a hand."

The outdoor theater erupted in applause and Elissa felt herself holding back sudden tears. To see such love between siblings was inspirational, but it also twisted her stomach into an unexpected knot. She realized that Nash was the only one not clapping. Instead, he was gripping the edge of the table until his knuckles turned white. His lips were pressed together so tightly they'd turned as white as his knuckles. At first, she mistook his expression as rage, but no—there was something deeper going on there.

The clapping subsided and dinner was announced. Brett leaned forward across the table, catching their attention.

"You should go over and thank them for racing because those delusional losers are the reason you won't be coming in last."

Nash's head turned slowly toward Brett like something out of *The Terminator*. Any deeper emotions he might have been harboring evaporated into pure rage as he stood up and stepped backward over the picnic table seat. Elissa quickly rose and grabbed his arm. She vaguely heard Fia beside her asking for calm as Nash quietly asked, "What did you just say?" His accent was on full display.

"Oh, did I insult you?" Brett leaned back, a smarmy smile on his face. Even Stacy looked appalled at his behavior and scooted away.

"Nash, let's—" Elissa started to direct him away but he completely ignored her.

"Nothing that comes out of your worthless hole could ever insult me. But I think you better watch your mouth when you're talking about those good folks, you fucking worm."

"You gonna make me, cornpone?"

"If that's what it takes."

Nash started around the table, Elissa hanging on his arm like a forgotten rag doll. "Nash, he's not worth it."

"Come at me, bro." Brett goaded him on.

Suddenly Fia was on Nash's other side. "Now don't go hitting him in the face. Number one, this shitehawk's just trying to get you disqualified. And number two, shite splatters and I just washed this dress."

Nash blinked as if coming back to earth. He looked from Fia to Elissa.

"It's true; he wants us to get disqualified because he knows we'll kick his sorry ass," Elissa said.

Nash looked at Jason, who was turning Cara's wheelchair to head for the buffet line. He clenched his fists and shook his head. Then he shook Fia and Elissa's hands off his arms and stormed off through the gathering crowd.

Elissa shared a quick look with Fia, who snapped her head to the side in a *go after him* gesture. She stuffed their info packets into her tote and started after him. She didn't have a hard time catching up, thanks to the wide wake he left behind him.

"Nash, come on," she said grabbing his arm again. She

steered him toward the entrance. "Let's go for a walk, huh?" This time he let her lead him as if he were the rag doll now. The absolutely bereft look in his eyes nauseated her.

She had a feeling it was time to finally ask about the flower tattoo.

FIFTEEN

Nash had always prided himself on his calm. It didn't matter if he was in another country under fire, or if he was Stateside driving in Los Angeles traffic that would test St. Peter, he kept things cool. Turned his anger into a joke. Buried the frustration in a deep hole.

Except when it came to situations like this one.

He let Elissa direct him to the entrance like he was a live grenade that she was deflecting from a crowd—which she was basically doing. They got wrist bands so they could get back in, then she steered them down Front Street. They'd walked a couple of minutes before he asked, "Where are we going?"

"To the beach. I think there's access to one down this way."

"Why the beach?"

"It's where I always go when I need to re-center myself. I figure it might work for you, too."

"I'm fine."

"You're not fine, Nash." She stopped walking and turned to him. "When you're fine, you're cool as a cucumber. I don't recognize you right now."

Anger swelled in his chest, a substitute for the pain he didn't want to feel. "You don't know me."

She flinched and he felt immediate regret, which he stacked on top of the huge pile of old regrets he'd built up over the past few years. "I'm sorry, shug. That was uncalled for."

She shrugged and started walking again, directing him to hang a right. "Truth hurts. I'm only realizing now that you're really good at hiding yourself behind your humor. There's a lot I don't know about you, Nash, and you distract me from digging deeper by making me laugh or suggesting we go do something fun. Tonight, you couldn't do that. So, we're going to the beach, we'll walk along the sand and watch the waves, and then maybe you'll come back to yourself enough to let me in and tell me why Brett's particular insult hurt you so bad."

His rage flared again, fueled by deep shame. "Any man worth his spit woulda done what I did. Son of a bitch had no right to go and insult them."

"Of course. I wanted to deck Brett over that. But the difference is, I wasn't personally hurt by it. You were." Her voice had gone soft and she grabbed his hand. Blue water crowned by the beginnings of a fiery sunset and framed by trees lay just ahead of them at the end of the road. Wondering what beach it was, he brought up a mental map and realized where they were just as he spotted the narrow spire of a pagoda jutting up from the trees on the left.

He stopped cold as a mix of dread, shame, and regret filled his gut.

Elissa stood watching him. "Okay, new plan." She tugged on his hand. "We're going in *there.*"

"No. I...I can't." His feet were moving though, straight toward the open gate covered with a Japanese-style roof of red-brown shingles and the words *Namu Amida Butsu* carved on the lintel and painted yellow. He stopped just before going through as though an invisible barrier blocked him.

Elissa sighed. "So, if we aren't going in, are you ever going to tell me about this?" She touched his shirt over his tattoo. "And how many times you've been to Maui? And with who? Obviously, something happened to you last time you were here that you haven't resolved—"

"No, it didn't. I've never been here."

Elissa stopped. "Never been right *here*, specifically?" She narrowed her eyes. "Or...?"

"I've never been to Maui. Or any other Hawaiian island." He was shocked by the shudder in his sigh. He hung his head. "This is my first time here."

Elissa stared at him looking bewildered. "But... you found that food truck park so easily on our first day. You know your way around like you live here. I figured you *had* lived here at some point, or at least visited a dozen times."

He only shook his head, afraid that if he tried to speak, he might break down. Elissa was right, he wasn't himself. And if he walked away from this place right now, he might never be again.

Nash owed her more than that.

And he owed Elissa more than that, too.

He gripped Elissa's hand and together they walked through the gate into the Lahaina Jodo Mission.

Instead of dread, peace immediately descended on him. They stood in a grassy courtyard crisscrossed with paths leading to the pagoda, a wooden temple, a bronze bell, and to their left, a giant statue of the Buddha on a platform.

Beside him, Elissa breathed in as she looked around. "It's beautiful," she whispered. "So peaceful." She looked up at Nash. "How could a place like this make you afraid?"

"Not afraid. Just full of regret." That was all he could

manage before he was unable to talk around the lump in his throat. Elissa nodded and together, they walked the paths in silence. The late sun shot golden rays through the mission, bronzing the structures and lining the palm fronds with gold. So beautiful, and so painful for Nash to see. He wrapped his arm around Elissa as they walked. She was there with him, having seen through his lighthearted façade, wanting to know the real him, to ease his pain.

He directed her to a gazebo beside the Buddha and they sat down. He hoped the words would come. She sat patiently as he sorted through his thoughts until he was ready.

"To answer your question about why I know my way around so well. I've researched the hell out of Maui because I was supposed to be here four years ago. And the person I was supposed to be with was my sister."

Her eyes widened. "You have a sister?"

"Had."

Elissa covered her mouth. "Oh, God, I'm so sorry." She dropped her hand and grabbed Nash's. "That explains why you left Jordan and Costello's party so suddenly when your mom called. Your poor mom."

He nodded. "She's better about it now, but every now and then Bonnie's death hits her fresh and she needs me there."

"What happened, if I can ask?"

He looked across the courtyard to the intricately-carved door to the temple. "Bonnie had a rare form of cancer. One in a million. Her prognosis was grim—three years on the outside. She stretched that into seven. Seven years, and we were supposed to do all sorts of things together.

"We did some of them—spent a week in Seattle seeing every single thing, then dropped down to Portland and stood in line at Voodoo Doughnuts for an hour. Best damn doughnut I ever had, and before I could grab another, she gave away half of them to some homeless guy. She was always a hippie." He chuckled as he wiped his eyes. "We gave each other shit about our life choices." He met Elissa's eyes and was not surprised to see them looking misty. "I wanted to do everything on her bucket list. But, I had to cancel a few plans because of my job. I wasn't always in the country, you know?"

Elissa nodded. "Her biggest bucket list item was Maui, wasn't it?" She touched his chest and he covered her hand.

"A friend of mine gave us matching tattoos a year before Bonnie passed, in honor of the trip." He looked over to their left. "She wanted to see the biggest Buddha statue outside of Japan. She thought this mission must be incredibly peaceful. I figured she wanted to find her own peace, come to terms with what was happening to her body. She wanted to come here so badly, but we had to save up. Most of my pay was going toward her treatments. She fought me on that, but as her big brother, I threatened to arm wrestle then noogie her into submission if she fought me too hard on it." He surprised himself with a laugh. "Bonnie just said a noogie would be good for polishing her bald head."

Elissa barked out a laugh then immediately covered her mouth, looking mortified. "I'm so sorry."

"Sugar, it's okay to laugh. My sister always did everything in her power to make people laugh."

"She got that from you." Elissa bumped her shoulder into his.

"We all said she got that from the Dolly side of the family. She woulda been tickled to see you laugh. Would have *loved* it. Would have loved you. Just like I do."

Elissa inhaled a sharp breath. "Nash? Did you just...say what I thought you said but without saying it?"

"I did. Because I'm not sure if you're ready to hear—"

"I love you, too." The expression on her face changed

from wonder to joy. "I do. I've never felt this way about anyone. I never thought I would."

Nash grabbed up her hands, brought them to his lips, and kissed her fingers. "Me neither. I always thought that was for other folks. Thought I would have felt it somewhere in my twenties, but I didn't. Reckoned love wasn't for me. I didn't take into account that I just hadn't met my match yet. A woman as brave and crazy and funny and smart and caring as you. Thought she was a dream. Thought *you* were a dream, first time I laid eyes on you. Goddamn, so pretty. I fell for you right then. Stone in love, just like the song. Perfect little California girl. Way out of my league."

"Oh, stop it," she said. "First time I saw you, I couldn't look away. I've always had a thing for cowboy hats. And then when you opened your mouth and that voice dripped out—"

Nashville threw his head back and laughed.

"Don't laugh, I'm serious! I looked down at your boots half-expecting them to be covered in honey."

"You know I was hoping to catch your attention with that."

"Well, you did. And you held it with your smile and your laugh and your big old—"

He smirked.

"Brain. Your big old *brain*." She tagged him lightly on the arm. "So I could barely string two words together around you. I was afraid you'd think I was some dumb blonde." She bit her lip. "And you made me nervous."

"Do what now? How could I make a little old thrill-seeker like you nervous?"

"Oh, you did. I was afraid I'd miss my chance if I said the wrong thing. And, well, considering that I was always with someone else, I hated myself a little for being attracted to you at the same time."

Nash shook his head a little. "Just means you have integrity." He squeezed her hand. "Much as it pains me, I may have to buy ol' Sneakerhead a real drink for leaving you high and dry."

"Ugh!" She pulled her hand out of his and covered her face with both hands. "Don't mention him here. God, now I understand why you were so upset when he insulted them." A sudden tear slipped down her cheek. "You saw yourself and your sister in Jason and Cara, didn't you?"

There it was. She went straight to the heart of it and it smarted. "I do. When I saw those two sitting there, I felt ashamed that I'd let my sister down when it came to her biggest dream. And then when that asshole opened his mouth, I lost it. I felt like he'd somehow *known*, so I was defending my sister's honor right along with theirs."

Elissa touched his cheek and he realized he was crying. He felt his cheeks heat with embarrassment and looked away. She slid her hand across his chin and turned his face back to hers.

"Don't you dare feel ashamed about any of this, Nash. You loved your sister. You paid for her cancer treatments. You gave her more time on this earth to enjoy life. So maybe you didn't make it here with her, but you did so many other things together. You're honoring her now by being here. And something tells me that somehow, some way, she knows."

"She's an angel in heaven, shug. I'm sure of that." He took her hands in his. "And I'm sure she sent you to me. I love you, Elissa."

"I love you too, Nash."

"I want us to be together after this. I'm not gonna turn tail and run once we get back to California."

"Good, because I will hunt you down if you do. And you know how fast I can run."

Nash laughed. "Can't escape by sea, either. You'll kayak me down."

"I'll swim you down. I'll surf you down." Her eyes gleamed with that mischievous look he'd come to adore. "There is no escaping me."

"Not that I'd try."

They watched the last of the sun's rays fade across the mission as the sky turned pink and orange. Nash knew it was traditional to leave something at the feet of the Buddha's statue, and a lot of people left behind things that symbolized what they wanted to let go of. Nash didn't have anything except his regrets. Yeah, could at least attempt to leave those behind. He'd try to remember this place, its peacefulness and serenity, whenever his regrets started to creep back in.

Though maybe all he had to do was look at Elissa's beautiful face.

"We should probably get a move on," he said. "Get back to the luau."

Elissa covered her face. "Don't remind me that I'm going to see Brett again."

"Yes, you are. And when you do, shug, you are gonna hold your head high and proud and show him what a dumbass he is."

She dropped her hands. "You know what? I don't give a shit what he thinks. I really don't." She grinned. "He is a wad of gum on the bottom of my shoe. Yeah, just a spot of gunky beach tar."

"Oh, now there she is. That's my girl." Nash pulled Elissa in and kissed the top of her head, luxuriating in her warmth and good, sweet smell.

They got quiet again and looked around at the grounds. A strong breeze blew through the palms, bringing with it the salt smell of the Pacific only a few yards away. A wisp of plumeria hitchhiked on the wind, a sweet counterpoint to the salt. Yup this was the most peaceful place Nash had ever been. Bonnie would have loved it.

Elissa pointed straight up. "Look." Nash followed her finger and saw two winged shapes riding the wind. "What are they?"

"Well, I'll be. Good eye. Those are called Magnificent Frigate Birds. Twelve-foot wingspan. They're a good sign."

"I'll take it." Elissa leaned into Nash and bumped her shoulder against his. "You okay?"

He nodded without looking at her. "Yeah, shug." He put his arm around her and pulled her close. "Better'n I've been in years. Now, let's get you where I am."

She gave him a quizzical look. "What do you mean? I'm good. Brett doesn't bother me."

"I'm not talking about Brett. I'm talking about your family."

Elissa sighed.

"I'm not saying you did anything wrong, because you sure didn't. But, I think if any moves are going to be made to heal the rift, you're the one who's gonna have to make them. Maybe you'll do it here, maybe back home. I'll back any play you want to make, you just let me know."

Her expression turned soft, her eyes filled with wonder. "You're taking my side."

"Of course I am. We're on the same team. Why should that surprise you?"

Sudden tears dampened her eyelashes. "It's not you, it's me. Of course you'd take my side because you're wonderful. I'm just...always surprised when someone does. Surprised and grateful and I never, ever take it for granted."

"Well, you can with me." He stood and pulled her up. "Now, we really do need to mosey back to the luau."

Elissa's smile looked impish. "We could." She patted her tote. "Though I have everything we need in here. So, we could also head back to the room."

Nash held back his laugh. "Right. Because you need to rest up for the race, is that it?"

She shook her head solemnly. "Oh, I never manage to sleep before a race. I just can't seem to get my mind to relax. It's a real problem."

Nash rubbed his chin. "Hmm. That surely is. How about we grab dinner at the luau for energy, then we head back and I'll show you a guaranteed relaxation technique?"

Mischief filled her eyes. "Sounds like a plan, coach."

SIXTEEN

The weather decided to turn the morning of the Maui Challenge. The dreaded trade winds that stirred up the Pacific waves had held off all week but were picking up just enough to change the kayak route from a long, straight shot to a circular one. Instead of starting out at a different beach and kayaking to a second one, they would begin at the same beach where the bikes waited for the second leg, go around a buoy, and circle back. The cycling would be harder too, and probably the run.

The competitors stood waiting on the sand, their racing kayaks beside them. Elissa's arm itched under the temporary tattoo of her racing number and she tried not to scratch it. She'd probably sweat it off by the end of the day anyway—the humidity was being as unkind as the wind, and the temperature was already rising.

Nash looked like he was trying to resist scratching his too, but something else was bothering him. He was surreptitiously scanning the competitors as well as the crowd gathering to watch. Sure, that was his job, but he seemed agitated. He'd woken up that way, or at least Elissa assumed he had since he was already up when she awoke. He'd been affectionate but close-lipped up until they got to the beach and unloaded their kayak.

"Will you tell me what the matter is now?" she asked.

He looked at her as if she'd startled him. A decision weighed heavy in his eyes. "All right, shug, I don't want to worry you right before the race, but I talked to Gina and I just... I trust her, but I also feel like she's hiding something."

"Her nickname's Spooky, right? That's kind of her nature."

"True."

"Did she say I'm in danger?"

"No. If she had, we wouldn't be standing on this beach. I'd have stashed you in some lava cave behind a waterfall by now."

"Ooh, new bucket list item. Where's the nearest waterfall?"

"Shug." Nothing but warning in his voice.

"What? It's not like I've had this fantasy all my life of skinny dipping in a pool with a waterfall. And a hot guy. I'm halfway to the dream." When he didn't smile, she changed tactics. "So what did she say?"

"Just that everything was under control."

"Okay..."

"Shug, she *never* says that. She just *has* things under control, know what I mean? If she has to say it's under control, then it's not."

"Maybe she's just trying to reassure you so we have a good race?"

He just shook his head and kept scanning the crowd.

"Everyone in the race checked out, right?"

"Yeah. Both Stacy and Fia. Stacy is a hairdresser from West Covina who almost qualified for Ironman last year." He cleared his throat. "Looks like Sneakerhead started sniffing around her about two months ago."

Elissa's eyes popped. "Wow. Yeah. He hadn't even met my parents yet." She couldn't help but glance their way as they looked over their kayak. They'd arrived about fifteen minutes after Elissa and Nash and the two parties had studiously ignored each other at least. "What about Fia?"

"She checks out, too. Signed up for the race months ago, flew in from Dublin a couple days after us. She's a waitress at a pub called Man of Aran in Tuam. It all checks out."

"Which is exactly what she told me at the cocktail party. So, I think we're okay, right?" Elissa ignored the hair on the back of her neck that had been imperceptibly rising since she'd asked Nash what was wrong.

Nash shook his head like a dog shaking off water. "Maybe I'm being paranoid." Something caught his eye and he touched her shoulder. "Back in a sec, shug." He jogged up the beach. Elissa watched him help Jason and Cara maneuver their kayak down the beach along with a couple other competitors, including Fia. Her heart clenched at the sight, especially when Nash smiled at Cara. She blinked back sudden tears, knowing how Nash must feel. When he jogged back to her, she immediately hugged him.

"I so freekin' love you," she said.

"Love you too, sugar."

"We gonna win this race today?"

"We've already won."

The chant started slowly with one voice, then another, until it was a chorus. "Elissa. Elissa. *Elissa!*" She turned around and couldn't believe what she saw.

Her parents and her brother's family stood at the front of the crowd. Knowing her father, they'd just elbowed their way up there. Her nephews were jumping up and down holding handmade signs with racing flags and her name beside the words *first place* inside a blue ribbon.

She couldn't help it. A smile spread across her face as she waved to them.

"Guess you don't have to make the first move after all," Nash said. He waved as his other arm went around her.

"Aloha!" a voice boomed over a loudspeaker. "Welcome to the ninth annual Maui Challenge! How's everybody today?"

A roar rose from the beach. Elissa's heart accelerated. *This is it, finally!* She barely comprehended the announcer's words as he went on about the rules, the weather, the route. Blood pounded in her ears as adrenaline amped up her excitement. She wiped her sweaty palms on her thighs and double-checked her regulation personal floating device and the leash that would keep her tied to the kayak. Everyone around her did the same. She caught Fia's eye and gave her a thumbs-up, which the woman returned.

"Now, let's bow our heads in a prayer of thanksgiving and to ask for our competitors to have a safe race." The beach quieted as the announcer asked for blessings on everyone gathered on the beach. "Mahalo! Thank you!" he ended.

The athletes tensed. They'd been divided into two waves that would leave ten minutes apart, and Elissa and Nash had qualified for the first wave. She knew that the first wave included Brett and Stacy, and she wasn't surprised to see Fia reading herself. So, they were competitors after all, but in the best way.

The starting gun sounded and her water shoes dug into the sand as she and Nash carried their kayak into the water. The first waves hit as they moved to deeper water and prepared to jump in. She was thankful the surf wasn't too bad today despite the wind—it helped them get farther out. They transitioned from carrying to riding and starting paddling, maneuvering around the other competitors all fighting for the lead. The announcer was a blur of sound to be tuned out as he narrated the race from the tall platform on the beach.

Elissa and Nash were in sixth place as they paddled as hard and fast as they could. Brett and Stacy were up ahead in third as they gained on the couple in second. Fia was somewhere behind them with the other singletons. Rescue boats flanked the course far enough away to keep from interfering, but close enough to assist with a rescue if needed.

The wind started to pick up, gusting hard and threatening to push everyone closer to the shore on their starboard side. Now they were fighting just as hard to stay the course as to move forward. Another starting gun went off, signaling the second wave to begin. Elissa hoped the other competitors would be all right, especially Jason and Cara. Their start was much harder than hers and Nash's had been.

Her attention quickly returned to paddling as hard as she could. They were gaining on the kayak in front of them. The promise of passing them spurred her on and soon they were drawing alongside number five. The others paddled faster but Elissa and Nash shot past. Number four wasn't too far ahead and seemed to be losing some speed. A gust of wind hit them and sent their kayak almost straight into Elissa and Nash's path. They did some quick maneuvering and managed to avoid a crash. Soon, fourth place was theirs.

Elissa tried her best to keep her mind on her own race and not on Brett and Stacy's position, though she knew they'd taken second. Her arms already ached from fighting the wind and sweat coated her back under her lifejacket. Her chapped lips tasted of salt and the corner of her mouth stung from cracking. She put all discomfort out of her mind and focused on taking third. The buoy was just up ahead. If they could take third place before having to make the turn, they'd have a better chance of overtaking Brett and Stacy. She didn't know what sort of chance she had at beating either of them in the next two legs, especially Brett, but if she and Nash could manage to hit the beach before they did, she'd declare herself victorious. His words came back to her. *Run your own race, Elissa.* Just being here and competing was a win.

The third-place kayak drew closer. It looked like they had used most of their energy to get there and they were losing the fight against the wind. They'd almost reached the buoy and were beginning to swing out for the turn when the wind hit, causing them to overcompensate. Elissa and Nash worked as one to tighten their turn, and passed between the other kayak and the buoy in a tighter radius, which gave them third place.

Up ahead, Brett and Stacy had taken the lead. The second-place kayak appeared to be having some sort of difficulty and one of the safety boats was approaching it. Yup, one of the competitors was holding up his paddle. Nash and Elissa steered around them, which cost them some time even as they took second. Brett and Stacy sped ahead, aided by the downwind current that was now with them. The gap widened.

No! She couldn't let them win, couldn't stand the thought of Brett gloating, telling her that he'd made the right decision abandoning her, that she was a loser and always would be. Her luck, he'd make sure to do it right in front of her family, who'd witness her lose to him. Her stomach knotted and her anger flared.

Come on! Convert that anger into energy. Paddle!

She and Nash acted as one, paddling as hard as they could to shorten the gap. The current carried them faster but they didn't dare let up. On the other side of the buoy, she was surprised to see Fia coming into the turn, in third place now ahead of some tandem kayaks. *Good for her!*

Elissa was faintly aware of passing other competitors on

their portside going the other direction as they made their way to the buoy. Her focus was on one kayak and one kayak only— Brett and Stacy's. Stroke by stroke, they drew closer until Nash could have reached out and touched the bow of their kayak. They were going to do it, they were going to pass them on the portside. Brett and Stacy had made the same mistake as the athletes now in fourth place and had used up their energy too soon to stay in the lead. With a fresh burst of speed, Nash and Elissa maneuvered around the other kayak's outrigger beams and *ama* that balanced it, and drew up beside them as Brett and Stacy lost speed. So tempting to yell *in your face* as they passed, but she wouldn't waste a drop of energy. They weren't worth it.

The wind gusted just before they cleared the kayak and suddenly, Brett and Stacy's *ama* hit their kayak on the starboard side. The hit seemed to Elissa to be a little excessive for the gust to have caused the collision alone. Brett and Stacy's kayak swung toward them.

"Port!" Nash yelled, and Elissa's attention was drawn to her left side as they swung out into the path of a kayak coming the other way. A single-person kayak pulling along a modified one that belonged to Jason and Cara.

Nash and Elissa tried to correct but it was too late. The three kayaks tangled and spun. The look on Jason's face was pure terror mixed with concern as he looked back at where Cara lay in her kayak. God, had it taken on water? Elissa heard an outboard engine as one of the rescue boats approached, but she didn't think it would get there soon enough. Without hesitation, she slid into the water and crossed the gap between her kayak and Cara's.

"Elissa!" Nash shouted at her.

"Cara!" she and Jason shouted at the same time. He was suddenly in the water next to her. Nash kept the kayaks from bumping into each other, allowing her and Jason to check on Cara. She was scared, but otherwise seemed to be okay. In what felt like another world orbiting around theirs, Elissa noticed that Brett and Stacy had untangled themselves and were speeding on their way while a different kayak approached and turned. Fia's. She helped Nash untangle the two kayaks as the rescue boat approached.

We're okay!" Jason shouted to the rescue boat as Cara gave a shaky thumbs-up. He looked at Elissa. "Go! You still have a chance!"

"You're both okay?" she confirmed as salty water splashed into her mouth. He nodded and she turned to climb back onto the hull. She grabbed her paddle that floated and bumped against the side of their kayak and off they went. Fia paddled off as well, now in second, with two other kayaks approaching fast behind them. If they couldn't recover, the best she and Nash could hope for was fifth place, but at this point, Elissa didn't care. Cara was safe, and that was the important thing. But that didn't mean she wouldn't give it her all. Again, she let her anger—now borderline rage—at Brett fuel her arms and heart and lungs as they passed Fia, retaking second place. The gap between them and Brett's kayak was impossibly wide as the beach drew closer.

Little by little, they closed the gap. But Brett and Stacy put out what energy they had left and made it to the beach first. They ran up the sandy shore toward the transition area where the row of bikes and gear bags waited.

"Go!" Nash shouted to Elissa when they reached the shallows. "I've got the kayak." Elissa jumped off and sprinted as best she could through the water. Behind her, Nash shouted, "Love you, shug! Give 'em hell!" Even though the crowd was roaring, his words carried over it.

Her legs pounded the ground as she reached the transition area. She was already stripping off the wetsuit over her one-piece tank and shorts combo. A volunteer held her gear bag as she tore off the water shoes and slipped into her light tennis shoes, put on her helmet, and jumped onto her bike. Brett and Stacy had already cleared the maze-like transition lane as she pedaled as hard and fast as she could to catch up.

A crowd stood behind the low walls cheering and she saw it again—the sign her nephews had made. It bounced up and down as they held it while jumping. She was going too fast to read her family's expressions, which was probably a good thing. She wouldn't have to see and contemplate their disappointment for the rest of the race.

Elissa bent over her bike and tried to envision becoming the most aerodynamic thing she could think of. *I'm a bullet fired from a gun. I'm a spear flying through the air. I'm a falcon diving from the clouds.* Brett had disappeared from sight but Stacy was still fair game. She was just ahead, pedaling hard, determined to keep her lead. Elissa heard cycles behind them and knew she'd eventually be passed by the male competitors but it didn't matter. They were running their own race and she was running hers.

At least I can finish this with a clear conscience, and knowing that I've done my very best.

The wind had really picked up now, threatening to blow them sideways into the foliage along the road as they raced north up Maui's coastline. It stole Elissa's energy just as the heat dehydrated her. She took the longest sip she could manage without her stomach rebelling from a straw attached to a water bottle mounted on the front of her cycle. The bag beside it held energy bars broken into bite-sized nuggets. *After you pass Stacy, you can have some* she told herself. She knew she had enough energy to do it, and she had the motivation for sure. Plus, it looked like Stacy was losing steam as they headed up a long incline. Brett had undoubtedly pushed her too hard in the kayak race. Elissa would have felt sorry for her, but the woman had made zero effort to help someone else.

Just before the crest of the hill, Elissa shouted, "On your left," and passed Stacy. The woman grimaced at her as Elissa put in a little more oomph and sped down the other side of the hill. So what if she was getting passed by a group of guys determined to overtake Brett in the lead? She'd overtaken Stacy and she was making her best time, she could just feel it. The energy bar nuggets tasted as good as the best chocolate in the world right then.

The miles flew by after that—not easy ones by any stretch, but Elissa had hit that delicious, delirious wall of endorphins. She was flying through paradise, the Pacific sparkling on her left, and rolling, mist-shrouded hills on her right. Rainbows appeared and disappeared, too frequent and numerous to count. She was in the prime of health, strong and capable. She had a good man who loved and respected her, one who she loved and respected right back. As for her family—the fact that they were there and (maybe?) cheering her on gave her hope.

She drank the last of her water and crunched the final oaty nugget of energy bar as she approached the transition point for the run. She'd been passed by a score of men and several women—including Fia, God bless her pointed Irish head—but not by Stacy. *So what? I'm running my race today.* Up ahead, she saw a figure waiting in the lane, ready to take her cycle and hand her the next gear bag.

The figure tipped his cowboy hat at her and she smiled. Nash of course.

She slowed just enough so she could jump off the bike and let him take it. "Love you," he said as she grabbed the next bag for her run. She gave him a thumbs-up as she took off down the lane, again lined with people. And there it was a third time—that handmade sign with her name in a blue ribbon. This time, she braved a closer look.

Her nephews were ecstatically cheering for her. Surrounding them was the rest of her family. Her sister-in-law smiled and clapped from beneath a straw hat with a comically-large brim that practically shaded the twins as well. Her brother's scowl looked a little less scowly as he clapped then fist-pumped the air. Her dad of course was yelling, "Ironman," much to the chagrin of the other people around him. And her mom blew her a kiss.

As to their sincerity? Well, they were trying, right?

* * *

Run your own race. Run your own race. The mantra played over and over through Elissa's head as she ran. This part of the Challenge was the hardest—the last leg, the hottest part of the day, and what felt like the slowest after the kayak and the speed of the bike. This was the loneliest stretch, too, the one that tested every athlete's spirit right along with their body. Every muscle in Elissa's body ached and begged for a break out of the sun. Her heart pounded and her lungs wanted to burst. She'd slathered on sunscreen as best she could while running, but the patches she'd missed turned to stinging red streaks on her arms that she knew would only hurt more tomorrow. Now wasn't the time to think about beating anyone else. Now it was all about finishing as strong as she could, about not giving up.

She wasn't doing this to show up Brett anymore. She wasn't doing this for her family. She wasn't even running for Nash. This was for her, to prove to herself that she could accomplish something big she'd set out to do and had worked hard for. To prove she was more than a quitter, more than just a thrill-seeker.

Run your own race. Run your own race. Run your own race.

So, on she ran.

The crowd that had thinned out to nothing in places along the running leg of the race was thickening up again. Elissa was almost there. She could hear cheers up ahead as competitor after competitor crossed the finish line. Not only was the crowd gathering again, but so were the runners. She had no idea what place she was in within the division; she'd been passed by runners whom she'd later passed. She'd watched some drop out entirely, stopping at the water stations and taking off their shoes or sitting or lying down in the shade.

Doesn't matter what place you're in. End strong.

Shocked, Elissa realized she still had enough of a reservoir left to challenge the runners up ahead and to keep the approaching ones firmly behind her. She put on a burst of speed. Her feet pounded the road harder than she'd ever run. She passed one woman, then another. A third one challenged her with her own burst but then flagged behind. She passed a skinny dude who looked pissed as she flew by. Elissa's heart banged against her ribcage, her lungs screamed for mercy but she kept on running.

The finish line was just ahead when she heard a runner thundering up behind her. No time to look back, she poured on her speed, determined to use up the last of her strength to stay ahead. But it wasn't enough. She'd used up everything she had to get this far, this fast. A figure drew up next to her as the crowd roared, excited by the close match right at the end. Long blond hair streamed in Elissa's peripheral vision as the runner passed her.

Stacy.

Up ahead, wearing a victor's lei, Brett stood beyond the finish line as someone stretched a fresh ribbon across it. Elissa swore he was somehow simultaneously cheering Stacy on and booing her.

Run your own race. Run your own race.

Oh, fuck it. Beat this bitch.

One last, bone-deep, soul-deep, spirit-deep burst of determination, and Elissa flew past Stacy, breaking the ribbon a good length ahead of her.

Sweat streaming down her face, gasping for air, Elissa closed her eyes and raised her arms over her head as she slowed to a jog, then a walk. Strong arms wrapped around her and her nose filled with the familiar, loved scent of pine, leather, salt, and the essence of Nashville Jones.

"You did it, shug. You won."

SEVENTEEN

Nash nuzzled into Elissa's hair as he held her at the finish line. She was shaky, drenched in sweat, half-laughing, half-crying, and completely his. He'd never loved her more. Just to watch her fight so hard for her dream, even if it didn't turn out exactly as she'd planned, made his chest swell with pride on her behalf.

She needed to keep walking to get the lactic acid out of her muscles or they'd really be hurting tomorrow. "Come on, let's get you walking some." Nash pulled back, then put his arm around her.

A volunteer came up to them carrying a lei and congratulated her as he put it around her neck. He handed her a printout with the breakdowns of each course and her final time and told her she'd receive an official certificate later. Elissa looked at the paper and smiled as she and Nash walked to the water station.

"It's my best time both on the bike and running," she said.

"Told you that you won." He pulled her in closer. "Probably woulda been our best kayak time too if that son of a bitch hadn't interfered."

She looked up at him. "You think Brett did it on purpose? That it wasn't just the wind or the water?"

He smirked. "Don't *you* think so?"

She grinned. "Yeah, okay, I do. I think he took advantage of a dangerous situation and made it worse. He used to tell me to use any advantage that I could, that the only ethics that counted in competition was winning. I used to argue with him about that."

Nash stopped walking. "So that's why."

"That's why what?"

"Shug, *that's* why he left you high and dry. It wasn't because he didn't think you were tough enough, or fast enough, or a good enough athlete. He knew he didn't have a chance of winning with you on his team because you wouldn't stoop to his level and screw someone else over, so he found someone who would. Because that's not you. You ran a fair race; hell, you helped someone else who was in danger. He dumped you because you are way too good for him and he knew it."

Elissa stood up on her toes and kissed him. "I love you."

"I love you too, but what was that for?"

"For what you said, you goof."

"It's just the plain ol' truth." He grinned. "But if it gets me your sweet kisses, I can tell you some more truths. Like how sexy you look right now."

"Oh, God, that is so *not* the truth." She laughed.

"Yeah, it is. It *always* is, shug."

She shook her head but she kissed him again.

"Does that mean you believe me?"

"Means I believe you're still a goof."

Nash noticed Brett and Stacy off to the side of the water station table covered with bottles and tamped down his rage. He'd watched that smug son of a bitch come in first and nearly ground his teeth to dust. Nash steered Elissa to the opposite side where several competitors gathered, rehydrating, eating, stretching, and getting checked out. Everyone was congratulating everyone else, laughing the half-delirious laughs of athletes who'd just given a race their all and the camaraderie was running high. But no one seemed to want to go anywhere near Brett and Stacy.

Nash grabbed a sports drink, opened it, and handed it to Elissa. "We need to keep you walking and stretching, but let's get some water and electrolytes into you first." She nodded and took a long drink, then joined in with the others, cheering every time someone new crossed the finish line.

The mood suddenly changed around them. Voices lowered except for two—Brett and Stacy stood toe to toe, arguing.

"You sucked there at the end," Brett said. "So fucking disappointing."

"Well, fuck you right back," Stacy answered as she put her hand on her hip.

"I should have never picked a loser like you."

"Well, maybe if you hadn't screwed up with the kayaks..." Her voice trailed off as they both realized they had an audience. She wrapped her arms around her torso and looked at the ground.

"Yeah, about that kayak incident," Nash said. Everyone's attention turned to him. "Cara could have gotten seriously injured or even killed. And off y'all went without a second thought as to anyone else. You should be disqualified." Voices murmured in agreement around them.

Brett smirked and spread his arms, palms up. "Not my problem if someone who doesn't belong in a race decides to be stupid and enter anyway. You wanna disqualify someone, disqualify her brother for being even stupider and agreeing to help her—"

Nash started to charge forward but Elissa had a hold of his arm, bringing him right back to himself. The look of terror in Brett's eyes was enough—for the moment. "I'm not talking about disqualifying you for being a douche nozzle; sadly, there's no rule against that. I'm talking about how y'all deliberately hit our kayak to keep us from passing."

Voices rose. One man said, "Yeah, brah, that looked way suspicious."

"Bullshit," Brett said. "Prove it. You're just a fucking loser." He looked around. "You all are." His eyes landed on Stacy, who was backing away from him, her arms still around her body, her gaze firmly on the ground. "Especially you, you aren't gonna back me up." He shoved her shoulder and that's when Nash lost it and ran forward—only to be passed by Elissa who stood between him and Brett.

But his sugar wasn't there to stop him. She was there to dish it out herself.

"I'll tell you who the loser is! You, you big fucking bully! You fucking loser coward! Anyone who would cheat and hurt other people just to win a goddamned race, who would disrespect a teammate. Who would..." she was panting now, tears filling her eyes, "who would lay hands on someone smaller and weaker than they are and try to hurt them, someone you're supposed to care about, *that's* the loser, you son of a bitch!" Before Nash could stop her, she reached out and ripped the lei off Brett's neck and tossed it on the ground. "You don't deserve aloha, you should be—"

Nash laid both hands on her shoulders and spun her away from Brett before she risked disqualifying herself. He wasn't worried that Brett would attack her because she was right—he was a complete and total coward and she'd shown him that she was a badass unafraid to kick his sorry dick into the dirt.

"Let's walk, sugar." He snagged another bottle off the table and aimed her at the finish line. "We can cheer on the other winners, how does that sound?" He ignored the rising voices behind them and the accusations flying at Brett. It wasn't their rodeo anymore. His concern was making sure his brave-ass woman had what she needed, whether it was another bottle of water or something to eat or a good old-fashioned roll in the hay.

Okay, maybe that last one was a little self-serving. But he'd make sure she enjoyed it even more than he did.

One thing was for sure though. Once she was calm and rested and recovered, they were going to talk about what really set her off about Brett shoving Stacy.

Who would lay hands on someone smaller and weaker than they are and try to hurt them, someone you're supposed to care about.

Yeah, he was going to get to the bottom of that one.

"Wait, please wait up," a voice called behind them. They turned and let Stacy catch up.

"What do you want?" Nash asked, none too kindly.

Stacy looked at Elissa. "I want to say thanks for sticking up for me. I don't deserve it."

Elissa folded her arms. "Don't ever say that. You don't deserve to have anyone lay a hand on you to hurt you. Especially not someone you trust."

Stacy laughed bitterly. "Oh, he's never someone I trusted, believe me. That's why I don't deserve it. We did try to sabotage you. It wasn't an accident at all. He told me before we even got here that that's how it was going to be if that's what we needed to do to win." She broke her gaze with Elissa and looked over Nash's shoulder at Brett, still the center of a mob, it sounded like. "I'm going to tell the judges what we did. I don't care if I get banned from every race from here on out. It was wrong. Cara could have gotten hurt for real. I just want you to know I never meant for that to happen. I didn't want to keep paddling, but I kinda..." She tipped her chin toward Brett, then sighed and shrugged. "You know?"

"What I know is that you need to get away from him ASAP," Elissa said. "He'll hurt you, especially now."

"No, he won't. You're right about him being a coward. I can see it now. I won't let him touch me again."

"I'm glad to hear that, Stacy. I really am. But please be careful."

Stacy gave her a sad smile before extending her fist. "Good race there at the end."

Elissa bumped fists with her. "Yeah, good race."

"See you around." Stacy turned and headed off toward the judges' booth.

Elissa looked up at Nash. "Do you think she'll be all right? Should we go with her, maybe guard her or something?"

Oh, my lady with the protective soul. "We can do that." He glanced at Stacy. "But I don't think she needs us." They watched as a couple of men and a woman caught up to her. The woman placed her hand on Stacy's shoulder as they talked. Stacy pointed to the judges' booth and they all took off together, the men flanking her like bodyguards.

Brett was making a quick exit. *Good riddance to bad business* Nash thought. "Shug, I need to ask you something."

"Yeah?" She looked up with hesitation in her eyes at his serious tone.

"The way you were talking, did he ever hurt you?"

She looked relieved. "Oh, no way. I don't put up with that shit, not from anyone. I had one boyfriend grab my arm once when he was angry and that was it. I buried him." Her eyes widened. "I mean figuratively, not literally. Don't arrest me."

Nash laughed. "I'm a bodyguard, not a cop." He leaned down and whispered in her ear, "I'm more likely to dig the hole for you."

"Cool, I'll remember that."

They continued walking toward the finish line. Nash was relieved that Elissa hadn't been physically abused by anyone. But still, he thought something was there. *Someone smaller and weaker, she'd said.* Maybe it was just her protective nature coming out.

He encouraged Elissa to keep pacing and stretching, and grabbed water bottles and food for her when she needed it. She answered a bunch of texts including one from her mom apologizing for leaving so soon after the race since they already had plans, but inviting them to dinner the next night since she and Nash were staying a few more days. She'd rolled her eyes, but answered that they'd love to have dinner with the fam.

Nash had a few of his own texts to answer and send, including one to Lachlan asking for a status report. Lach texted back that there was no change so stay the course, and congratulated Elissa on her race. He'd already heard the news through the grapevine, further proof that Watchdog was a sieve when it came to gossip. Of course, it was no mystery how he'd heard—Elissa had called Elena to tell her, and Elena had obviously told Camden, who blabbed it everywhere.

There was no text from Gina, good or bad.

Which to Nash's mind was bad.

They spent the evening cheering on the rest of the competitors as they completed their races. And when Jason pushed Cara's wheelchair across the finish line well ahead of a dozen others, Nash and Elissa cheered the loudest.

EIGHTEEN

"Am I dead yet?"

"No, shug."

"Are you sure?"

"You wouldn't feel this warm curled up against me if you weren't among the living. Probably wouldn't be talking, either."

"Then did you at least get the license plate of the cruise ship that hit me?"

Elissa felt Nash's body shake as he suppressed a laugh. *Victory.* "Cruise ships don't have license plate numbers, shug."

"Well, they should so that we can report them when they hit innocent victims like me."

More shaking. "Hate to break it to you, but you did this to yourself."

"Crap. I think you might be right."

Elissa stretched her leg out straight under the sheet and felt the ache of tired muscles. The truth was, she felt nowhere near as sore as she thought she would the day after the race. Nash had seen to that. He'd kept her hydrated so well that she didn't need to use the IV kit with the bag of saline she'd brought—a sure-fire cure after a race and a really good hang-over-preventer as she'd learned in her paramedics' training. Nash fed her, kept her moving, and scrubbed her down in the shower until her skin tingled.

Then best of all—he'd given her a full-body rubdown in the privacy of their lanai. The wind had died down to a delicious breeze that kissed her body as he poured warm, tropical-scented oil onto the small of her back. His hands glided over her skin, waking up all her senses. He rubbed her arms and legs in long, hard strokes that eased the knots and made the aches disappear as if he were draining the pain right out of her fingers and toes. By the time he got to her shoulders and back, she was moaning in appreciation, ready to worship his hands.

Nash wasn't nearly finished with her. When she turned over and lifted her arms over her head, he let out the sexiest little groan as he looked at her breasts. He straddled her thighs and poured a stream of oil into his palm. He rubbed his hands together and then placed them on her breasts, rubbing and kneading and pulling on each nipple, sending delicious currents of pleasure straight to her core until she was grinding against him. He ran his hands down her belly and circled her belly button with one finger, sending the butterflies underneath into flight. Then down over her mound until he found her hard and swollen clit aching to be touched. More oil, more gliding fingers circling, circling. One deep plunge into her aching walls and she was arching into his hand and moaning out her pleasure while he bent and kissed her throat.

She paid him back for the massage when they got to bed, wrapping her lips around his thick, hard cock while playing with his balls until he begged to be inside her. She grabbed a condom from the dwindling pile on the nightstand and tore the wrapper open.

As soon as she'd worked the condom down his length, he flipped her onto her back and sank deep inside. Instead of moving right away, he stared down into her face with a mixture of wonder and familiarity. No one had ever looked at her the way he did, as if he wanted to memorize what he saw, lock the memory of her away in case she disappeared.

Elissa had no intention of disappearing. For the first time, she didn't feel like she was settling for good enough until she could find real love. Nash was it. He felt like home.

"I love you," she whispered.

"I love you, too," he answered. "Can you feel it?"

She grinned and squeezed around him. "You tell me."

He gave her the soft, tender smile she'd come to recognize as serious and said. "I mean, can you feel how much I belong inside you?" He shifted his hips. "How every time we're together, it's like coming home?"

Her heart stuttered. "I thought Costello was the psychic."

"Like he always says, there aren't psychics, just good observers." He started moving inside her as he lowered his head to her neck. "We're home when we're together. We fit. I don't ever want to leave. I don't ever want to be without you. Just the thought of it hurts too much."

"I don't ever want to lose you, either," she answered. "Now that I've found you."

The rest was lost in pleasure.

Elissa stretched her arms over her head. "The truth is, I feel pretty good this morning, and I have you to thank for it." She blinked at the light coming in around the curtains. How late did we sleep in?"

Nash grabbed his phone from the nightstand and looked at it. "It's almost ten."

"God, that's half the day gone."

He chuckled. "We're on vacation."

She propped herself on her elbow. "Are we still? No word from Gina?" Even as he smiled and shook his head, she saw his eyes darken.

"We're good, shug. You're still off the radar."

She arched an eyebrow. "Your lips say yes, but your eyes say no. You're worried."

"It's my job to worry." He sat up and stretched. "Let's get up, have some breakfast, and get moving. The more you keep moving, the faster those aches will go away."

"So we'll go for a run, maybe find a good surfing beach now that training and the race are over, though it is kinda late in the day already. Or we could snorkel because that was so much fun. Oh! Maybe we could rent paddleboards."

He laughed and caught her face in his hands and kissed her. "Indecisive much?"

"I just want to do all the things, as usual. But what do you want to do?"

"A run sounds perfect. If you were up to it, I was thinking a helo ride but I'd rather be the one flying it myself."

"Wait, you know how to pilot a helicopter? Duh, of course you know how to pilot a helicopter! Will you teach me?" She batted her eyes.

Nash chuckled as he shook his head. "And of course you'd want to learn to fly. Hell, I'm surprised you don't already have a license."

"Oh, it's on the bucket list." She pursed her lips and nodded. "So, will you teach me?"

He grinned. "I'm not a certified instructor, but I'll give you pointers."

"Yes!" She fist-pumped the air. "So, what do *you* wanna do instead?"

"So much, shug. The road to Hana's one thing, but it's

over on the other side of the island and it'd take all day to drive it. It's already late morning."

Elissa crinkled her nose. "Yeah, I'm just not in the mood to sit in a car all day and look out at a landscape I could actually *be* in."

"The whole point of the drive is to get out and be in all that beauty. There are waterfalls and rock climbing and jungle hikes and ocean views."

"Waterfalls?" Her eyes took on a funny light.

"Yeah..." he said, starting to grin.

"Any waterfalls on *this* side of the island?"

"I imagine we could scare one up. Why?"

She immediately turned neon pink. "Oh, no reason."

"I don't believe you."

"Well, it's not like I'm thinking about my fantasy of maybe skinny dipping in a pool with a waterfall. And a hot guy."

"Oh, shug. Yeah. Yeah, I think we need to find one."

In the end, they stuck close to the resort and took it easy. Despite that, the day felt full of anticipation, as if a storm were brewing out at sea and the air carried the tension from it building up. There were three reasons for that. One, she had the dinner with her family to worry about. They hadn't run into each other—her mom probably had everyone scheduled to the gills and they were out and about somewhere—but she still kept thinking she'd bump into them and that it would be just as awkward as the meeting at the elevator. Number two, Nash seemed preoccupied but insisted everything was fine when she pushed him.

Number three was a text she'd gotten from Fia.

She'd been surprised and disappointed that Fia was nowhere to be found after the race. Then when she received the final race results in an email that morning, Fia's name wasn't listed, which meant she'd dropped out somewhere along the way. Elissa didn't remember seeing her at any of the water stations getting first aid. She'd seemed fine—hell, better than fine—but accidents did happen sometimes. It didn't take much to twist an ankle or pull a muscle, and it was super-easy to get heatstroke.

Then she got the text:

It's Fia. We make a grand team, don't we? Hope to catch you surfing today.

Elissa texted back:

Fia! Girl are you ok? I didn't see your name on the finals. Where you surfing? Love to catch up.

She texted back:

You'll find me in the usual places.

Yeah, that really narrowed it down. How many places could you surf on Maui? Oh, yeah—all of them.

LOL! Can you be more specific?

No answer. Well, at least she was well enough to surf, so who knew? She was probably out catching a wave already. Maybe she'd text again when she was done and they could go out the next day.

Two other names had disappeared from the finals list too —Brett and Stacy. No surprise there.

She was happy to get an email from Jason and Cara, too. It turned out they lived in the Los Angeles area and wanted to know if she and Nash would be interested in training with them for Ironman. Elissa had texted back that no way was she ever going for that, but she'd love to train with them.

Nash happily agreed. "You just make friends everywhere you go, don't you, shug?"

"I do my best. Now, if I could just get along that well with my fam."

He pulled her in for a hug. "We'll see how tonight goes with all them. Maybe they'll surprise you."

They arrived at the resort's restaurant after everyone else was already seated. True to form, the minute her dad laid eyes on her he was up out of his seat and cheering for his Ironman. Her mom and sister-in-law smiled and clapped too and her nephews were their usual hyper selves, bouncing up and down in their seats. Stefan just stared at the empty plate in front of him and fiddled with the napkin in his lap. At this point, she thought maybe a crab had crawled up her brother's butt and made its home there. Took one to know one.

"It's the Maui Challenge, Dad. Not Ironman," she said when they got to the table.

He glanced around at the other patrons. "Well, I'm sure you'll win *that* one next."

Lord, give me strength. Nash laid a comforting hand on the small of her back as he pulled out her chair. "I didn't win and I'm not going for Ironman. The Maui Challenge was great, and I proved what I needed to—to myself."

Undaunted, her dad went on. "Well, you still have plenty of time to think about it. I'm starving, let's order."

She appreciated Nash when he grabbed her hand under the table and squeezed.

Dinner was par for the course. She made chit-chat with her mom and sister-in-law, cracked her nephews up with funny faces and fart jokes—scoring bonus points every time her mother frowned and cleared her throat—and tried to engage Stefan in conversation, which he returned in grunts and one-word responses.

Fine. What-fucking-ever.

Nash was the perfect gentleman without being fake about it the way Brett had when they'd gone to dinner with her parents. He mostly ran interference with her dad. Nash was wise enough not to namedrop Dolly Parton or mention that he lived in Laurel Canyon or else her dad would've loudly transformed him into some sort of country music star before dessert. He talked about his work with Watchdog, again careful not to name names of famous clients, and that he'd served his country overseas. Not a word about being a SEAL.

"How about family?" her dad asked. "Any brothers or sisters?"

Elissa laid her hand on his knee and squeezed when Nash hesitated. She wanted him to know it was okay to say something or not. "Just one sister in heaven, sir. Lost her to cancer four years ago."

She braced for her father to somehow turn Nash's admission into a show. Instead, he nodded and quietly said, "I'm sorry for your loss, son."

Wow.

"Thank you. That means a lot, sir," Nash replied.

Elissa was proud of both of them.

After dinner, her dad suggested drinks by the pool and Elissa surprised herself by saying yes. They agreed to meet in half an hour after going to their rooms.

Nash's phone rang and Elissa braced herself for word from Gina.

Reading her mind, Nash said, "It's my mom. I, uh, told her where I am."

Her heart ached at his expression. "I'll cancel downstairs."

"No, no. You go on ahead and I'll catch up."

"I can stay if you need me."

He hit the receive button. "Hi, Mama, give me one sec." He put her on mute, then smiled at Elissa and her heart melted like shave ice. "I got this. It'll be fine. You go make things right with your brother."

"You noticed that, huh?"

"Kinda hard not to."

"When we get back, I'd love to meet your mom."

Now it was Nash's turn to look like his heart was a sweet, dripping mess of melted sugar. "I surely would love that. I'll tell her. She'll be tickled, shug."

She hugged him and he told her he loved her.

Elissa pushed the glass door to the pool area open and saw only one person sitting at a table, a half-empty glass of something frozen, frothy, and undoubtedly potent sitting in front of him. Stefan looked like he'd been sentenced to death.

Elissa walked over to the tiki bar at one end of the patio. She pointed at her brother.

"Two of whatever he's drinking, STAT."

She carried the drinks back to the table thinking they had to make them frozen because the amount of alcohol in each one was definitely a fire hazard. Her brother glanced up at her, then at the drinks, and promptly downed the rest of his first one in a single gulp.

"Careful, don't give yourself an ice cream headache," she said as she set the drinks down and took the chair beside him.

"Maybe one will duke it out with the migraine I already have."

"Sorry to hear that," she said, and she was. Stefan's migraines were legendary. "That why you're being such a poop?"

He glared at her over the rim of his glass as he started on his second drink.

"No? So it *is* me? Mind telling me what I did so I can either apologize or sock you in the arm, depending?" She took a drink. *Wowza. Better not exhale near an open flame.*

Instead of answering, Stefan asked, "So what's up with you and the bellboy?"

"Oh my God, Nash is not a bellboy! He's a freakin' Navy

SEAL. I should tag you in the arm just for that." She took another fortifying gulp. "And for trying to change the subject. What's really going on?"

"You schooled him well, not telling Dad that." Stefan's words were slightly slurred. "He's not coming?"

"He'll be down later. Where's everyone else?"

"Claire's putting the boys to bed and probably not coming down. Mom and Dad, who knows?" He shrugged, then picked up his glass and gestured to the few people scattered around the rest of the pool area. "Not much of an audience for them."

"Yeah, right?" she agreed.

Stefan drained the second drink to the dregs and lifted the empty glass at the bartender along with two fingers. "Catch up, sis. Next one's coming at ya. They never let up."

"All right. Last chance. What's. Going. On?"

He looked her in the eye and she was impressed that his weren't crossed. "You know we come here every year, right? Only, we go to Lanai."

"Yup." She finished off her drink. "Later in the year though, right?"

He nodded. "To see the whales. Claire and the kids travel all over the place throughout the year when she tours and takes them. Lanai's my only chance to get away and relax."

Elissa's stomach clenched. "And Mom talked you into changing your plans."

He nodded.

"Because they were already going and thought it'd be a hoot to have you along."

Another nod.

"And you're mad at me because it's all my fault. And I ended up here anyway so you needn't have changed your plans. Got it."

This time, he shook his head.

"What? Totally my fault. I sincerely apologize for being a flake and messing up your life." Two more drinks appeared on the table and she grabbed one, later bed-spins be damned.

"You don't get it," Stefan said. "You know how you walked into the restaurant tonight?"

"Yeah? What about it?"

"Dad did that to me, too, when I was still a med student. Remember when I came home from college that first year?"

"God, how could I forget? If you weren't dead-asleep, you were grouchy as hell."

"Yeah, part of that was because the second I stepped out of airport security still in my student scrubs, with my stethoscope around my neck because I'd literally gone straight from a test simulation to the airport, Dad was there greeting me with, 'Hey, doctor! How many people did you save today?'"

"Seriously? Like, he meant it?"

"Seriously. Not only that, but he looked around to see how many people were watching us—the happy reunion of a proud, successful dad and his life-saving doctor son."

"Oh, God." Elissa rolled her eyes.

"That's not the worst part though." Her brother shook his head. "The worst part is that I played along."

"You did *not*." Elissa covered her mouth.

"Yes, I most certainly did. As I approached him, I said just as loudly, 'I saved a baby today.' Forget that the baby was a silicone and plastic model hooked up to a machine recording my clumsy efforts to resuscitate it while my three instructors watched behind a mirror, either laughing or crying at my incompetence. Probably both. Nope, I played along, hugged Dad, and we never said a word about it. As far as he was concerned, I'd done my job of making him look good.

"This is why I'm not actually mad at *you*, I'm mad at myself. I admire you, Lis."

"Admire me? Pffft."

"Yeah. Admire you. Because when Mom and Dad pull their shit with you, you don't take it. You don't play along. You've always chosen your own path."

That shocked her. "What do you mean? My life has been a mess. I've started and quit so many things. I mean, look at you; you *are* a successful surgeon now who saves lives for real, you've got your own amazing family, you've got a beautiful house. Sometimes I think I should have listened to them tell me what to do with my life."

Her brother held up his hand. "Stop right there, little sis. You have no idea what kind of a bullet you dodged. Yeah, no regrets I love my wife and kids, I'd die for them. But sometimes, I feel like I've given up my life for our parents, do you know what I'm saying? I let them push me into changing my vacation plans for Hawaii, but that's nothing. They pushed me into medicine, then they pushed me from wanting to go into family practice into becoming a surgeon. And no shit, they still call me to this day asking if I've cured cancer yet and when I'm winning the Nobel. Surgeons don't even cure cancer." Red-faced, he stopped to gulp his drink and for some reason his words made Elissa laugh. "What?"

"I'm sorry," she said and then doubled over laughing even harder. "But, oh my God, they want you to *cure cancer*." She snorted. "Singlehandedly, probably."

Stefan cracked a grin that turned into a chuckle.

"And here I was feeling sorry for myself because Dad wants me to win freekin' Ironman for the bragging rights, but you, you need to *cure cancer*."

By now Stefan was laughing too, harder than Elissa ever remembered seeing him laugh. She was vaguely aware that the door behind them had opened and someone was walking to their table. She recognized her father's footsteps.

"It does a father good to know his kids get along so well. Look at the two of you; you were always the best of friends and that still holds true today. I raised you right," her dad said loud enough for it to carry across the entire pool area. Hell, any passing ship probably heard it out at sea. He patted them both on their backs, setting off another round of laughter.

"I have the best, the brightest, the most talented kids in the world," he added, obviously pleased at the attention from the few people around the pool.

That made them laugh all the harder. "Yeah, Dad. Yeah, you do," her brother said.

"And the drunkest!" Elissa shouted as she held her glass up over her head and to her astonishment, her brother reached up and clinked his glass against hers.

Their dad smiled awkwardly and backed away. He disappeared into the resort.

"God, I love you," Elissa said as she threw her arm around her big brother's shoulders.

"Back atcha, little sis," he said, leaning over to kiss the top of her head.

"We're never gonna change them, are we?"

"Our parents? Not at this point." He clinked his glass against hers again. "But you know, I think I'm going to take a page out of your book and try to laugh about it more. That I *can* change."

Elissa never thought she'd hear that. "So tell you what. To make up for this debacle, when we get back, why don't you drop the twins off with me, and you and Claire can take a long weekend together? I know it's not a week in a tropical paradise but." She shrugged.

Stefan waved her off. "I can't impose on you like that."

"It's not imposing! I love the little twerps and I'll have time off anyway since I'm unemployed." She snorted. "Am I still your hero?"

"Always, little sis."

Out of the corner of her eye, Elissa saw the glass door open again and Nash walked through, eyeing the two of them and looking bewildered. She smiled and waved him over, savoring his confused but cautiously optimistic look.

"Hey, y'all." He pointed his thumb back over his shoulder. "Thought I saw your dad heading for the elevators. What'd I miss?"

"Oh, nothing. Your timing is perfect." She gestured to the chair next to her. "Have a seat. Doctor Cancer-Curer was just about to buy the next round."

Her brother sobered and pulled back, looking pissed. "Excuse me? I think it's Ms. Ironman's turn."

"Uh! I don't think so." She whipped her head around to face Nash, giving him her best mock-offended glare even as her lips twitched from holding back her smile. "You gonna defend my honor?"

Nash's confused look warped into a grin. "How 'bout the SEAL buys this round?"

Her brother locked his serious gaze on Nash and nodded. He nudged Elissa. "I like the bellboy."

"I like him too. Think I'll keep him."

"Cure cancer? Are you teasing me?" Nash asked Elissa later in the elevator on the way up to their room.

"I am not. My parents honest to God ask him every time they call if he's cured cancer yet."

"Are *they* teasing?" The elevator opened and he gestured for her to precede him.

"I seriously don't think so." She threw her hands in the air as they walked down the hall to the room. "All these years, I had no idea. I thought they only made unreasonable demands on me. God only knows what they expect out of my sisters. Probably world peace from Tamara and a colony on Mars from Katheryn. In retrospect, I've gotten off easy. They had no idea what impossible feat to command me to do since they never knew what I was going to do next." She giggled. "My flakiness has saved me."

Nash swiped the keycard against the lock and opened the door. He immediately stiffened at the darkness inside the room.

Elissa sobered faster than she thought possible. She stretched up and whispered into his ear, "What is it?"

"I always leave a light on," he whispered back. His hand went to his waist and his Sig appeared in his hand. He gently pushed Elissa behind him and flattened himself against the wall at the side of the door, gun at the ready.

Inside their room, a dog sneezed.

They looked at each other and said, "Gina?"

NINETEEN

"Sorry about turning off the lights, I have a horrendous headache and light just makes it worse," Gina said as she readjusted the folded washcloth covering her eyes. She was sitting on the couch with Fleur's head on her lap. Nash noticed the patio door to the lanai was closed, the drapes shut, and the light on the device that scrambled other listening devices was on and blinking green.

"Where have you been?" Nash demanded as he stood over Gina. "And why in the hell haven't you contacted me through the phone like a normal person?"

"What I want to know is how you got both Fleur and Reggie here," Elissa added from the floor where she was busy running her hands through the Lab's thick fur.

"Questions are like light," Gina mumbled. "But, you need answers. And, I need your help." She peeled the damp washcloth off her face and squinted in the low light coming from the lanai.

"So, y'all *don't* have everything under control." Nash gritted his teeth and tried to ignore Elissa's sudden perkiness at Gina's request.

She blew out a breath. "No."

Elissa stood up ever so slightly wobbly but no less enthusiastic. "Let me get some water and aspirin. I've got an IV kit, too." She walked to the minifridge, Reggie on her heels.

"I've already taken some migraine medicine, but water would be nice."

"Oh, well, the aspirin's kinda for me, too." She opened the minifridge and pulled out two bottles of water, then brought them over to Gina who took one, looking grateful. Elissa took a seat on the couch beside Gina while Reggie curled up at her feet. Elissa opened her purse and shook two aspirin from a bottle into her palm. "Hangover prevention. If I had time, I'd set up the IV saline I brought, but honestly, just seeing you has sobered me up. Now, how can we help?"

"Elissa," Nash warned.

She raised her hand, palm out. "Nope, if I can help, I'm gonna help. I've said so from the start, Nash."

"Fuck," he muttered under his breath as he studied the resolute expression on his stubborn woman's face.

"Hear me out," Gina said, scratching Fleur's head. "We did everything we could to keep you guys out of this, but it's impossible. We need Elissa's hacking skills—"

"Great, that's fine, but she can just as well hack from a safehouse as she can from out in the open where it isn't safe."

"No, she can't. Not in this case," Gina said, shaking her head.

Realization dawned on Elissa's face. "The server's not connected to the internet, is it?" she asked. "You need me to physically go wherever it is and hack straight in—"

"Over my dead body," Nash growled.

"Over *a lot* of dead bodies if you say no," Gina growled back. "We know what this thing is now, and it's dangerous if it gets out. I'm not exaggerating—people will die. Innocent civilians—men, women, and children all over the world if we don't shut it down first."

Elissa covered her mouth. "Is it some sort of nuclear thing?"

"No, nothing as straightforward as that." She squeezed the bridge of her nose. "Though, it could become a possibility if this thing isn't stopped."

"No fucking way," Nash said. "Send me in. Hell, send in all of Watchdog, but Elissa is not going anywhere near wherever the hell that server is."

Gina grinned bitterly. "Too late for that, because it's right here on Maui."

Oh, hell no! Nash grabbed Elissa's arm and pulled her up. Reggie got to his feet, ready to follow Nash's lead. "We are getting the hell out of Dodge, now."

"No!" She pulled away from him. "Half my family's here, and as much as they try my patience, I'm not abandoning them to some sort of danger."

"Then we'll get them out of here, too and someone else can fix this."

"Not possible," Gina said. "Elissa is only one of two people who can access the server. Believe me, we...already tried." The heaviness in her voice stopped him cold. "Pretty sure Capitoline did, too."

"No. No, this just gets worse and worse. We're—"

"Gina, what happened?" Elissa sat down again.

"I should have been with them," she murmured, shaking her head, all her concentration focused on Fleur. "My entire team is gone."

Elissa gasped. "Gone...gone?"

"We aren't sure. We lost contact with them twenty-four hours ago."

Nash bit the insides of his cheeks. "Look, I'm sorry about

that. But what makes you think Elissa has a chance if a trained elite team went missing?"

"Like I said, she's the only one we have who can access the server."

"So an evil maid attack," Elissa said.

"A what?" Gina asked. When Nash smiled grimly, she looked to him for clarification but he let Elissa continue.

"It's when a server has to be breached on-site and you need to physically get someone in to do it, like in a movie when an operative goes undercover as a maid to sneak into the enemy base. Evil maid attack."

Gina pursed her lips in thought. "All right then. It's an evil maid attack."

"No fucking way. Y'all aren't sending her in like that."

"She wouldn't be going in alone," Gina said. "I'll be coming with you, and so will Malcolm. Camden and Psychic just got in. And I doubt I could stop you from coming too, Nash." She glanced up at him. "And Elissa is not just any civilian. She's got an amazing skill set. Under other circumstances, I'd be actively recruiting her."

"Whatever you've got, I'll join," Elissa said.

"Elissa—"

"Nash, please, I love you but just shut up, stand down, and *listen* to me. I *need* to do this." She turned to Gina. "What am I hacking into?"

"A server belonging to a group of anarchists calling themselves Loki."

Elissa's eyes brightened. "As in the Marvel villain?"

"Marvel?" Gina tilted her head.

"Yeah! The comic books." Gina still looked confused. "The movies?" Elissa looked at Nash for help. "She doesn't get out much, does she?"

"I'm kind of busy trying to keep the world together," Gina said.

"Like a superhero," Elissa said, nodding.

"*Not* like a superhero," Gina retorted. "Like a very overworked woman. May I continue?"

"Of course."

"They've set up a sort of sick game." Gina shook her head, a look of disbelief on her face. "Did you catch the news story about that borough in New York going dark for no discernable reason?"

"Yeah, but what does it have to do with this?"

"The original server you hacked into, the one with the video, was traced to that borough. It was located in an abandoned building that consequently went up in flames not long after you logged out the first time. And then that night, everything went dark for twenty-four hours."

"Which is why I couldn't get back into the server when you asked me to," Elissa whispered, her shoulders jerking like a chill just ran down her spine.

Gina nodded. "You and Ulysses22 were the only ones who had access to that video," Gina said. "And since the server was immediately destroyed, no one else could go in and find that clue to discovering the location of the next server."

"The server that's offline?"

"Right. But my team was able to analyze the view from the video and locate the camera. It was set up in a resort not far from this one, in room three-one-two. We rented the room, searched it, and found the next clue." Gina pinched the bridge of her nose. "A hidden message from Loki that told us where the second server was, and what was on it."

"And it's here on Maui," Nash said.

"It is. This Loki group has been playing a long game. In the jungles to the north, there's a plot of land owned by what amounts to a Matryoshka, a Russian nesting doll set of shell companies, one nestled into the next that circles back to the first, impossible to track the actual owner. Though we have our suspicions." She waved her hand. "Not important right now. What is important is that there is a remote lava cave on this land with a hatch inside that we can't crack. It's bio-coded to you and Ulysses22. My team figured that out and reported back in once they'd reached the surface again. And then they went dark. We're assuming mercenaries from the Capitoline Group were waiting for them. But God only knows. It could have been Loki fucking with them. The other thing my team was able to tell us is what's on the server. Your twisted prize for hacking the first one."

Elissa raised her eyebrows. "Something tells me it's not a timeshare."

"Nope. Your prize is a digital skeleton key that can take down any municipality in the world. It can lock up finances, take down power grids, halt water treatment plants. Anywhere. That section of New York? They were flexing, showing us what they can do. What the news didn't report was that the power grid had been compromised via malware that also sent the mayor a one-word email when it struck: Loki."

"They can hold entire cities ransom," Elissa said.

"States, too," Gina added. "Some smaller countries, where it could spread by exploiting weak points in outdated security programs in other systems. Even launch missiles." She stood up and started pacing.

"There was another news story like the one from New York," Elissa said. "Part of London went dark—electricity, the tube, water."

"That was in retaliation for our team attempting to breach the room containing the server. Loki indicated that if that happens again, it will trigger copies of this skeleton key to disseminate to random targets around the world. And there won't be any ransom to pay and no chance of reversing it."

"Game over," Nash said.

Elissa shuddered and Nash put his arm around her. "I don't understand why they would do this," she said.

Gina stopped and looked at Elissa. "Some people just want to see the world burn. For others, it's a power play."

Nash glared at Gina. "This is why Elissa needs to go into hiding now. Instead, y'all are gonna dangle her out there like Loki did, helpless bait for any and all comers."

"Weren't you listening to what I said? We would send her into hiding *if* we didn't have Ulysses22 out there. We have no idea what he might do. The key is too important to risk falling into the wrong hands." She looked at Elissa. "Are you positive you don't know this person, that you have no idea who or where he could be?"

Elissa shook her head. "No idea whatsoever. But the good news is, he doesn't know who I am, either."

"Are you positive about that?"

"I am. We never traded personal info. My VPN is top-notch. No way he could have traced me. My server address bounced everywhere. And I couldn't trace *him*. I tried, of course. We all do." She grinned. "So, let's go crack this server."

Elissa may not have been able to trace Ulysses22, and maybe he hadn't traced her. But Loki had found both of them —and somehow obtained retina and fingerprint data. That knowledge froze his heart.

"Shug, no. You don't—"

Elissa lifted her hand to stop him. "I don't what? Need to help? I do. Or, do you think that I don't understand?" She sighed. "Please, don't underestimate me. Not you."

Nash blew out a breath. "Never."

She shook her head. "I've never told anyone how I got into hacking and why. So this is why I'm perfect for the job. I know how to get to the bad guys, and not just through a computer but in person."

"What do you mean?" Nash's gut twisted. It was the look on Elissa's face that did it. The same look she had when she confronted Brett after the race. *A wounded warrior, that's what it is. My woman has seen some shit.* "Sugar, what is it?"

Reggie dropped his chin onto Elissa's lap and she smiled at the dog and scratched his ears. "Thanks, buddy." She took a deep breath and started talking. "When I was a teenager, I used to babysit this really sweet kid down the street in the summertime. But he would get out of control easily, just suddenly lash out, and I never understood why. There was something there that I just couldn't put my finger on. His parents shared custody and he went back and forth between their houses. When his dad had custody, that's when I'd babysit during the day while he was at work."

Elissa's hands twisted together. "The whole neighborhood thought he was a great guy. He showed up at every single school event. He encouraged his kid to do his homework. They went to movies and they played a ton of video games together. Whatever the kid wanted, he got immediately. All the same...the guy never quite sat right with me. You know what I mean? But since he was friends with everyone in the neighborhood, I was pressured into setting my gut feelings aside."

Gina looked like she was going to throw up. "I know where this is going."

Elissa nodded. "I had a bad feeling and one day I just got too curious. They had every last video game console you can imagine. I ended up tinkering with one that looked like it had been tampered with. I opened it up and found the secret memory storage." Elissa's eyes watered. "There are some things in my life that I wish I had never seen. What I found in that memory storage is one of those things. The looks on the kids' faces..."

Nash felt his legs go weak. He picked Elissa up and sat her on his lap, his arms around her as she leaned back into him. Reggie laid his head on her lap again and she scratched his head.

"I completely understand," Gina said. "I've seen a lot of those things too, and they stay with you. I suggest talking to someone about it, if you haven't already."

Elissa nodded. "I didn't tell my parents. Instead, I immediately contacted the police. Turns out, he was already on the FBI's radar." She stopped petting Reggie and clenched her fist. "They'd been watching him for a year. Just watching, not *doing* anything. How could they...?" She wiped her tears and Nash held her tighter. "The hardest thing that I ever had to do was walk away from that little boy. All I wanted to do was sweep him up in my arms and take him with me, but the police told me I had to leave him there. They were building a bigger case. They said I'd ruin it if I didn't walk away. So I quit."

"Sugar. You don't have to say anything else."

"But I do. The dad called me one morning. He begged me to come over for Tim but he wouldn't say why. Of course I knew what was happening and I raced over there. Police cars were parked everywhere in his driveway, up and down the street. Just everywhere. I marched up the drive. Went into the house. And that son of a bitch stood there in his living room looking like he was stunned, like they had the wrong guy. He looked right at me and told me that I needed to take Tim to school. I mean, my God. Instead, I took him home with me and we waited until a social worker got there to take Tim to his mom. The minute they walked out of my house, I went into the bathroom and I threw up."

Nash kissed her head. She leaned into him, but she kept talking. "I went to every single one of his hearings. But he hired an expensive lawyer who specialized in this shit and so he had the best justice that money can buy. He saw zero jail time. Just had to wear an ankle bracelet and go see a probation officer for a year, and he wasn't allowed to live near a school."

"It makes me sick how often that happens," Gina said.

"So what did he do? He moved to a different neighborhood and bought a house that was literally twenty-five feet outside of the range of a school. He could see the playground from his backyard. There were a lot of kids who went to that school who lived in his neighborhood. It made me sick. I couldn't sleep at night. I kept seeing those images over and over."

"You don't need to keep going, shug." Nash felt his heart tearing up into little pieces at Elissa's words. His sweet, innocent woman had layers to her he'd never suspected.

Elissa wiped her tears away. "That 'justice' wasn't good enough for me. So I took matters into my own hands. He was a computer programmer. Do you know that hacker group, the one called FawkesAnon?"

"Yeah everybody who codes knows them," Nash said. "They're the ones who go after predators online. I wouldn't exactly call them white hats, but they sure do a lot of good work."

Elissa nodded. "You know how they wear those Guy Fawkes masks, right? Whenever they announce they've taken someone down?"

"Of course."

"He told me once he was afraid of them. I didn't understand why at first, but then of course it became clear. He was the type of predator they love to target. I contacted them but they never responded. So I targeted him online instead. I wasn't a good enough hacker back then. There was nothing that I could do to stop him. But I could do something more... immediate. I waited until Halloween that year and bought a Guy Fawkes mask, a cape, black pants, and platform boots.

"Then I went to his neighborhood disguised in my costume, looking like I was somebody from a Halloween store passing out flyers. I went up to every single door in that neighborhood and slid a sheet of bright orange paper between the screen and the regular door. That paper had his mugshot on it with his criminal record. It had his history. And it had his current address. I wanted everybody to know exactly who was living among them and how close he was to their school."

"Damn, shug. You doxed him on his own street." Nash glanced at Gina, who was smiling like a wolf.

"And when I was done with that, I went to the end of his driveway and I faced his house. I looked in his big picture window and I saw that the drapes had been pulled shut, except for one little crack. I stood there and I stared through that crack knowing he was staring back. I wanted him to think I was with FawkesAnon. I wanted him to know that he was targeted, that he was being watched, that I was the predator and he was the prey. That since justice wasn't in the courts, it would be served on his own goddamn street in his own goddamn face and his neighbors would know who he was and what he was."

Elissa took a deep breath. "They chased him out, but each time, he found a new neighborhood near a school. So I did that three years running. In the meantime, I got better at hacking. I helped bring him down, but I did it anonymously. And you know how much it mattered? In the end, not very much.

Same situation. And all they gave him was another slap on the wrist.

"He eventually moved out of state but I kept at him online, finding and outing him wherever he went. He amassed another collection of...well, you know." Elissa smiled grimly. "I exposed him again, and that time he finally saw justice. He's locked up now, at last.

"So I'm the perfect person for this. I can harass somebody online and I can harass them offline. And I'll be damned if I'm going to stand by and do nothing. If I can help save one single person, I will do it. Please, please let me do this." She stood up. "Actually, I'll do it whether you let me or not. I've gone rogue before."

Gina gave Elissa a warm smile that transformed her face. Nash had never seen Gina look so unguarded. So open. He felt sorry for every time he'd thought of her as somehow inhuman, as cold. "You don't need to go rogue, Elissa. I would be honored to work with you. We do need you; now I'm convinced more than ever that we picked the winner." She grabbed Elissa's hand.

Elissa pulled the woman up and into a tight hug that Gina didn't hesitate to give back.

"Thank you," Elissa said.

"Thank *you*," Gina answered.

"We'll talk sometime, okay? When all of this is over and we're back in Cali." Elissa pulled back and fixed Gina with her gaze. "First, just you and me, and then we'll do girls' night out or something. You need to come drinking with us, with me, Elena, Delia, Rachael, and Jordan. Oh, and Arden when she's in town. Just one of the girls."

Gina's smile was as sad and wistful as her previous smile had been happy, like a distorted reflection in a carnival fun house Nash's mom had taken him to as a kid. "I'd like that," she said, her voice low as she nodded. "Just...be a little patient with me? I don't have a lot of friends."

"Well, that's gonna change." Elissa put her hands on her hips.

Gina put her mask back on before she looked at Nash. "I need you on board with this mission, Nashville, or I'm going to have to call someone else in."

He looked at two of the strongest women he'd ever known. "You know I'm in. So what's our next move?"

Elissa's phone buzzed in her purse. "Hang on, that might be my brother. I want to try and get my family out of here." She looked at the name on the screen with puzzlement in her eyes and Nash's instincts pinged.

"Fia? What's—"

TWENTY

The voice that cut off Elissa was not Fia's. It was a man's voice running through a modulator that made him sound inhuman and robotic.

"Hey, Surfboi, good to speak to you at last. I guess you're not a dude though, huh?"

"Who the hell is this?" Elissa asked, though she already knew. *God, I've been so stupid. So stupid and naïve.* She put the phone on speaker and watched Nash and Gina's faces.

The voice over the phone laughed. "Come on, you know your old friend."

"What did you do with Fia, Ulysses?"

"She's here and she's safe, for now. But for how long, well, that's going to be up to you."

Gina was digging furiously through her tote while Nash scribbled on hotel stationery: *Keep him talking.* Sure, they were going to trace the call. "Where are you? Why are you doing this? Like you said, we're friends. Well, at least up until you decided to kidnap my newest bestie."

Ulysses22 laughed, an unnerving sound through the modulator. "Things have changed a lot in the past couple of weeks, haven't they? I caught your race. You have a tender heart, just like I thought, so I think I can still trust you."

"If you hurt Fia you can trust that I'll hurt you right back, old friend or not."

"Fia will be just fine so long as you come to see me and we talk. I promise, one surfer bro to another. We have a lot to discuss."

Surfer. Elissa closed her eyes. Fia had been trying to send her a distress text. She wasn't talking about literal surfing, but online surfing. Had Ulysses kidnapped Fia directly from the race? *But why not cut to the chase and take me?* Her answer was watching her like the protective hawk he was. Ulysses didn't dare grab her with Nash so close. But Fia had no one to protect her, and now she was in serious danger just for befriending Elissa.

"Where are you?" By now, Gina had found her phone and sent a text; Elissa presumed it was to someone who could trace the call. "I'll come talk to you, but I'm gonna need proof of life first. Put Fia on the phone, now." She glanced at Gina who gave her a thumbs up while Nash looked fit to be tied and shook his head violently.

"You can talk to Fia on one condition. You come to me alone without your watchdogs, know what I'm saying? I know two of them are sitting right there with their ears perked up. You've kept me talking more than long enough for Gina to trace this call, so you know where to find me now. I'll expect you within the hour. Come alone or I guarantee you won't see her again."

Ulysses disconnected. Elissa realized she was shaking, but it wasn't with fear for herself. She was enraged both at the dude she'd trusted and at herself for endangering someone innocent.

"Elissa? Shug, we traced the call." Nash laid his hand on

her shoulder. His touch and his words brought her back to the room.

"Where? Where is the bastard?"

Gina put one finger up for silence. She picked up Elissa's phone, took off the cover, and removed the battery. "I'm pretty positive your friend was listening to us through your phone somehow."

"So where is he?"

"Where else? Room three-one-two, Mahalo Aina Resort," Gina said. "Where we found the camera Loki set up. Ulysses figured it out, too."

"Cool." Elissa looked back and forth between Nash and Gina. "What are we waiting for?"

Nash looked shocked. "You aren't going to fight us on not going alone?"

"Like I'd even win. No, of course not. I know you're going to shadow me, and I imagine Ulysses does too. He's not stupid. I think he's playing chess here, or else he would have simply grabbed me from the race, not Fia. He wants to talk to me alone, so I'll give him that, knowing that you guys have my back if things go sideways."

Nash shook his head. "You trust me that much."

"Well, duh." She grinned. "I know you'll always have my back. You too, Gina. That's what teams do, right?"

Gina nodded, the ghost of a smile briefly crossing her lips. "I think you're right about the chess-playing. Malcolm and Camden are already in position at the Mahalo Aina Resort. Nash and I will cover the other exits. Take this." Gina handed Elissa a necklace with a pendant. "I'm borrowing it from a friend. There's a tracking device in the pendant. Put it on and under no circumstances do you remove it again, understood?"

"Roger."

Nash took the necklace from Elissa and fastened it around

her neck. Then he handed her the keys to the Jeep. "This is killing me, shug," he said.

She closed her hand around his. "Not me. I know I'm going to be safe because my coach has my back." She kissed him, trying her best to hide any trace of worry. She let her excitement take its place instead.

He cupped her face. "We aren't going to let him touch a hair on your head. I love you."

She nodded. "I love you, too. Let's roll."

E lissa parked in a visitors' spot at the Mahalo Aina Resort. She got out and started across the parking lot to the entrance which faced away from the ocean. Was Ulysses22 watching her from a different vantage point? Was there a gun pointed at her as she walked into a trap?

Stop it. If there is a gun pointed at your head, it's too late to do anything about it. You've got to trust your team. And yourself.

She took several calming breaths as she walked into the lobby. This resort was way nicer than the one they were staying in. She passed by the check-in desk with a smile and a wink at the guy behind the counter as she headed for the elevators. To her right was a freestanding bar surrounded by couches and low cocktail tables. She studiously ignored the big man sitting in a chair facing the entrance and Malcolm ignored her in turn. Camden was nowhere in sight but that didn't mean he couldn't see her, unless he was up on the third floor.

Elissa hit the up button and entered the elevator alone. She punched number three and waited. Her stomach was a mass of writhing snakes as the car lifted. She swallowed rising bile as images of an injured or—God forbid—dead Fia filled her mind and she pushed them away. The doors opened on an ominously quiet hall. Elissa followed an arrow pointing left on a sign saying Rooms 300-315. Her legs felt shaky like she'd just finished a race. She was thankful she'd had a couple of drinks with her brother or else she'd need one right now. She stopped at the door numbered 312 and wondered if she should knock or what when she noticed the keycard sticking halfway out of the bottom of the door.

Deep breath, Elissa. She stooped and picked it up, then inserted it into the lock and watched the light turn green. She grabbed the handle and opened the door without stepping through. She wasn't about to let herself get coldcocked if Ulysses was standing off to the side.

Straight ahead, she saw a standing figure backlit by the dim light coming through an open patio door.

Fia.

"Dear God, you're grand for coming!" Fia said. "It's all right, Ulysses isn't by the door."

"Fia? What the hell? Are you all right?"

"Close the door. Please." She sounded on the verge of panic. "Please, just drop your bag, toss your phone to me, and come in."

Against all her better instincts, Elissa closed the door behind her but stayed where she was. "I'm so sorry this is happening to you. I never meant to get anyone involved." She looked around the room. "Where is he? In the bathroom?"

"Please, just toss me your phone, all right?" Her voice was shaky.

Elissa complied and Fia caught it. "Now, you are to sit down across from me at the table, and then I can give you a message." Fia backed up and pulled out a chair at a small table. Elissa swallowed hard. If she took the seat, anyone outside could see her. Target her. What if Ulysses was hiding somewhere out there, waiting to see her through a scope mounted on a rifle?

No. If he wanted me dead, he could've done it already. He needs me alive.

Elissa crossed the room and sat down opposite Fia. In the meantime, Fia removed the battery from Elissa's phone and placed both on the table. The woman looked like a ghost with her long dark hair streaming down either side of her face, her pale blue eyes round and huge. She sat with her hands folded in her lap under the table. "Any other listening devices I should know about? This is life and death."

Elissa shook her head. "No, I promise. Are you all right? I'm sorry I didn't understand your texts." Elissa repeated. "Where is he?" She glanced around, though she didn't feel anyone else in the room. Was he right outside on the balcony?

"Ulysses22?" Fia said. Then she smiled as she tucked her chin into her throat and raised something to her mouth. "I'm right here, bro." Her voice came out distorted and robotic. She dropped her hand and added, "Your man isn't the only one who can lose his accent at will." She'd deepened her voice and all trace of an Irish lilt was gone.

"Oh my God, I *trusted* you." Elissa fought to keep from yelling. "I thought you were a friend, both as Ulysses22 and as Fia."

"I *am* your friend, Elissa." Her accent was back, so at least she actually was Irish. Maybe. Okay, God only knew at this point. "I needed to know if you'd be my friend, because I'm completely fooked otherwise. So, I entered the race. It wasn't hard to fake and backdate everything." She smirked. "The hard part was making it believable enough, knowing your man would have Watchdog look into my background. I needed to get close to you, to see what kind of person you were and if you'd help me. When I sent you those texts, I was hoping you'd put two and two together, figure out I was Ulysses, and agree to meet me online. "This," she gestured at the room, "was my crappy plan B."

Elissa shook her head. She glanced out the patio doors, positive she was being watched now. "All you had to do was tell me you were Ulysses from the start."

"Sure and I know that now but I had to be certain. I see you looking out those doors. I placed you there as an act of trust. Your people can see you clearly and know that you're safe. I'm not aiming to hurt you. Do you believe me?"

"You know I'm not here alone?"

"You think I'm daft?" Fia grinned. "Course you're not alone They'd never let you come here all on your own. But I just wanted a private word with you first, and this was how to get it."

"Fine, you've got me, so talk." Elissa felt a bead of sweat trickle down the back of her neck. "But make it quick because my friends get pretty impatient."

"Then I'll cut straight to it. You're going to fail if you try to get into the server alone. I know because I already tried and it nearly cost me my life."

"You were there?" Elissa's heartrate ticked up. "What happened? Is it rigged? Did spikes come out of the cave walls or something?"

Fia actually laughed. "It's not quite that Indiana Jones, but close. No, nothing related to the server tried to kill me. My employers did." She watched as the penny dropped for Elissa.

"You're working for Capitoline, aren't you?"

Fia's expression turned grim. "Yes, though I didn't know who they were, I swear on my Mum's Bible. If I had, I would've disappeared. They're big, and they're powerful.

They hired twenty of us to try and crack that first server. All
the best. Except one. You."

"Why not me?"

Fia looked incredulous. She gestured to the patio and the
darkness beyond. "You don't reckon it's because of your team
out there, do you? That if Capitoline had so much as sneezed
in your direction, they'd bring down their wrath?"

Elissa glanced outside as if she could somehow magically
see, who? Gina? Camden? Nash? "I'm not really part of
Watchdog. Just a friend."

Fia raised an eyebrow. "Don't kid a kidder, girl. You're all-
in with them. So here it is. I succeeded with your help to hack
that server—"

"*We* hacked that server."

Fia rolled her eyes. "Potato, po-tah-to. Once we did it, I let
my handler know and he told me that there'd be a lot of
money in it for me if I could hack the second. Of course I said
yes. So they flew me out here, first-class and everything. Put
me up in this room and I found the next clue. Then didn't
they whisk me away again to get to the hacking? And didn't I
do as asked, only to find that damn hatch is keyed to the both
of us? Which is when they thought I was lying and threatened
to kill me. I managed to convince them I was telling the truth.
And then I convinced them of one more thing."

"Which was?"

"That I could talk you into working with me to get in."

Elissa folded her arms. "I will never work with them."

Fia nodded quickly. "I know, I know. Which is why I'm so
fooked. Because if you don't help me, they *will* kill me. But I
had to give it a try, didn't I?"

Elissa growled as she rested her forehead on the tabletop.
"I can't say no and let you die, either."

"Well, now, you *could* let me die. Because full disclosure;

if I do talk you into helping, then I'm supposed to kill you once I have the key."

Elissa's head shot up. "Would you actually...do...that...?" Her words trailed off when she saw the two red laser dots, one on Fia's chest over her heart and the other square in the middle of her forehead. "Oh, God, Capitoline's watching us right now."

"Guess again. That's your side, girl. I don't think they liked it when you put your head down all of a sudden." Fia looked down at her chest then met Elissa's gaze again. "There's another one on my forehead, isn't there?"

"I'm afraid so."

Fia bit her lower lip. "Could you maybe?" She gestured with her head at the open doors. "It's really distracting."

"Oh, sure." Elissa waved and gave a thumbs-up sign to let them know she was all right. The red dots disappeared.

"Thank you. And to answer your question, no, I'd never kill you. I've never killed anyone and I don't intend to start now. That includes myself, so I'm begging you, please, help me. They're afraid of Watchdog and its connections, and that's saying a lot. *Nothing* scares these people. They've got the life of Riley, I tell you—rich, powerful, they own governments. I stand no chance on my own. So I'm asking you to please tell your friends that I'm on your side while I tell Capitoline I've fooled you into working with me. We can get in, hack the server, I don't kill you, and I'm under Watchdog's protection. I'll owe all of you."

"What's to stop Nash from coming into the room once we've opened the hatch? He could stand there with a gun to your head the entire time."

Fia shook her head. "The instructions are written on the hatch. Only you and I go in once we've opened it, or else it'll trigger the damn thing to hit random cities. They're completely bonkers. This Loki group encouraged the powers that be to find whoever hacked in and, I quote, 'Do what you will to the winners. Treat them like truffle-sniffing pigs to find the prize or kill them outright to keep the key hidden; the choice is yours.'"

Elissa shuddered and ran her hands through her hair in frustration. "So what happens when we get the key? You're not going to give it to Capitoline, are you?"

"God, no." She narrowed her eyes. "Are you planning on giving it over to your people?"

"I..." *Am I?* She realized she didn't want to give anything that dangerous to anyone. How could she really trust what would happen to it after that?

Fia read the hesitation on Elissa's face and heard it in her voice. "I have another idea," she said.

Elissa smiled. "I hope it's the same one I have."

"This thing...I don't trust it in anyone's hands," Fia said quietly.

Elissa couldn't help glancing outside. "I trust Watchdog. I trust Nash of course. And I trust Gina. But, I don't know the people she works for." Her voice had dropped to a whisper.

"Then what say we work together, hack in, and destroy the server along with the key?" Fia drew her eyebrows down. "Unless you think your people wouldn't forgive you for that?"

"*My* people would." *But would Gina's?* she wondered.

Fia nodded. She reached across the table and grabbed Elissa's hand. "Please. I've been honest with you tonight and I know you're a good person. Help me. Or if not me, then do it to protect the innocents who'll suffer if this thing gets out."

Dammit.

Elissa squeezed her hand. "Okay. I'll help you. I'll see that we all help you."

TWENTY-ONE

T he Maui jungle was sweltering, even at night, which was not a new situation for Nash. He'd been in so many jungles he'd lost count. He knew it was the same with Camden, Psychic, and Gina, and he figured Malcolm was no stranger to the danger either.

What was new was the dread in his gut every time he thought about the fact that his woman was here with them on Operation Evil Maids and that the objective was to keep her safe, even when she would be beyond their reach and alone with a woman Nash found impossible to trust. Fia, or whatever her real name was, had manipulated Elissa—hell, had manipulated his entire team—into guaranteeing her protection on this mission and beyond if necessary, and that left him as jumpy as a long-tailed cat in a room full of rocking chairs.

They'd wasted no time after Elissa had signaled to them that she and Fia were coming down from the room. Psychic met them at the hotel room door, still on the alert for Ulysses22 and thinking that Fia must be working with him. Then when they'd all gathered at the rendezvous point and Fia told her story, Nash was ready to throttle her for putting

Elissa in danger. Capitoline knew exactly where they were and what was happening. All they could do was trust that Fia would keep her word that she wouldn't harm Elissa, and there wasn't enough trust in the world to convince Nash that she wouldn't.

So he was left having to trust Elissa and that she could take care of herself once they got past that hatch and into the server.

But first, they had to get her to the hatch.

"Psychic reporting in," Nash heard over his comm. "No change." His teammate was in the lead with Anubis, a black Malinois that suited him perfectly. The dog was smarter than some humans. Anubis would silently neutralize any threat to their team. Reggie was with Nash, Elissa, and Fia, his nose twitching and his ears perked up for any sign of danger.

"Joker reporting in. No change." That was Camden behind them with Toby, a formidable German Shepherd.

"Watchtower reporting in. No change." Malcolm was several yards to their left.

"Spooky reporting in. No change." Gina flanked them on the right. She'd left Fleur behind. She was a great dog and Gina's constant companion, but she was a rescued street dog, never trained for this work.

"Garth reporting in. Payload secure." Yeah, Nash hated his handle. He probably had that in common with Gina.

He shifted his backpack to a more comfortable position. He was carrying an array of survival items like collapsible water bottles and energy bars, and a fair number of weapons, including explosives. The jungle teemed with life all around them, the sound of insects and small animals filling the air along with the high-pitched, irritating whine of mosquitoes trying to eat them alive. At least they didn't need to worry about snakes since there were none on Maui. Nash *hated* snakes. Their biggest threats from nature were wild pigs and accidents from falling. The hatch was about four miles from the road. They had to cross streams with slippery rocks and do a fair amount of hiking in the dark. Even with their night-vision goggles, the terrain was challenging. Thank God that Elissa and Fia were in such good shape and able to keep up the pace.

So far, there was no attack from their true threat—other mercenaries sent by Capitoline. But they were out there. The occasional snap of a broken branch or low whine from one of the dogs alerted the team to their presence. Moving between the trees, Nash had caught sight of a man-shaped figure on his infra-red scanner about fifteen yards away, shadowing them. He'd alerted Malcolm, who was the closest, but his teammate already had the man in his sights. Nash was sure it goaded Malcolm as much as it did him not to take the shot and neutralize the threat, but that would just bring on an unnecessary attack from the rest of them. No, the time to fight would be on the way out after Elissa and Fia had done their jobs. He hoped Gina's extraction plan would work or else they were all just sticking their heads right into a tightening noose. He tried not to think about the team that had disappeared before them.

The sky opened and rain poured down. The jungle steamed.

"We're getting close," Fia whispered. "Your man up front should be almost on it."

Sure enough, Psychic reported in a couple minutes later. Though his voice sounded staticky, Nash could make out the word, "Closure."

"Copy," Nash replied, followed by everyone else.

They jogged up to the cave entrance, little more than a hole in the ground surrounded by mud. Gina said something over the comm but her voice was garbled.

"Spooky, come back," Nash said, but her voice remained garbled. *Fuck. It couldn't just be the rain.* Something was scrambling their signals. They knew this would be a possibility, since TAC had lost contact with the first team. Sure enough, Nash's goggles went dark. "Fuck," he said as he tore them off. When he saw Psychic, Elissa, and Fia remove theirs, he asked, "Y'all's went dark, too?" They each nodded.

Fia touched his arm. "This happened when I was here before." She took her earbud out and handed it to him. "These are rubbish now."

"Keep it, just in case," he said. His gut turned to ice water. He had no way of knowing if her tracker pendant was still working, and he'd hoped to at least stay in contact with Elissa via the comms, but of course they weren't allowed nice things on this mission. Then again, they had the dogs, who didn't have to depend on electronics to know when an enemy was near. He smiled grimly at what he hoped would be an advantage against their targets.

More garbled messages came in from Gina, Camden, and Malcolm. He assumed they'd taken their places around the cave entrance. Maybe they were far enough away from whatever dampening field they'd found themselves in that their equipment still worked. The official plan was for Psychic to stay topside with the dogs while Nash accompanied Elissa and Fia to the hatch. Nash's unofficial plan was to go into the server room with them. He wasn't about to leave Elissa alone with Fia again.

He took out his flashlight and turned it on. At least that still worked. "Let's go," he said against every instinct that told him they were crawling into their graves. "You first, Fia, since you know the way. When you get to the bottom, do not move, understood?" They'd searched the woman for weapons, but there was no guarantee she or Capitoline hadn't stashed one at the bottom of the cave.

"I understand," she answered. Her flashlight in hand, the woman slipped into the hole. "There's a metal ladder but it's slippery with rain," she warned before her head disappeared.

Nash held onto Elissa as she found the first rung. She smiled up at him. He looked for any sign of fear but all he could see was excitement in her eyes before she disappeared into the darkness.

Nash climbed down after them. Fia hadn't lied; the rungs turned treacherous as muddy water poured in, making them slicker than pig shit. Fia had made it to the bottom and was shining her flashlight up to help Elissa and Nash. *You may be on your best behavior, but I don't trust you as far as I can throw you* Nash thought. The sound of squishing mud told him Elissa had stepped off the ladder, and then he made it to the bottom. True to her word—at least for now—Fia had done as asked and stayed put.

Nash shined his flashlight around the cave. Black lava rock drank in the light like the mouth of hell, broken up only by patches of mossy greenery here and there that looked like infected sores. Past the 'stairwell' they'd have to stoop because the ceiling couldn't have been more than five feet high in most places. He took three headlamps out of his pack and handed them out.

"The hatch is this way," Fia said, pointing into the darkness. "It's not a fun walk and the ceiling gets even lower than this until the passage opens up again. We'll be on our hands and knees before it's over."

"Fantastic. Lead on," Nash said.

"Thanks, Fia," Elissa said.

"We're all in this together, aren't we?" Fia responded with a smile.

"For now," Nash said. Elissa scowled at him.

"I'm planning on keeping it that way," Fia said as she moved forward, carefully avoiding the sharp rocks. "I can only trust you are, too."

"All up to you," Nash said.

"Of course we're keeping it that way," Elissa said as she followed Fia.

The first thing Nash was going to do when they got out of this mess was school Elissa on trusting strangers. No, actually the first thing he was going to do was ask her to marry him, *then* they'd have a talk about her sweet, trusting nature.

Fia hadn't lied. The cave grew smaller as they went on until they were crawling on their hands and knees through several inches of water. Water dripped around them, filtering down through the porous stone. At one point, Nash felt the walls scrape against both shoulders at the same time. Thunder rumbled somewhere far above them; Nash almost felt it more than heard it.

"I can't believe there's a server down here," Elissa said. "How the hell do they keep it dry and powered up?"

"We'll find out, won't we?" Fia replied. "Just the hatch itself is impressive, you'll see."

Nash swallowed a growl. If Gina's team hadn't confirmed the existence of the hatch, he'd think Fia was leading them straight into a trap—which was still a possibility.

"Almost there," Fia said after they'd been crawling for fifteen minutes. "The ceiling gets higher from here until we get to the hatch chamber."

"Thank God," Elissa said. "This is doing nothing for my claustrophobia."

"Here we go." Fia started duck-walking as the cave's ceiling lifted, until they could almost stand upright again. Another few feet, and they exited the tunnel into a cavern about ten feet high with a floor that sloped toward them. At the higher end of the cavern stood a door-sized hatch embedded in a perfectly smooth, metallic wall.

"Damn." Elissa started toward the wall. "How in the hell did they build this?"

"Elissa, wait," Nash said as he grabbed her arm. "Let me check it out first. You," he pointed at Fia, then at the cave wall to the left, "go stand over there and keep your hands visible."

"Yes, sir," Fia said as she backed up toward the wall, her hands lifted palms out in front of her.

Elissa was right, the wall and hatch were impressive pieces of work. A red light glowed steadily next to a retina scanner. Below that was a panel with the outline of a hand drawn on it. That was disturbing enough, but worse was the etched metal plaque with Elissa and Fia's names on it and instructions on getting in, with a warning that the scanner would detect if the eyeballs had been removed and the hands severed, and that if anyone else entered the chamber, the server would alert Loki and random cities around the world would shut down soon after.

Fuck. There had to be some way to get around it. There was a window in the hatch at least. Nash tried to shine his headlamp, then his flashlight into it, but the darkness was complete.

Elissa took a deep breath beside him. "Things just got real," she murmured.

Nash took out two comms and gave her one. He put the other in his ear. "Let's give this a try."

She put in the comm, took a few steps back, and turned away from him. "Can you hear me?"

Nothing but static filled Nash's ear. "Dammit." He ripped it back out of his ear and Elissa handed him her useless comm.

He could only assume the pendant tracker around her neck wouldn't work down here, either.

"Sugar, we can turn around now. I can keep you safe."

"No. Not that I don't trust you can keep me safe, but think about it. God only knows how many people are gunning for me right now. There'd be a target on my back and on Fia's for the rest of our lives. You and I would have to stay on the run, and as much as I would love to globetrot, that's not what I had in mind. We need to do this. I can't walk away knowing that I left behind something so dangerous."

Nash studied her face. He cupped his hands around his mouth. *"You're going to destroy it, aren't you?"* He mouthed the words so that Fia and any listening devices couldn't pick up what he said but Elissa could read his lips.

"Yes," she mouthed back, her hands similarly cupped around her mouth. He thought he made out the words *Fia is too* but couldn't be sure.

"Sugar, please be careful. If it's a choice between you and the world, I choose you. I love you."

She blinked back tears. *"I love you, too."* She signed the words along with saying them, then cupped her mouth again. *"I have to do this."*

Nash nodded, his heart filled with reluctance.

"You'll keep us safe."

He nodded again.

Elissa smiled and kissed him. She turned to Fia. "Ready, partner?"

Fia grinned and approached the hatch. "Ready, partner."

Nash drew his Sig and looked at Fia. "I'll wait for y'all right out here."

"As expected," she said. "Just remember our deal."

"You, too."

Elissa blew out a breath. "Okay, now that we're done

swinging dicks around, I'll go first." She stepped up to the retina scanner and placed her hand on the panel. The light turned green and a computerized voice said, "Surfboi-sixty-five recognized." Then the light turned yellow and the voice started counting down from ten.

"I think that means you're next." Elissa stepped aside for Fia.

"Last time, it counted down to zero and the light turned red again. I reckon since you weren't here to log in." Fia looked into the scanner as she pressed her palm against the panel.

"Ulysses-twenty-two recognized. Login complete." A metallic clank sounded and the hatch opened. Bright bluish light shone out around the edges and through the little window in the hatch.

"Here goes nothing," Fia said as she grabbed the edge of the door and opened it wide.

Nash readied to dash in after them but when he got a look past Fia his heart dropped. He could recognize an airlock when he saw one. Just beyond the hatch was a body scanner built into a short manmade hallway and another sealed hatch at the other end of it. There was no getting past that.

The computerized voice said, "Scanner will activate when hatch one is closed." Then it began another countdown from twenty.

"We need to hurry," Fia said as she stepped inside.

Elissa looked back at him. "See you on the other side."

"Elissa, wait." But she'd already closed the hatch behind her.

TWENTY-TWO

F eeling like she was the newest character in a *Mission: Impossible* movie, Elissa stood under a flood of LED lights and watched as Fia stood in the body scanner while the countdown continued.

"Pervs better not be looking at my drawers," Fia said. The scanner chimed and the red light above it turned green. She stepped through and turned around. "Your go," she said.

Elissa turned around to see Nash's face behind the window in the first hatch. The expression on his face damn near killed her. She turned back around and vowed not to look at him again until she was through the second hatch or else she'd find herself banging on that window to be let back out.

Elissa stepped into the scanner and waited to either be approved or instantly evaporated. When she heard the chime, she continued on through. The second hatch opened with a whoosh and the sharp, clean smell of ozone filled the cool air.

"Well, here we go," Fia said.

The second hatch had a window like the first. If Nash remembered the sign language she'd taught him on the plane, they could communicate, so long as the light stayed on. *Don't look back yet.* Elissa followed Fia into the room. Before the hatch could close, Elissa impulsively wedged her backpack in the doorway to keep it open.

Like the airlock, there was nothing even remotely cave-like about the room housing the server. The manmade walls were painted white like the tiled floor. An air purifier hummed quietly and a panel on the wall read sixty-eight degrees F, humidity thirty-five percent. As she watched, the humidity rose three percent and she heard something kick on —presumably a dehumidifier—until the number returned to thirty-five percent.

"Fancy pad," Fia said, looking around. "Someone has deep pockets."

"This is what I'd expect from Capitoline."

"Me, too. Or your people maybe?"

"That would be above my paygrade," Elissa answered.

Fia glanced at Elissa, then gestured at the table positioned in the middle of the room. Sitting on it were two keyboards and two monitors, all hooked to an innocuous-looking black server sitting on the floor beside the table. "Shall we?"

"Let's do this."

"To activate the server, please step away from the door," the computer's voice commanded. Fia and Elissa looked at each other, then at the backpack.

"It was worth a shot," Fia said.

Elissa picked up her backpack and the hatch swung closed with an ominous click. Now she looked through the little window and took hope when she saw Nash's face through the second window about ten feet away. He quickly signed letters spelling out CAN U C ME and she nodded vigorously. She blew him a kiss before turning back to the table.

The monitors flickered to life as the computer's voice

intoned, "Welcome, Surfboi-sixty-five and Ulysses-twenty-two. You have one hour to breach the partition containing Skeleton Key. If you succeed, Skeleton Key is yours to copy to the provided thumb drives and use at will. Once you have successfully copied Skeleton Key you are free to go."

"And if we don't?" Elissa asked. There was no answer.

Their plan was to fool the server into thinking the partition was still intact after they'd destroyed it along with what they hoped was the only copy of Skeleton Key. There was no guarantee that this was the only copy, but they tried not to think about that.

Run your own race. The words came back to Elissa. This was no different. She could only do her best and hope it was enough.

A timer appeared in the corner of each screen and started counting down. Elissa and Fia took their seats. Elissa's heart sped up with excitement. She couldn't believe she'd been giving her brother shit about curing cancer when little did she know she'd literally be saving the world hours later.

"Everything all right?" Fia asked.

"Yeah, peachy. So weird, hacking with you sitting right here."

"Same." Fia laced her fingers together and stretched her arms out until her knuckles popped. "I brought the root kit that allowed us to get into server one. Shall we begin there?"

"That's what I was thinking. I doubt it'll be that easy, but it's a start."

For the next several minutes, the clicking of computer keys played against the hum of the climate controls adjusting the temperature, humidity, and air purity. The computer screens filled with lines of code. Fia was the first to swear when their initial attempt failed.

"Here, let's try this." Elissa deleted a line of code then

typed in a new one, taking a cue from the words on the sign in the video.

"Oh, smart," Fia said. "We are dealing with a group of jokers, aren't we?"

The second attempt got them into another partition closer to the jackpot. Now the server was attacking back in earnest. Their fingers moved faster, Fia modifying code to attack while Elissa mapped the system with the intent of creating a phony partition that would hopefully fool the server.

"Shite buckets," Fia said when her next attempt failed.

"Anything from the clues you found in the room?" Elissa asked.

"Yeah, let me try..." Fia's fingers flew over the keyboard. "Ha! That helped. It's like they half-want us to succeed."

"Coulda fooled me. Ok, now let me..." Elissa paused her work on the partition and added to the attacking code. She disabled one of the attacks, only to have a new firewall pop up blocking the next partition. "Shit!"

"No, you're grand," Fia said. "It's progress."

Despite the cool air, a bead of sweat formed on Elissa's forehead and tickled its way down her temple. She shook her head and then apologized when her sweat hit Fia.

"No worries, I'm fairly covered with it myself. Besides, we'll be taking another swim on our way out, won't we?" She grinned at Elissa.

Elissa wished she had Fia's confidence right now. Thirteen minutes had ticked by and God only knew if they were being watched. How ridiculous was it that she couldn't even see the enemy she was fighting? Elissa pictured a bunch of evil nerds with a giant bucket of popcorn gathered around a screen showing the two of them sitting there, clicking away. The ridiculous cartoon image helped calm her nerves.

Until the computer announced, "You have forty-five minutes left. If you fail to hack the partition in that time, the router will be activated and Skeleton Key will be disseminated to random cities around the globe and executed. Any attempt to access and disable the network interface card will trigger the router."

"Fuck!" Elissa wiped the sweat off her forehead. "Where's the router? Maybe we can smash *that*."

"It's not in here."

Run your own race. The words that sustained Elissa through the Maui Challenge came back to steady her.

"Relax," Fia said. "We've got this. And *you* at least will be getting out of here alive. Your man will make sure of it."

"He'll keep his word to you, Fia." *So long as you keep yours* she added silently. Fia had shown no signs of going back on her promise. *Yet.* Elissa wanted with all of her heart to trust the woman, because she really did feel like a friend. *Please, let's keep it that way.*

Another fifteen minutes went by. Elissa was close to finishing the phony partition, then she could test it. Fia had defeated the firewall and was into the next partition but was being attacked by a new bot.

"What do you think the final password is?" Fia asked.

"Let's just get into the next partition first," Elissa answered. The attacking bot was hellbent on keeping them out, threatening to overheat the system—possibly after the server sent out the message to trigger Skeleton Key. The good news was that if they could overtake the attacking program, they could use it to melt the server after they'd secured the partition with Skeleton Key, destroyed the malware, and won this twisted race.

"You have thirty minutes to retrieve Skeleton Key. Any attempt to destroy the server or the partition containing

Skeleton Key will result in Skeleton Key's dissemination to random cities around the globe for execution."

"Hmm. That might be a problem," Elissa said.

And that's when she noticed it.

"Oh, shit, Fia, the climate controls are tied in." She looked away from the screen.

Fia's stark expression met hers. "So, if the computer overheats..."

"There's a good chance we might, too."

"Well, that's a bucket of shite." Fia turned her attention back to hacking. "Guess we'll deal with it when we get in, eh?"

Yeah, right.

Elissa typed faster. The phony partition had to be *perfect*.

The minutes ticked by as they spun their code, one minute winning the battle against a new attack, the next having to retreat. Elissa tested the new partition while Fia outwitted the next attack.

"You have fifteen minutes to retrieve Skeleton Key." Elissa and Fia both growled at the voice.

"Okay, my part is finished and tested. How are you doing?"

"Grand. Help me out here."

Elissa changed her screen to show Fia's attacks. "How about this?" With a few keystrokes, they were back on the offense.

"Excellent work," Fia said.

"We're almost there."

And then they had it. The last attack ended. All that stood between them and Skeleton Key was one login and one password each.

"All right. If they're as twisted as I imagine they are, I think I have a good guess for mine," Elissa said.

"Same."

"You have five minutes—"

"Shut *up*!" they both shouted at the computer.

"Okay. Here we go." While Fia typed in her handle, Elissa typed in Surfboi65 then hesitated on her password. What if she only had one chance and guessed wrong?

Run your own race. You've done the best you can.

"Four minutes until Skeleton Key launch."

She typed in one word: Ironman.

"Partition breached. Skeleton Key available for download."

"Shraaa!" Fia exclaimed. "We did it!"

"Oh my God!" Elissa high-fived her hacking partner, then ran to the door. She signed SUCCESS to Nash who gave her a huge smile and a thumbs-up.

"You have three minutes, thirty-two seconds to download two copies of Skeleton Key or it will be launched."

"No!" She ran back to her seat in time to see Fia downloading a copy of Skeleton Key.

"We're still destroying this, right?"

"Of course." She pulled out the thumb drive. "Your turn."

"First download complete," the computer said. "Two minutes to download a second copy."

"Shit!" Elissa fumbled with taking the cap off and she dropped the thumb drive on the floor.

"Argh!" She swooped it up and then inserted it. She executed the command to download. "Come on, hurry up!"

"One minute until Skeleton Key launch."

Fia grabbed Elissa's sweaty hand. Both women held their breath.

"Second download complete. Skeleton Key launch aborted." The hatch behind them swung open, though the outer one past the scanners remained shut.

They whooped and hugged each other. Then without saying a word, they placed the thumb drives on the floor and each raised a foot to stomp down. Fia looked pale and nervous. She glanced back up at Elissa then at the open hatch.

"Fia, please. We're going to be fine. *You're* going to be fine. I promise."

Fia gave her a smile that wavered at the edges.

Bits of plastic flew everywhere as they ground the drives under their heels. Elissa felt like she could finally take a truly deep breath. Fia had kept her promise and Elissa looked up and through the hall to make sure Nash witnessed it through the hatch window. He gave them two thumbs up. Fia looked somewhat relieved.

"Okay. Now comes the tricky part," Elissa said as they sat down again.

"*Now's* the tricky part?" Fia's laugh sounded damn near unhinged. But her hands were steady on the keyboard as they prepared to fool the computer.

Elissa waited to hear the demonic voice announcing that Skeleton Key had launched while Fia typed. But Fia's root kit was excellent voodoo and Elissa just had to have faith that she'd secured the server with it and that the phony partition would pass for real.

"Almost," Fia muttered under her breath. "Come on, love." She pushed her chair away from the desk. "Got it!"

"All right." *Now to destroy the partition housing the key.* She looked at Fia. "You subdued that burner bot, right?"

"I did. I used it to damage a partition holding a different attacker. But we have a bit of a wrinkle."

Elissa closed her eyes. "Of course we do." She opened her eyes again. What is it?"

"Remember that connection you found to the environmental system? Guess exactly where it's hooked into."

"But if it didn't go off before..." That's when they noticed the room's fan had stopped humming and that what they were hearing was the computer's fan trying desperately to keep the server cool. They looked at the panel on the wall, which now read eighty-two degrees, humidity at fifty-eight percent. The temperature rose as they watched.

"I thought this was just flop sweat." Elissa wiped her forehead.

"Yeah, me, too." Fia blinked rapidly.

"Assholes!" Elissa whipped her head around to look at their only way out. "What happens if we can't get that second hatch to open? What if it's tied in as well?" Another glance at the panel told her the room's temperature was now ninety degrees—much warmer than the night outside.

Ninety-one degrees.

For the first time, panic threatened to overwhelm her.

"We may still be grand though, considering this door opened," Fia said as she laid a reassuring hand on Elissa's arm. "Maybe all we have to do is go through the scanners to open the second."

Elissa nodded and took a deep breath, keeping the panic at bay. She needed to think. She pulled out two water bottles and handed one to Fia who downed half the water in one long swig and poured the rest over her head. Elissa did the same. She felt better.

Leaning in close to Fia's ear and speaking low, Elissa said, "New plan. Now that the computer thinks the phony partition is the one holding Skeleton Key, we can launch an attack that'll overheat the server. I can disable the computer's fans to make it overheat even faster as the temperature climbs in here. Even if the computer realizes it's melting and tries to launch Skeleton Key, it'll be trying to access it in the phony partition. Skeleton Key and the rest of the server will melt down before the computer can find the right partition again, if it even knows to look for it. In the meantime, we're getting the hell out of here."

"Grand. How are you disabling the fans?"

"Like this." Elissa reached into her backpack and pulled out the dog-eared paperback she took with her everywhere and had read so many times she knew it by heart. She bit her lower lip, then cringed as she tore out the page signed and inscribed to her and stuffed it back into her backpack. She held the book up to the server's intake vent, blocking it, then duct-taped the book into place.

"Riley Edwards to the rescue."

Fia laughed as she typed. "Should have taken you for a Riley's Rebel, too." A few more clicks, and she stood up. "That should do it. Let's get out of here. I'm feeling nauseous."

So was Elissa. The panel on the wall read one hundred and four degrees with one hundred percent humidity. The clean ozone smell was gone, replaced by rank sweat and fear.

Fia went through the door to the adjoining hallway, which was just as miserable as the server room. Elissa watched Nash's face through the tiny window in the second hatch. He looked calm, though the tight skin around his eyes betrayed his worried mind. She gave him a thumbs-up as Fia stopped under the scanner's arch. It came to life and the light turned green at the top as it chimed.

Elissa's turn. She waited what felt like forever for the scanner to recognize her. Maybe it couldn't read her through the sweat. It felt like it was two hundred degrees in the little room. The scanner finally chimed—the most beautiful sound in the world.

And then the room went pitch black.

TWENTY-THREE

When the light in the scanner hallway went dark, Nash slammed his fist against the unbreakable glass. He'd never felt so helpless.

"No. No, God dammit, this is not over!"

He'd be damned if he'd let Elissa die like this. They had a future together. He looked at the handprint panel embedded in the wall. He'd been working on trying to hack it from the moment they'd passed through the scanner, just in case the whole thing was a trap. He'd thought about blowing the damn door open—he had more than enough C4, det cord, and a blasting cap ready and waiting in his backpack—but he didn't even have to calculate psi versus distance to know there was no way he could blow that door off without giving himself a TBI and probably bringing the entire cave down.

And now he didn't have eyes on Elissa and she was trapped in the dark with Fia, who he still didn't trust.

A faint light shone through the window. He looked up again to see Elissa's face illuminated by her headlamp. She was shining the light straight up under her chin to avoid the glare.

"Elissa!" Nash ripped his headlamp off and did the same.

She mouthed his name as sweat poured down her cheeks. He touched the window. It felt too warm. Her hands moved rapidly as she signed. Somehow, they'd triggered the environmental control and now the rooms were heating up. *Wish I had my IV bag* she added with a sad smile.

IV bag... That's it.

He stood close to the window so she could read his lips. "I'm getting you out of there. I tried to hack the panel but it's gone dark. I need you and Fia to go all the way back against the far wall in the other room. Close that door as far as you can but put something to prop it open a little just in case. Shield your head with your arms. Do you understand?"

Elissa nodded and turned to Fia, who he could see in the halo of her headlamp, and relayed what he'd just told her. The other woman nodded and Nash's gut twisted as he watched them dash into the other room, their lights growing dimmer. Now he could barely make out any light shining through the second window. He had to trust they were in place.

Nash tore open his backpack and rummaged inside. He found the coiled-up detonating cord, duct tape, a half-full collapsible water bag, and a second, empty one. Working fast, he filled both bags from the water pooling on the cave floor. He lined the det cord along the hinge-side seam of the door and duct-taped it in place. Next, he flattened a pinch of the putty-like C4 into two thin sheets. He approximated where the two hinges were and adjusted the C4 sheets and bags over each one to direct the blast.

He'd done something similar in a hostage situation in Afghanistan when his team wasn't sure about the location of the hostages in the building they were breaching and couldn't just blow the door up and risk fragging everyone. He wished he had two of the pre-made, neatly measured IV breaching bags he'd used before, but beggars couldn't be choosers. Nash had to trust his makeshift tamp charge bladders would work this time, too, without sending shrapnel everywhere or disturbing the cavern too much.

Nash unwound the rest of the det cord and backed into the narrow cave entrance as far as he could, thankful the stuff was waterproof.

"Fire in the hole," he repeated three times needlessly, but protocol was protocol. He took out his lighter and ignited the fuse.

The explosion was nearly instantaneous. Nash's ears rang and he prayed the second hatch was enough of a shield to protect Elissa. He crawled out of the tunnel to see how well he'd done. The light from his headlamp showed nothing but kicked-up dust and smoke. The cavern felt at least twenty degrees hotter. He covered his mouth with the top of his shirt and felt his way to the door.

And walked right through.

"Elissa!" he shouted, barely able to hear his own voice over the ringing. He pushed aside the twisted door and loped through the dead scanner.

"We're all right," she called back.

Thank you, Almighty Lord.

The room was hotter than hell and Nash was instantly drenched in sweat. He helped Elissa up. Fia was already standing.

"Go, go, go. We need to get the hell out of here. I'm sure Capitoline is waiting up top."

The women practically moaned with pleasure when they hit the cool water in the cavern. The trip back through the narrow tunnels felt like it took twice as long going back as it did coming in. But soon enough, they were able to crouch and then stand. Nash got ahead of them, his Sig drawn in case the worst had happened and Psychic had been overpowered. No one stood in the stairwell. Nash put his comm back in and tried to raise someone—anyone—but the communication was still garbled. He put his finger to his lips and motioned for the women to put in their comms for when they managed to get out of the dampening field or whatever it was that was monkeying with the electronics.

Lightning flashed and thunder boomed. Water still poured down the ladder. With any luck, the storm hid the sound of the explosion and they could sneak on out of there through the jungle before the mercenaries knew what was happening.

Stay down here until I flash my light down for you to come up Nash mouthed to Elissa. She nodded and he started up the ladder, his headlamp turned off. Halfway up, he whistled and waited for Costello to come back that everything was safe. He didn't have to wait long. Psychic gave the all-clear whistle back. Nash turned his flashlight on and signaled down to the women who started climbing behind him.

Costello gave him a hand up once he got to the top, and then both men helped Elissa and Fia out of the hole. Anubis was nowhere in sight—patrolling, Nash had no doubt—but Reggie was there silently wagging his tail. Elissa went to her knees in the mud and loved on him before Nash gently placed his hand on her shoulder to remind her that Reg was on the job. Nash had yet to meet the dog who could sniff out the enemy better than Reggie.

Costello motioned for them to get a move on toward the rendezvous—originally, a nearby clearing surrounded by trees. They had a helo coming in, but with the strong winds blowing and the rain making visibility low, they'd have to go to the secondary extraction point, a larger field about a mile away.

"What's the good word?" Nash asked him.

"Enemy's out there, waiting. The storm's a mixed blessing. At least it's covering us, and the dogs—"

Lightning blinded them momentarily as thunder crashed. Fia shouted.

Fuck. She was trying to alert the Capitoline mercenaries to their position. Nash grabbed her and covered her mouth.

"You traitorous—"

"No, Nash, she's hurt," Elissa said, trying to pull his hand away from Fia's face. Fia moaned against his palm and tried to nod. Her legs gave out and he lowered her to the ground. A man's howl of pain came from the underbrush a few yards away, accompanied by snarls. Anubis had found his target. Psychic took off in their direction. Reggie stood guard.

"How bad?" Nash asked as Elissa tore the collar of Fia's long-sleeved tee to get to the rapidly expanding dark stain on the sleeve. "Nash, they shot her when the lightning flashed. I need some light."

"No can do. It'll give us away."

"I'm all right," Fia gasped. "Just nicked me. Scared me more than anything."

Elissa examined the wound as best she could. She tore off the sleeve, wrapped it up, and handed the wad of cloth to Fia. "Keep this pressed against it."

Nash heard footsteps returning and raised his Sig. Anubis emerged from the brush first, followed by Costello.

"Friendly here," he said. "Target neutralized."

"You okay to move?" Nash asked Fia, though the truth was he'd leave her there if it meant getting Elissa to safety. But he'd given his word, and his objective with Operation Evil Maids was to get both of them out in one piece. He didn't care about Skeleton Key just as long as Elissa was safe. Fia nodded and they started off, the dogs acting as sentries as they continued down the hill.

More garbled words came over the comm just as a figure appeared ahead. Nash could just make out Malcolm's voice and matched the large figure to the man approaching them on the goat trail masquerading as a path.

"Comm's acting bitchy," Malcolm said when he joined them. "Spooky and Joker are dead ahead. We've got another half mile to go." He looked at Fia, who was pressing the wad of cloth against her arm. "What—"

More shots fired ahead. It was impossible to say who was firing at who.

They took cover in the undergrowth. Nash threw his body over Elissa's while Malcolm shielded Fia. Psychic aimed into the dark night punctured by lightning. The dogs were nowhere in sight.

Something came at them low and fast. Camden's dog Toby penetrated the undergrowth and paused long enough to determine they weren't the threat, then sped on. Nash didn't dare shout out, even when he heard Toby barking and more men shouting.

"Let's move," he said, hoping to catch up to the others. The helo would be there soon and they couldn't afford to miss it. If the damn thing couldn't land or they weren't at the extraction point right on time, they'd have to keep on foot and fight their way out. That was going to be harder with Fia wounded.

"You should leave me behind," Fia said as if she'd read his mind. "You saved me from the hatch, it's enough."

"Hell no, that's not the objective," Nash answered, silently adding *I'll be damned too if I let you run off with your lords and masters shooting at us out there.*

"I can make it. I can hide—"

"I said no," Nash growled.

"We'll all get out," Elissa said.

Gina's voice came over the comms, clear as a bell. "Garth, report."

"Asset acquired. Quarter mile from the extraction point."

A dog yelped to their left and the vegetation rose around them as three men in ghillie suits appeared to grow out of the ground. One grabbed Nash, who was trying to make heads or tails out of the man's body through the thick, hanging jute covering his form. Psychic and Malcolm fought off the other two, when a fourth mercenary dashed in, grabbed Fia, and took off.

TWENTY-FOUR

Elissa whirled in confusion when the shaggy man-shapes appeared and hemmed them in. One tried to grab her arm but she ducked, spun, and kicked, somehow making contact with a kneecap. Nash was struggling with another mercenary, as were Costello and Malcolm. When the fourth man came at them, Elissa braced to fight, but he dodged and grabbed Fia by her wounded arm. The woman shrieked before he picked her up and made off with her.

Elissa had no choice. She'd made a promise, so she went running after them.

"Jesus Christ," Nash swore somewhere behind her. But then she heard him speak the magic words that sent a dark shape shooting past her faster than she could ever hope to run. Reggie leaped onto the mercenary's back and took him down. He let go of Fia to defend himself from the dog's attack just in time for Reggie to be joined by Anubis, who, judging from the strangled screams coming for the man, showed no mercy. Fia took advantage of the situation to try and escape into the jungle.

"Fia!" Elissa shouted. But Fia continued in the opposite direction. Elissa took off after her until she'd nearly caught up. Fia slowed down to a stop, panting heavily and gripping her wounded arm.

"Back this way." She pointed toward the others.

Fia shook her head. "Thank you for all your help, truly. But, I'm not coming with you."

Elissa's stomach flipped. "You have to. You can't go back to them."

She shook her head. "I'll not go back to Capitoline. But I'm sure Gina has plans to interrogate me and I'm not keen on that either. Here." Fia pressed something small into Elissa's palm. A thumb drive. "She'll find some of what she wants on there, but if she wants any more information, she's out of luck with me. She'll have to find someone else."

"Fia, she wouldn't harm—"

Fia looked Elissa square in the eye. "Gina might not harm me. But I can't take the chance that the people she's beholden to won't."

That sent shivers down Elissa's spine. She tucked the thumb drive into her pocket. "All right. I'll make sure she gets it *and* I'll let her know you were totally on the up and up the entire time."

Fia grinned, then spoke quickly as they heard Nash and the others approaching. "Thank you. I owe you big. Cheer up. I'm sure we'll meet again. We make a grand team. But for now, I need to disappear. Sort things out. I need to tell you something else to pass on to Gina, something that's not on the drive. Call it a good-faith measure and my insurance that she'll at least try to stop her people from coming after me, and that I can depend on her protection in the future."

"Okay, what is it?"

"Tell her that her man is still alive."

Her man? Before Elissa could ask, Fia disappeared into the jungle.

When Nash, Malcolm, and Costello reached her, all she could do was tell them that Fia had disappeared.

"I knew she would. That woman was crooked." Nash looked back toward the path. "Dammit, Toby's injured and we need to get you out of here, but we need to secure Skeleton Key. Psychic—"

"She's not crooked, Nash, and she doesn't have a copy of Skeleton Key."

"How do you know?"

"She smashed her thumb drive back at the server." Elissa took a deep breath. "We both did."

"What?" Malcolm said.

"It's too dangerous for *anyone* to have." She stared at Gina's friend, hoping he wasn't about to do something horrible to her. Nash followed her gaze and locked eyes with Malcolm, who stared back impassively.

"We're getting out of here," Nash said. "Come on."

All the way to the field, Elissa listened in vain for Fia's running footsteps behind them. She prayed the woman would change her mind and trust them. She also prayed that she wouldn't hear Fia's screams or shouts for help. But only the sound of the rain falling on the palm trees followed them to the open field where a helicopter swiftly appeared and carried them to safety.

They didn't return to the resort, but instead flew to Lanai across the channel. After they landed, Gina whisked them off to a swanky private residence in the island's only town. Clean, dry clothes were waiting for all of them.

Camden was the only one who didn't bother changing right away. Instead, he tended to Toby's wounds, which were mercifully superficial.

"Tina would never forgive me if I let something happen to you, big guy," he told the dog. Toby thumped his tail on the floor at his little girl's name.

Anubis and Reggie were unharmed but looked just as miserable as their buddy every time Camden poked too hard and Toby whimpered. Fleur was waiting for them at the house and she joined the other dogs in sympathy for Toby. Costello did his best to distract the dogs with treats and pets while he talked with Jordan on his cell. From what Elissa could gather from his side of the conversation, she was telling him about her latest plans for another community garden in an underserved area.

Elissa sat as far away from Gina and Malcolm as she could. She kept waiting for the big man to snitch on her. She trusted that Gina wouldn't ever harm her, but Fia's words came back, just as chilling as they'd been when she spoke them.

Gina might not harm me. But I can't take the chance that the people she's beholden to won't.

She waited for Gina to pull her into one of the bedrooms for an interrogation, especially after she confessed to destroying every known copy of Skeleton Key. But Gina never did. Instead, she told Malcolm to check the news for any cities suffering from any weird shutdowns and calmly typed a report into her laptop. Malcolm surfed his own computer. His only comment was that it looked like the Cubs might make it back into the World Series.

"Is that weird enough for you?" He smirked at Gina.

"Hey, I like an underdog," she said without looking up, but she smiled all the same.

Elissa was on a white couch facing the pool and cabana outside the back patio doors, where Nash had swept her into his lap and wrapped his arms around her. The sky was turning light blue streaked with pink, but Elissa was anything except tired. She was so wired she wasn't sure if she'd ever sleep again.

"You okay, shug?" Nash murmured in her ear.

She nodded. "I am." She shifted in his arms so she could look into his face. "Is it always like this?"

"Is what like what?"

"Is it always this weirdly quiet and normal after a mission?"

He shrugged a shoulder. "Sometimes, yeah, especially when it's successful."

Elissa frowned. "But it wasn't, not entirely. Fia's not here."

"No, but she did give you that thumb drive. Gina seems pleased by whatever's on it."

Yeah, we'll see how she acts when I give her the other news Elissa thought. She lowered her voice as she glanced over his shoulder at Malcolm and Gina across the wide room. "I didn't bring back a copy of Skeleton Key. I destroyed it instead. I kinda thought Gina's *friends* would be here waiting to string me up for that."

Nash tried unsuccessfully to hide a wince. "It's feeling a mite stuffy in here. Let's go check out the pool." Only Costello looked up when Nash lifted Elissa off his lap and led her to the sliding glass doors and the pool beyond.

"Should we be outside?" Elissa asked. "Do you think..." She looked around at the manicured hedges surrounding the pool area.

"No one's watching us, shug. This place is secure, trust me." When they'd gotten to the house, they'd all removed their shoes at the front door as was the custom, so when Nash and Elissa sat down at the edge of the pool, they let their bare feet dangle in the water.

"Are Gina's friends securing it? I mean, they seem to be able to do anything. Even fly a pack of dogs to the middle of the Pacific Ocean without going through quarantine."

Nash smiled without looking at her. "They can accomplish a lot that us mere mortals can only dream of, I'll give you that."

DO U TRUST THEM? She surreptitiously signed the letters.

He took her hands in his. "I will trust anyone who keeps you safe."

Even if it's a deal with the devil? She wondered. "Will I still be safe when they get that report Gina's writing up? The one that says I destroyed Skeleton Key?"

"It was your call in that room and you followed your conscience."

"Mine and Fia's, don't forget."

She watched him try not to roll his eyes. "Yours and Fia's. It's the best any of us can do. As far as I'm concerned, you made the right choice. I'm hoping they see it that way, too. That their objective was to study it so that they could stop future attacks, then destroy it."

"You look doubtful though."

He shook his head lightly. "You did them a solid, Elissa. They won't forget that. And if they do, Gina will remind them."

She looked back toward the house. The rising sun was just beginning to reflect golden against the glass, blocking her view of the inside. "Will I have to hide for the rest of my life?" She looked Nash in the eye. "Will Capitoline come after me?"

He looked grave. "I can't say either way until we know

more. But no matter what happens, I'm going to be there with you." He stood and pulled her up with him.

Then, he went to one knee.

Elissa covered her mouth. "Nashville Jones, what are you doing?"

"What does it look like I'm doing?" He smiled up at her. "I'm asking you to marry me."

Her heart stuttered and butterflies flew throughout her body. "No. I can't marry you."

Nash sighed, though the smile didn't leave his face. "This feels like Jordan and Psychic's party all over again. So why are you telling me no this time?"

"Why? Because what if they come after me? I can't condemn you to a life on the run."

"Are your ears still ringing from when I blew the door off its hinges? Didn't you hear what I just said? I'm going to be at your side no matter what happens. But I'd really love to do it as your husband."

The world shrank down to the two of them. Nash was absolutely serious. *I can't imagine my life without him in it anymore.*

"If you think you can keep up with me, coach, then yes. I'll marry you."

A look of pure joy spread across Nash's face. He whooped as he stood and picked her up and spun her around.

The patio doors opened and Camden led the others outside. "That looked suspiciously like a marriage proposal," he said.

"That's because it was," Elissa said, beaming. "And don't you *dare* tell Elena until I've talked to her first."

"She's going to be so mad either way that I knew first. So where's the ring?" Camden smirked at Nash.

"No ring yet," Nash said. "Not all of us have Bette Collins

at our beck and call to help hunt up an engagement ring right after a mission."

Red crept up Camden's throat but he laughed. "You know about that?"

"Hello?" Elissa said. "Elena told *everybody* that story."

Gina's phone buzzed and she looked at the screen. "Congratulations, but I need to take this. It's news about my other team." She turned and jogged into the house, a hopeful look in her eyes. Malcolm followed, looking equally hopeful.

Sudden exhaustion hit Elissa like a tidal wave.

"You okay, shug?"

"I don't know. I'm suddenly really tired."

"Your system's gone through its adrenaline and you're crashing," Costello said. "Rack out and you'll feel better after."

"Great idea. Pardon us." Nash carried Elissa past Costello and Camden, past the dogs, and into the farthest bedroom in the house. Eventually, they slept.

When Elissa woke early the next morning, it was to good news.

Gina's original team had walked unharmed out of the jungle and onto HI-340 with fuzzy memories of captivity. A high amount of Propofol—Milk of Amnesia—was detected in their systems. The most they could remember was that they'd been ambushed right after emerging from the cave, drugged, and taken to a secondary location. They hadn't been questioned or tortured, but had been sedated and kept in bed with restraints until they woke up in the jungle. One man remembered being told 'your side won, so you're going free now' before he blacked out and woke with the others later.

Apparently, the captured Capitoline team had not fared as well and were still missing.

The best news was that with Skeleton Key neutralized, Capitoline had no interest in Elissa.

"But how do you know?" she asked Gina.

"We'll talk about that once we get home," she answered. "You'll need to come into Watchdog for a debriefing with Lachlan and me. But I assure you, you're safe." She handed Elissa two tickets. "These are for the ferry between Lanai and Maui. You'll find the Jeep parked at the landing and all your things are still at the resort. Go enjoy the next couple of days. Go surfing." She smiled. "And there are some nice jewelry stores in Lahaina so tell Nash to put a ring on it."

Tell her that her man is still alive. Fia's voice rang in her head. But with so many people around...no, she'd wait.

Elissa laughed. "I will. And you and I are definitely going out for a girls' night."

Gina nodded and turned her attention to Fleur.

E lissa and Nash were walking into the resort when they ran into her brother's family on their way out, pushing a bellman's cart heaped with luggage.

"Ah, here's a bellboy when I need one," Stefan joked.

"That's brother-in-law bellboy to you." Elissa held up her left hand to show off the engagement ring they'd picked out in Lahaina an hour before.

Stefan's jaw dropped. "Congratulations." He hugged Elissa then shook Nash's hand while Elissa showed her ring off to Claire.

"So you guys are headed back to California?" Elissa asked Stefan.

He grinned. "Actually, since Mom and Dad left last night, we decided to extend our vacation. We're heading for the airport to catch a flight to Lanai for a few more days."

"Oh, great! It's so beautiful." *Oops.* "I mean, if it's anything like Maui."

"I was hoping to catch you for a meal before we left for Lanai, but we haven't seen you," Stefan said. "Where you been?"

"Oh, you know. Off saving the world, as expected," Elissa joked back. Nash raised his eyebrows and she winked at him. "So you'd better be over in Lanai finding the cure for cancer."

Stefan's laugh carried across the lobby. "I'm on it, Ironman."

They hugged again. "Love you, big brother. Have a wonderful time."

"Love you too, little sis. Claire and I will take you up on the long weekend of babysitting next month. I've decided to start scaling back and taking it easy. Well, *easier.*"

"Awesome! See you then."

As Elissa and Nash waved goodbye, someone else slinked into the lobby with a suitcase in one hand and his phone in the other. He almost sneaked past Elissa but she'd gotten into the practice of constantly scanning her surroundings and caught him out of the corner of her eye.

"Well, hello, Brett." She smiled and waved obnoxiously at her ex with her left hand, making sure her new diamond caught the sunlight.

Brett ignored her and instead looked back and forth between his phone and the portico, waiting for his ride to pull up.

Elissa elbowed Nash, who'd been watching her antics with an amused smile. "Look, Nash, it's Brett."

Nash smirked as he tipped his hat. "Howdy. Off to cheat in the next race?"

"I didn't cheat. Stacey lied to the judges because she couldn't admit she was such a loser."

"Huh." Elissa pretended to ponder that. "Wanna race now? I bet I could beat you to that palm tree and back."

Brett rolled his eyes. "Fuck off."

"Come on. For old time's sake." She pointed at his bright blue sneakers that clashed violently with his shirt. "I bet those make you run really fast."

"These cost more than six-months' rent on your shitty little apartment, so no, I'm not fucking them up in a stupid race with you that I already know I'd win."

Elissa held her fingers in an upside-down triangle shape, index fingertips touching with her thumbs touching to make the line across the top. She then placed her hands over her abdomen.

"What *are* you doing?" Nash asked, trying hard not to laugh.

"This is my pussy detector. See how it's pointing down at mine?" She gave him a surprised look. "Oh, wait, what's it doing?" She made a beeping sound as she moved the triangle until her index fingers were pointing at Brett. "Wow! It really works!"

Brett looked like he wanted to punch her. He took a step forward before glancing at Nash and stopping. A car pulled up and parked. "That's my car so you're in luck. I won't kick your ass today."

Nash tipped his hat again. "Keep dreaming."

"You couldn't even begin to kick my ass," Brett said as he tossed his suitcase into the trunk.

"Well, sure I could. But it'd be way more fun to watch my woman do it." He wrapped his arm around Elissa, who wanted to kiss him then and there. "But we got better things to do. Come on, shug, trash just took itself out."

They turned and headed for their room.

After two days of surfing—and one memorable afternoon of finding a secluded waterfall and pool—Elissa and Nash headed home. While Nash dozed beside her, Elissa watched the deep blue ocean out the airplane window, her body relaxed but her head full of worry. Sure, she was engaged, and Elena, Rachael, Delia, and Jordan planned to ambush her the minute they landed to start on wedding plans, and that made her happy. She had Gina's assurance that she was safe and that held true so far. But she had no job and no prospects lined up. She also felt strangely let down after her adventure. The thought of another boring, pointless job after what she'd accomplished made her sick to her stomach, but what choice did she have? Her 'shitty little apartment' wasn't going to pay for itself, and even after she moved in with Nash, she didn't want to freeload.

She also had her debriefing with Lachlan and Gina to look forward to—not. Would they chew her out for destroying Skeleton Key? Maybe a bunch of men in black would be waiting outside the conference room door afterward to disappear her.

No. If they hadn't taken her by now, they wouldn't ever. At least not over this.

Maybe she could turn the meeting around to her advantage. The more she thought about it, the better she felt.

E lissa walked down the hall toward the conference room at Watchdog on Monday morning, the confidence she'd felt on the plane suddenly evaporating now that she was here. Nash had kissed her and assured her that everything would be all right before he headed off to his office. She paused outside the door, hearing voices inside. Lachlan and Gina seemed to be deep in discussion.

"...none of us do," Lachlan was saying. His usual rough tone sounded warm and mellow. "Especially me. Gina, I was...I was worried about you the entire time. They're—"

"Hang on," Gina said quietly, then louder, "Is someone there?"

"Knock, knock. Am I early?" Elissa said as she rounded the doorway. Lachlan and Gina were standing close together. Lachlan's face looked flushed and he cleared his throat as he took a step back.

Gina smiled and walked toward her. "No, you're right on time. Come in. Have a seat." She closed the door behind Elissa as she pointed to one of the chairs beside the head of the table. Lachlan took his seat at the head where three folders lay and slid one in front of Elissa. He started to hand a folder to Gina, who'd remained standing, and she waved it off.

"When will you learn not to waste paper on me?" she said. And was her tone teasing for once? *Wow.*

"Right." Lachlan pointed to his temple. "All up there already."

"Mmm-hmm."

He smirked and shook his head, turning his attention back to Elissa. "So. You had an exciting vacation."

"Sure, I guess you could call it that." She bit her lip. "Let's just get to it. How much trouble am I in for destroying Skeleton Key instead of giving you a copy?"

"Straight to the point. I like that," Lachlan said. He glanced at Gina. "You were right. As usual."

"So?" Elissa asked. "How much?"

"Absolutely none." Another glance at Gina before he returned his gaze to Elissa. "I would have done the same thing."

Elissa should have felt relieved but she had a feeling that Lachlan's approval didn't extend to Gina's friends. She turned to look at Gina to confirm.

"I would have as well," Gina said. "And I've explained that up the chain. If you'll open your folder, you'll see a secured website address where you can fill in the details of what happened in the server room and that should suffice."

"Baby's first paperwork," Lachlan added.

"Oh, I'm no stranger to paperwork," Elissa said.

"You haven't met paperwork until you've filled something out for the alphabets and-or the military. Get used to it."

Elissa looked up from her folder. "Get used to it?"

"Lachlan," Gina scolded. "You're getting ahead of yourself."

He snorted. "What? Just look at her." He gestured at Elissa. "It's written all over her face. Do I have to tell you again that you were right?"

"It never gets old, I'll admit."

"Excuse me, can you fill *me* in?" Elissa asked.

"Gina has suggested that you would be a good fit here at Watchdog. And that you would be interested in pursuing a career with us as well." Lachlan smiled and leaned back in his chair.

Elissa's jaw dropped. "I...uh. Yes, actually." She'd been thinking of ways to convince them to give her an interview ever since her flight home, and here they were already offering her a job. And now that they had, she was sitting here second-guessing. "Do you really think I could work here? I don't even know what I need to do to be qualified to do...um, what?"

Lachlan chuckled. "We know what you're capable of or you wouldn't be here. We know you kicked Capitoline's ass last week and we need all the help we can get to stop this menace. Because to me, Capitoline is the biggest threat to our safety, not some other country. The US can negotiate with other countries."

Gina smirked and shook her head.

Lachlan narrowed his eyes. "Don't patronize me."

"Then don't make naïve statements and I won't have to."

"Woman..."

Gina rolled her eyes. "Don't 'woman' me."

"What do you mean I kicked *Capitoline's* ass?" Elissa interrupted. "I thought it was Loki that created Skeleton Key."

Gina pressed her hands against the conference table beside Elissa. "Yes and no. Turns out, we got caught in the middle of a power play. Someone at Capitoline didn't like the way things were being run and Loki became a splinter group as a result. Skeleton Key was their way of testing Capitoline's strengths and weaknesses while seeing if there's anyone out there still able to challenge a group of powerful billionaires."

"And that was us?"

Gina nodded. "Capitoline lost, we won, and now my friends have gained an ally."

"Wait. You're telling me Loki's on our side?"

"For now. But who knows for how long?"

Elissa shook her head. "That's crazy."

"The *world's* gone crazy, Elissa," Gina said. "There are terrible people out there who just want to see the world burn. You've tangled with them already, and if you choose this life, you'll be going toe to toe with them all the time. If you join

Watchdog, what you'll be doing...some of it will haunt you the rest of your life."

"I know. Everything you say is true. I was scared shitless out in the jungle. But I was worried about my team more than I was worried about myself. And then when that clock started ticking and suddenly I had the entire world to think about..." she shook her head to rid it of the memory. "I'm already haunted by that, by what could have happened. But you know what? I'll shake it off. Because we won. But what will haunt me more, in the long run, is if I don't do something about it. So I accept the position, whatever it is."

Lachlan smiled wide. "Someone with your various talents, it'll take a little time to figure out where you'll fit in best. We'll start training you up in the basics, and you tell us what you want to do. I have a feeling you'll create your own position before it's all said and done."

"Thank you," Elissa said, bowing her head. "I think this is going to be a good thing."

"She says before she does the paperwork," Lachlan said. He gestured at the folders. "First, let's debrief. Then we'll get you started on the forms. At least you're not the only FNG. I just hired Malcolm McCoy."

"Seriously? Watchtower?" She looked at Gina.

"He'd like a change, and he thinks this might fit." She shrugged.

They spent the next hour debriefing and Elissa realized they weren't kidding about the paperwork. But she didn't care —she was just excited to be starting the latest phase of her life.

"Glad to have you aboard." Lachlan stood and shook her hand. "Now if you'll excuse me."

After Lachlan left, Elissa stopped Gina. "There's something else I need to tell you. But, I wanted to do it in private."

Gina turned more serious than Elissa had ever seen her. "What is it? You've gone pale."

"It's Fia. She told me something before she disappeared." Elissa took a deep breath. "She said to tell you that your man is still alive."

Her expression didn't change but something flashed in Gina's golden eyes.

"Gina?"

"I...don't have a man," she said. "I haven't for a long time." She shook her head. "Thank you. I need to make some calls now." She turned away, effectively dismissing Elissa.

"Girls' night."

Gina turned back around. "What?"

Elissa smiled. "We're doing a girls' night, like I said before."

Gina looked genuinely perplexed.

"I'll kidnap you if I have to. I can do that."

She gave her a doubtful grin. "Sure."

"Tonight? Or sometime this week at the latest." Elissa winked. "Don't make me show up in your living room unannounced."

That cracked Gina up. "No need. I'll...I'll let you know."

"You'd better, girl." Elissa turned for the door.

"Elissa?"

She stopped. "Yeah?"

"Welcome aboard. And thank you."

"You bet."

Elissa found Nash in his office. She closed the door behind her. He looked up from his computer and his smile said it all.

"So you know already," she said.

"I know already. Congratulations, shug."

"This place really is gossip central." She walked slowly to his desk as his eyes roamed up and down her body.

"Scuttlebutt. It's called scuttlebutt."

Elissa slipped into his arms and sat on his lap. "So, let's give them some scuttlebutt to talk about," she said. And then she kissed him long and slow and deeply.

"I love you," he whispered against her lips.

TWENTY-FIVE

The thing about working at Watchdog? There were so many parties compared to working for the FBI and, well, for other entities. And not just basic, drink-a-beer-eat-a-burger-off-the-backyard-grill parties. No, you could find yourself standing in the grill line waiting for one of those charred burgers behind an elf and a superhero, listening in as they talked about the host—who also happens to be a psychopathic villain married to a stuntman—and her latest charity gala.

So, this is life in Holly-weird.

Malcolm McCoy suppressed a grin as listened to the hot elf go on about the dress she wore and how her ex turned practically green when he saw her dangling off the arm of her latest co-star, and what a great laugh they had about that later because her co-star had zero interest in women. The obviously bored superhero abruptly changed the subject to his latest art acquisition and how he couldn't be positive that it wasn't stolen during a recent coup in an African country whose name he couldn't remember. Mal couldn't believe the level of compromising intel just free-floating in the air. If he had no scruples, he could make a mint off just the last ten minutes' worth of blackmail-worthy gossip.

Of course, he'd been to some swanky parties in Chicago as an undercover FBI agent, but his fellow Midwesterners tended to keep their business to themselves. He'd had to be charming and witty, and always with an extra drink in his hand to pass on to his target to loosen up their lips. And even then, he didn't always get everything he needed.

This party? This would've been a cakewalk.

Gina Smith, his co-worker in the alphabets and now at Watchdog, walked up to him, drink in hand, Fleur trotting at her side.

"I know that look," she practically sub-vocalized.

"What look?" he said back just as quietly. Some habits were hard to break.

"The look that says you are a dog with a tasty new bone. Down, boy. Keep in mind we're not on duty and that we're actual guests here."

Mal eyed her drink. "Is that actual alcohol?"

She gave him a puzzled frown as she lifted her drink and inspected it. "Yeah, last time I sipped it. Why?"

Because the Gina I know is never off-duty he thought to himself. She'd changed since becoming embedded with Watchdog Security. Or was this just another mask she put on for her latest assignment? He tried not to study her too hard, because then she'd be asking him about *that* look, too.

"I'm not used to seeing you relax is all," he answered.

The tiny shrug she gave him spoke volumes. "To everything there is a season."

The elf and the superhero reached the head of the line, got their food, and moved on. Malcolm and Gina stepped up to the grill master. Grant was a retired stuntman happy to be home and flipping burgers. He was married to Bette Collins, who would never dream of giving up her acting career. Most people speculated that she hadn't even reached her peak yet—an astonishing feat for an older woman in a young woman's game. Malcolm was a big fan and could hardly believe he was an actual guest in her home. But that's what came of working with their son, Jake Collins, a profiler among other things, at Watchdog.

"How do you like your burger?" Grant asked Malcolm, a huge smile on his face. He turned that radiant look on Gina. "I know exactly how you take yours."

Gina smiled back, big enough to make her eyes crinkle at the corners—something Mal rarely saw her do in the field unless she was working someone, and never in private. "Grant, this is Malcolm McCoy. He's new at Watchdog."

"Pleasure," Grant said, extending his hand. "Welcome to your first Bette's Backyard Bash. Jake's mentioned you, Malcolm. Former FBI like him?"

"First, please call me Mal. Second, I take my burgers medium-rare with American cheese, and third, yes, that's right. Former FBI." *Technically.*

Grant chuckled. "Mal and medium-rare it is. Have you met my wife yet? She's off socializing as usual." Grant brandished his spatula like a scepter toward the vast backyard until he spotted Bette on the patio. "There she is."

Mal followed where Grant pointed the spatula until he recognized the actress sitting at a table with a few other guests. While he should've been dazzled by the star so obviously holding court, his gaze was drawn to the gorgeous woman sitting to her left. When she tipped her head back to laugh, her dark brown hair caught the sun in its glossy waves. The arc of her throat made his mouth water. Love of God,

he'd never reacted to a woman so immediately like this. But
her face was so open, so honest and carefree that he wanted to
know her just so he could bask in that feeling.

"I...haven't. Met your wife," Mal said as he managed to
tear his gaze away from the dazzling brunette.

"She's a stunner, huh?" Grant smiled lovingly toward
Bette. He handed Gina her plated cheeseburger with bacon
and barbeque sauce, along with a plain burger patty that Mal
assumed was for Fleur.

"Thanks, Grant," Gina said. She tipped her chin at Mal
and headed toward a table where Elissa sat with Elena,
Rachael, Jordan, and Jake's younger sister, Samantha. And
holy shit, was Gina actually sitting down? *With* them?

Yup. Either she's gone native or her cover is flawless.

That unguarded smile, though. Mal was leaning toward
Gina going native. *God help her.*

Grant flipped another burger and covered it with a slice of
American cheese, then placed it onto a waiting bun. Then he
plated up a second one. "If you wouldn't mind, could you take
this over to Bette?" he asked Mal. "She'll forget to eat, otherwise. She loves her people and gets distracted. It'll give you a
chance to introduce yourself."

Grant, you are my new wingman Mal thought, glancing
back at the brunette seated beside Bette. "Of course," he said.
Grant handed him the plates. "Nice meeting you."

"And you," Grant said. "Don't be a stranger."

My life is nothing but being a stranger. "Thanks," he said.
He gave Grant a chin lift and headed for Bette's table. The
most powerful actress in Hollywood looked up when he
stopped to her right, and Mal found himself face to face with
one of the most recognizable women in the world—known
best for playing a brilliant psychopath.

Her keen stare locked onto his, studying him like a master

interrogator, boring into his soul. Time slowed as her mouth took ages to open, until finally, she said, "Oh, my thoughtful husband's looking out for me again, isn't he? Did he send you over here with that burger? What sweeties, both of you."

Bette adjusted her motorized wheelchair until she'd backed up from the empty chair to her right far enough to pull it out. She patted its cushion and said, "Have a seat. I don't know you yet. I'm Bette."

Mal swallowed the lump he didn't realize was in his throat and sat down. "I'm Malcolm. Mal. McCoy. I work with Jake. Nice to meet you, Ms. Collins."

"Yes, Mal, of course! Jake's said nice things about you. And please, with friends it's never Ms. Collins, it's always Bette."

Friends?

But there he was, sitting next to Ms. Collins—Bette—chatting away between bites like this was an everyday thing. And he *was* chatting, telling her he'd been in Los Angeles less than a year, and that it sure beat Chicago winters, even if the traffic was hell on earth.

What am I doing? Which one of us is used to gathering intel again?

Part of it was Bette's piercing yet warm gaze incongruously paired with her remarkably disarming demeanor. But the other not-insignificant reason he was blabbing like he'd just mainlined sodium pentothal was that the gorgeous brunette was also listening to him with a rapt look on her face. He realized he'd spew out his social security number, the passwords to his three secret bank accounts, and the name of his childhood stuffed walrus if he could keep her deep-brown eyes trained on him like that.

He only stopped when a little girl ran up to Bette—

Camden and Elena's daughter, Tina. She had a Barbie doll wearing a white wedding dress in one hand and a...*seriously?* An honest-to-God Oscar in the other. Yup, on closer inspection it was an Oscar all right—wearing what looked like a G.I. Joe sailor suit.

"Bette," Tina said in the commanding voice only a little girl can wield. "You promised we'd play wedding today."

"Oh, goodness." Bette glanced at her watch. "It's past three already, isn't it?"

"Yes. I have to make sure everything is just right so we have to practice."

Bette leaned conspiratorially toward Mal. "Among other talents, Tina is a master wedding planner," she said loudly enough to make the girl beam. "Very exclusive though. She's planning just one, very important, wedding."

"Mama and Daddy's," Tina supplied. "I just hope Mama's not sick for it."

Bette looked suddenly concerned. "Why would she be sick? Is your mama all right, Mermaid?" Bette turned and she, Tina, and Mal looked at Elena, who was taking a big bite out of her burger.

Tina shrugged a shoulder. "I asked her and she says she's fine, but she keeps throwing up first thing in the morning and whenever she cooks broccoli, even if she plugs her nose. So broccoli is not going on the menu for the reception because she'd better not throw up on her wedding dress. It's dry-clean only."

By now, Bette's eyes had gone wide as saucers and she'd covered her mouth. Then she laughed. "I think your mama's going to be just fine, dear. I'll sneak her some salty crackers and sour plums and maybe that'll help settle her stomach. I know they certainly helped mine back then." She patted her lap and Tina climbed aboard. Bette turned her wheelchair around.

"It's been lovely getting to know you," she told Mal. "But I have some very important business to attend to." She looked at the other woman. "Annalie, why don't you scooch on over and you and my dear friend Mal can keep each other company."

Bette raised her arm in the air and both she and Tina said, "*Allons-y,*" as they sped away into the house.

Annalie—lovely name—turned to Mal and her smile dazzled him. "Those two are thick as thieves. I guess it's just you and me now. Like Bette said, I'm Annalie."

"And I'm Malcolm." He shook her soft, warm hand as he studied her face. He didn't think she was as young as he'd initially guessed when he saw her across the patio, and that was just fine with him. In his late forties, he didn't need to be chasing down a twenty-something. There was a calm wisdom in her eyes that spoke of life experience and he found that very attractive. From the way she was looking back at him, he thought maybe she liked what she saw, too.

He'd already checked her hand and was pleased to see her left ring finger bare.

"Hi, Mal," Annalie said. They were still holding hands. Her cheeks flushed slightly as she pulled hers back. "I guess you and Bette go way back," she teased.

"Oh yeah. All of, let's see," he checked his watch, "twenty minutes. What about you?"

She chuckled at his joke before she answered. "Actually, Bette and I do go way back." She looked as if her own words had taken her by surprise. "About twenty years now. Wow. Time flies."

Twenty years? Mal had her pegged around thirty-five

years old. Either she was just a kid when they met or Annalie looked young for her age.

"So, are you an actress, too?" he asked. She was more than beautiful enough. "Is that how you met?"

Annalie shook her head dismissively. "No, I'm more..." She pursed her lips, thinking. "In the machinery behind the scenes, I guess you could say."

"Oh? What do you—" A hand landed on his shoulder, surprising him.

Mal looked up into Gina's face. She always was good at sneaking up on someone. "Sorry to interrupt, but I need to talk to you inside." She smiled at Annalie but Mal recognized the seriousness just underneath the surface.

Dammit. So much for being off-duty.

He grimaced at Annalie. "Sorry. I hope this won't take long."

But they both stood and her body language said she'd decided to leave the party. Maybe he'd only imagined they'd had a connection. Weird, since he was so good at reading people. Of course, he wasn't used to getting blindsided by such an immediate attraction.

"It was nice talking to you," she said, avoiding his eyes as she looked around the backyard. "I need to find my ride. He sneaked away when I wasn't looking."

Oh. She wasn't here alone. No, of course not. How could someone that attractive be single? Then again, if the guy was stupid enough to let her out of his sight without falling to his knees and putting a ring on her finger first, well...how serious could the relationship be?

"Mal?" Gina slipped her hand around his arm with a hidden force that said she was losing patience quickly.

"Yeah, okay."

A clean break was always best so he didn't look back at Annalie as they headed into the house. No sense looking too long at what he couldn't have.

"So what's this about?" Mal asked, barely keeping the growl out of his voice as Gina led him through the house.

She gave him a look he couldn't read—not for the first time. "Impromptu client meeting. Well, more like a potential client."

"Here at the party?"

"He's one of the guests and approached Lachlan. You're the expert consultant on this. But God, I hope we don't actually need you."

"Need me on *what*, Gina?" They were approaching a room at the end of a hallway.

She checked for other guests over her shoulder. "Your expertise from your early FBI days."

The burger in Mal's stomach turned to concrete. "No."

"Like I said, I hope we don't need you."

Mal walked through the door into a library. Jake and Lachlan were already there, seated in wingback chairs facing a man who looked to be in his seventies sitting on a couch. His gray hair was neatly trimmed and his suit immaculate though a few years out of style. A fedora sat on the couch beside him. The guy was definitely old-school, wearing that to a party where everyone else was dressed casually.

"Hey, nice to meet you," the man said in a thick New York accent as he stood. His nicotine-stained fingers twitched when he reached out to shake Mal's hand. "Sorry to pull you away from such a nice party. Bette's just the best. I'm Murray Ackerman, of Ackerman Literary Agency." He reached into his jacket and pulled out a business card. "Do you ever write, Mr. McCoy?"

The question took Mal by surprise. "No, not beyond my reports, and the random grocery list."

Murray chuckled. "I had to ask. I ask everybody that question, but you being FBI, you got a lot of stories up here," he tapped his forehead, "and thrillers are a hot market."

Seriously? He'd been pulled away for *this* guy? "What exactly do you need me for, Mr. Ackerman?"

"It's Murray. And I'm not here for myself. I'm here on behalf of one of my clients. My best one. The kiddo has attracted some attention lately and I don't like it."

Mal's stomach clenched around that ball of concrete, formerly a hamburger. He sat down in an empty chair as Murray returned to the couch. Gina remained standing though she laid her hand on the back of Lachlan's chair.

No use in dancing around. "So your client is getting death threats?" Mal asked.

Murray's eyes shifted to Lachlan. "It's both more and less than that."

"After what you told me, I'd err on the side of more," Lachlan said. Gina and Jake both nodded in agreement. "Though technically they aren't death threats, they are escalating."

"From a fan? Don't creative people get those all the time?"

"Right, they do," Murray said. "And God knows the kid's had fans and detractors since day one who just love to be goblins."

"Goblins?" Mal asked.

"Er, no, they aren't goblins, Jesus." Murray shook his head. Then he snapped his fingers. "Trolls, that's what I'm trying to say. Always wanting to stir up trouble and controversy. Attention-seekers who get angry when an author doesn't become their best friend, or when they don't like a book. Nothing new there, hell, Shakespeare had his. A rose by any other name is still a shithead. So yeah, the kiddo's had plenty of trolls who usually go away when they don't get the attention they want. But this one." He pressed his lips together into a thin line. "This one's a doozy. But the kid's not taking it seriously, which is why I'm here on my own."

"Anonymous sender? Do you need me to track down the identity?" Mal glanced at Jake and he wondered why they needed both of them since Jake could handle that on his own. Pretty much anyone in his department could, but Jake had been a phenomenal agent before he jumped to Watchdog.

Gina started pacing. "The messages are signed, Mal, and that's why you're here. If this person is who he says he is, then we're dealing with one of your cold cases."

Oh, shit. "Which case?" he asked, though, by the sudden freezing of his heart, he knew exactly which one. He hoped to God he was wrong or else whoever this author was, his days were numbered.

"Murray!" a voice called from the door. "What the hell are you doing?"

Everyone turned to see a woman standing in the doorway, a look of exasperation on her face as she studied each person in the room, ending with Mal. Her expression turned to anger. *And no wonder.*

"You?" she asked.

Murray got to his feet. "Now, now, kiddo, I'm looking out for you like I always do."

"No, you're overstepping again, like you always do."

"Annalie, please," Murray said. "Just come have a seat. These people are for real and after what I told them about those letters, they have some concerns. Please, just five minutes, kid." He sat back down again and picked his fedora up off the couch and set it on his lap.

Annalie huffed but she crossed the room and took a seat

beside Murray. Those deep-brown eyes flicked to Gina before they locked onto Mal's.

"Five minutes," she said. "And that's all."

R ead about Malcolm McCoy and Annalie Givens in More Than Words Can Say, Book 6 in the Watchdog Security Series.

AFTERWORD

Los Angeles and Hawaii are real places, obviously, though I've taken huge liberties with the geographies to suit the purposes of my fiction. The Maui Challenge is something I made up, though there is a kayak race every year that runs between Maui and Molokai, and of course, the Ironman Triathlon on Oahu is a real thing, and damn impressive.

Same deal with any people (or dogs) depicted—everyone is a product of my imagination and no character depicts any real person. That goes for the computer hacking, the hackers, any government organization, and the Capitoline Group too. All fiction.

In every book, I've tried to depict as accurately as possible military working dogs and service dogs—their training, their challenges, and their devotion to their people. There is an amazing program called Puppies Behind Bars (PBB) that trains prison inmates to work with dogs who become services animals that can do anything from detect explosives to helping wounded veterans and first-responders with PTSD. This is a win for everyone! I've known a couple of dogs trained in the program and they are simply amazing. So are the people who make PBB happen. For more information, check them out at https://www.puppiesbehindbars.com/

OLIVIA'S LOVELIES

Never miss a release from Olivia Michaels by signing up for the Olivia Michaels Romance Newsletter. Be the first to read advance excerpts, see cover previews, and enter giveaways at https://oliviamichaelsromance.com/

Follow on Amazon at https://amzn.to/3sECMCk

Follow Olivia on BookBub at https://www.bookbub.com/authors/olivia-michaels

Follow on Instagram at https://www.instagram.com/explore/tags/oliviamichaelsauthor/

Want more? Come be one of Olivia's Lovelies on Facebook. I can always use another ARC reader or two... https://www.facebook.com/groups/639545290309740/

https://www.facebook.com/oliviamichaelsauthor

ALSO BY OLIVIA MICHAELS

Romantic Suspense

Watchdog Security Series

More Than Love

More Than Family

More Than Puppy Love

More Than Paradise

More Than Thrills

More Than Words Can Say (Coming Soon)

More Than Beauty (Coming Soon)

More Than Secrets (Coming Soon)

More Than Life (Coming Soon)

Watchdog Protectors Series

Protecting Harper

Protecting Brianna

Special Forces Christmas Anthology – Buster's Christmas

ACKNOWLEDGMENTS

Thank you, Caitlyn O'Leary, Riley Edwards, Susan Stoker, Trinity Wilde, Ophelia Bell, Godiva Glenn, Emily, Becca Jameson, Sara Judson Brown, Marsha McDaniel, Rayne Lewis, and Jo West. Love and gratitude to you all!

As always, thank you, Reader, for giving me a chance. I hope you enjoy reading both the Watchdog Security and Watchdog Protectors series and that I can give you a fun little escape from reality for a while. My goal is to create a world that you would love to live in, because those are *my* favorite kinds of books.

ABOUT THE AUTHOR

Olivia Michaels is a life-long reader, dog-lover, gardener, and a certified beachaholic. When she's not throwing a Frisbee for her fur-baby, harvesting tomatoes, or writing, you can find her playing in the surf, kayaking, or kicking back on the sand and cracking open a romantic beach read.

Made in the USA
Coppell, TX
22 April 2022